Dolores Claiborne

ALSO BY STEPHEN KING

NOVELS

Carrie
'Salem's Lot
The Shining
The Stand
The Dead Zone
Firestarter
Cujo
The Dark Tower: The Gunslinger
Christine
Pet Sematary
Cycle of the Werewolf
The Talisman (with Peter Straub)
It
Eyes of the Dragon
Misery
The Tommyknockers
The Dark Tower II: The Drawing of the Three
The Dark Tower III: The Waste Lands
The Dark Half
Needful Things
Gerald's Game

AS RICHARD BACHMAN

Rage
The Long Walk
Roadwork
The Running Man
Thinner

COLLECTIONS

Night Shift
Different Seasons
Skeleton Crew
Four Past Midnight

NONFICTION

Danse Macabre

SCREENPLAYS

Creepshow
Cat's Eye
Silver Bullet
Maximum Overdrive
Pet Sematary
Golden Years
Sleepwalkers

STEPHEN
KING
Dolores
Claiborne
Viking

VIKING
Published by the Penguin Group
Viking Penguin, a division of Penguin Books USA Inc.,
375 Hudson Street, New York, New York 10014, U.S.A.
Penguin Books Ltd, 27 Wrights Lane,
London W8 5TZ, England
Penguin Books Australia Ltd, Ringwood, Victoria, Australia
Penguin Books Canada Ltd, 10 Alcorn Avenue, Suite 300,
Toronto, Ontario, Canada M4V 3B2
Penguin Books (N.Z.) Ltd, 182–190 Wairau Road,
Auckland 10, New Zealand

Penguin Books Ltd, Registered Offices:
Harmondsworth, Middlesex, England

First published in 1993 by Viking Penguin,
a division of Penguin Books USA Inc.

1 3 5 7 9 10 8 6 4 2

PUBLISHER'S NOTE
This is a work of fiction. Names, characters, places, and incidents either are the product of the author's imagination or are used fictitiously, and any resemblance to actual persons, living or dead, events, or locales is entirely coincidental.

LIBRARY OF CONGRESS CATALOGING IN PUBLICATION DATA
King, Stephen.
Dolores Claiborne / Stephen King.
p. cm.
ISBN 0-670-84452-7
I. Title.
PS3561.I483D65 1993
813'.54—dc20 92-15467

Printed in the United States of America by
Arcata Graphics, Martinsburg
Set in Garamond No. 3 • Map by Virginia Norey
Designed by Amy Hill

For my mother, Ruth Pillsbury King

"What does a woman want?"

—*Sigmund Freud*

"R-E-S-P-E-C-T, find out what it means to me."

—*Aretha Franklin*

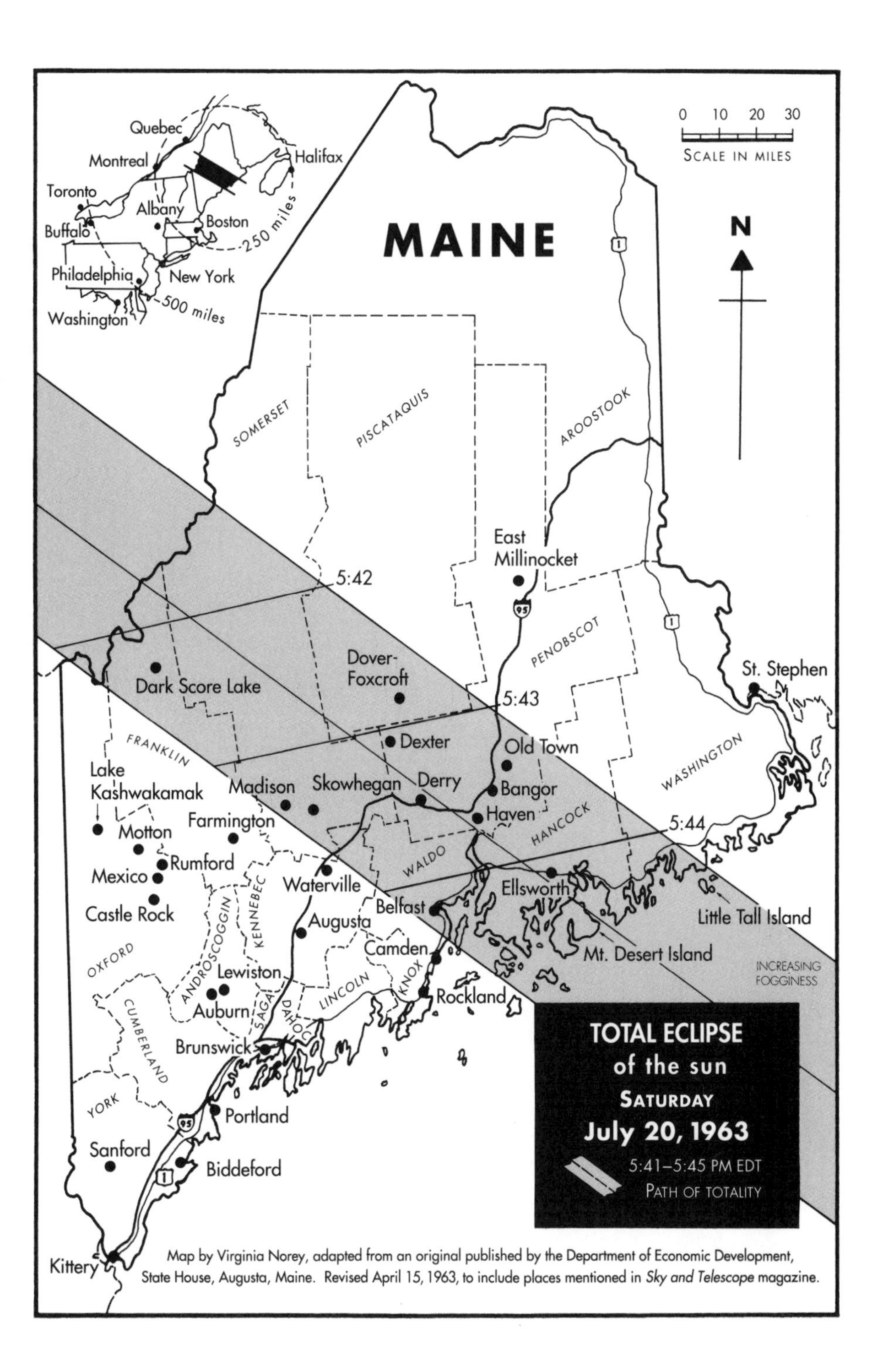

Map by Virginia Norey, adapted from an original published by the Department of Economic Development, State House, Augusta, Maine. Revised April 15, 1963, to include places mentioned in *Sky and Telescope* magazine.

Dolores Claiborne

W*hat* did you ask, Andy Bissette? Do I "understand these rights as you've explained em to me"?

Gorry! What makes some men so *numb*?

No, *you* never mind—still your jawin and listen to me for awhile. I got an idear you're gonna be listenin to me most of the night, so you might as well get used to it. *Coss* I understand what you read to me! Do I look like I lost all m'brains since I seen you down to the market? That was just Monday afternoon, in case you lost track. I told you your wife would give you merry hell about buying that day-old bread—penny wise and pound foolish, the old saying is—and I bet I was right, wasn't I?

I understand my rights just fine, Andy; my mother never raised no fools. I understand my responsibilities too, God help me.

Anything I say might be used against me in a court of law, you say? Well will wonders never cease! And you can just get that smirk off your face, Frank Proulx. You may be a hot-shot town cop these days, but it

hasn't been too long since I seen you runnin around in a saggy diaper with that same foolish grin on your face. I'll give you a little piece of advice—when you get around an old biddy like me, you just want to save that grin. I c'n read you easier'n an underwear ad in the Sears catalogue.

All right, we've had our fun; might as well get down to it. I'm gonna tell you three a hell of a lot startin right about now, and a hell of a lot of it prob'ly *could* be used against me in a court of law, if anyone wanted to at this late date. The joke of it is, folks on the island know most of it already, and I'm just about half-past give-a-shit, as old Neely Robichaud used to say when he was in his cups. Which was most of the time, as anyone who knew him will tell you.

I *do* give a shit about one thing, though, and that's why I come down here on my own hook. I didn't kill that bitch Vera Donovan, and no matter what you think now, I intend to make you believe that. I didn't push her down that frigging staircase. It's fine if you want to lock me up for the other, but I don't have none of that bitch's blood on my hands. And I think you *will* believe that by the time I'm finished, Andy. You was always a good enough boy, as boys go—fair-minded, is what I mean—and you've turned into a decent man. Don't let it go to your head, though; you grew up same as any other man, with some woman to warsh your clothes and wipe your nose and turn you around when you got y'self pointed in the wrong direction.

One other thing before we get started—I know you, Andy, and Frank, accourse, but who's this woman with the tape-recorder?

Oh Christ, Andy, I *know* she's a stenographer! Didn't I just tell you my Mamma didn't raise any fools? I may be sixty-six come this November, but I still got all my marbles. I know a woman with a tape-recorder and a shorthand pad's a stenographer. I watch *all* those courtroom shows, even that *L.A. Law* where nobody can seem to keep their clothes on for fifteen minutes at a time.

What's your name, honey?

Uh-huh . . . and whereabouts do you hail from?

Oh, quit it, Andy! What else you got to do tonight? Was you plannin to go over to the shingle and see if you could catch a few fellas diggin quahogs without a licence? That'd prob'ly be more excitement than your heart could take, wouldn't it? Ha!

There. That's better. You're Nancy Bannister from Kennebunk, and I'm Dolores Claiborne from right here on Little Tall Island. Now I already said I'm going to do a country-fair job of talking before we're done in here, and you're going to find I wasn't lyin a bit. So if you need me to speak up or to slow down, just say so. You needn't be shy with me. I want you to get every goddam word, startin with this: twenty-nine years ago, when Police Chief Bissette here was in the first grade and still eatin the paste off the back of his pitchers, I killed my husband, Joe St. George.

I feel a draft in here, Andy. Might go away if you shutcha goddam trap. I don't know what you're lookin so surprised about, anyway. You know I killed Joe. Everybody on Little Tall knows it, and probably half the people across the reach in Jonesport know it, too. It's just that nobody could prove it. And I wouldn't be

here now, admittin it in front of Frank Proulx and Nancy Bannister from Kennebunk if it hadn't been for that stupid bitch Vera, gettin up to more of her nasty old tricks.

Well, she'll never get up to any more of em, will she? There's that for consolation, at least.

Shift that recorder a little closer to me, Nancy, dear—if this is going to get done, it'll get done right, I'll be bound. Don't those Japanese just make the most *cunning* little things? Yes indeed . . . but I guess we both know that what's going on the tape inside that little cutie-pie could put me in the Women's Correctional for the rest of my life. Still, I don't have no choice. I swear before heaven I always knew that Vera Donovan'd just about be the death of me—I knew it from the first time I saw her. And look what she's done—just look what that goddamned old bitch has done to me. This time she's really stuck her gum in my gears. But that's rich people for you; if they can't kick you to death, they're apt to kiss you to death with kindness.

What?

Oh, *gorry!* I'm *gettin* to it, Andy, if you'll just give me a little peace! I'm just tryin to decide if I should tell it back to front or front to back. I don't s'pose I could have a little drink, could I?

Oh, *frig* ya coffee! Take the whole pot and shove it up your kazoo. Just gimme a glass of water if you're too cheap to part with a swallow of the Beam you keep in your desk drawer. I ain't—

What do you mean, how do I know that? Why, Andy Bissette, someone who didn't know better'd think you just toddled out of a Saltines box yesterday. Do you think me killin my husband is the only thing the folks on this island have got to talk about? Hell, that's *old* news. You, now—you still got some juice left in you.

Thank you, Frank. You was always a pretty good boy, too, although you was kinda hard to look at in church until your mother got you cured of the booger-hookin habit. Gorry, there were times when you had that finger so far up y'nose it was a wonder you didn't poke your brains out. And what the hell are you blushin for? Was never a kid alive who didn't mine a little green gold outta their old pump every now and again. At least you knew enough to keep your hands outta your pants and off your nuts, at least in church, and there's a lot of boys who *never*—

Yes, Andy, *yes*—I *am* gonna tell it. Jeezly-crow, you ain't *never* shook the ants out of your pants, have you?

Tell you what: I'm gonna compromise. Instead of telling her front to back or back to front, I'm gonna start in the middle and just kinda work both ways. And if you don't like it, Andy Bissette, you can write it up on your T.S. list and mail it to the chaplain.

Me and Joe had three kids, and when he died in the summer of '63, Selena was fifteen, Joe Junior was thirteen, and Little Pete was just nine. Well, Joe didn't leave me a pot to piss in and hardly a window to throw it out of—

I guess you'll have to fix this up some, Nancy, won't you? I'm just an old woman with a foul temper and a fouler mouth, but that's what happens, more often than not, when you've had a foul life.

Now, where was I? I ain't lost my place already, have I?

Oh—yes. Thank you, honeybunch.

What Joe left me with was that shacky little place out by the East Head and six acres of land, most of it blackberry tangles and the kind of trashwood that grows back after a clear-cut operation. What else? Lemme see. Three trucks that didn't run—two pickups and a pulp-hauler—four cord of wood, a bill at the grocery, a bill at the hardware, a bill with the oil company, a bill with the funeral home . . . and do you want the icing on the goddam cake? He wa'ant a week in the ground before that rumpot Harry Doucette come over with a friggin IOU that said Joe owed him twenty dollars on a baseball bet!

He left me all that, but do you think he left me any goddam insurance money? Nossir! Although that might have been a blessin in disguise, the way things turned out. I guess I'll get to that part before I'm done, but all I'm trying to say now is that Joe St. George really wa'ant a man at all; he was a goddam millstone I wore around my neck. Worse, really, because a millstone don't get drunk and then come home smellin of beer and wantin to throw a fuck into you at one in the morning. Wasn't none of that the reason why I killed the sonofawhore, but I guess it's as good a place as any to start.

An island's not a good place to kill *anybody*, I can tell you that. Seems like there's always someone around, itching to get his nose into your business just when you can least afford it. That's why I did it when I did, and I'll get to that, too. For now suffice it to say that I did it just about three years after Vera Donovan's husband died in a motor accident outside of Baltimore, which was where they lived when they wasn't summerin on Little Tall. Back in those days, most of Vera's screws were still nice and tight.

With Joe out of the pitcher and no money coming in, I was in a fix, I can tell you—I got an idear there's no one in the whole world feels as desperate as a woman on her own with kids dependin on her. I'd 'bout decided I'd better cross the reach and see if I couldn't get a job in Jonesport, checkin out groceries at the Shop n Save or waitressin in a restaurant, when that numb pussy all of a sudden decided she was gonna live on the island all year round. Most everyone thought she'd blown a fuse, but I wasn't all that surprised—by then she was spendin a lot of time up here, anyway.

The fella who worked for her in those days—I don't remember his name, but you know who I mean, Andy, that dumb hunky that always wore his pants tight enough to show the world he had balls as big as Mason jars—called me up and said The Missus (that's what he always called her, The Missus; my, wasn't he dumb) wanted to know if I'd come to work for her full-time as her housekeeper. Well, I'd done it summers for the family since 1950, and I s'pose it was natural enough for her to call me before she called anyone else, but at the time it seemed like the answer to all my prayers. I said yes right on the spot, and I worked for her right up until yest'y forenoon, when she went down the front stairs on her stupid empty head.

What was it her husband did, Andy? Made airplanes, didn't he?

Oh. Ayuh, I guess I *did* hear that, but you know how people on the island talk. All I know for sure is that they was well-fixed, *mighty* well-fixed, and she got it all when he died. Except for what the government took, accourse, and I doubt if it got anywhere near as much as it was probably owed. Michael Donovan was sharp as a tack. Sly, too. And although nobody would believe it from the way she was over the last ten years, Vera was as sly as he was . . . and she had her sly days right up until she died. I wonder if she knew what kind of a jam she'd be leavin me in if she did anything besides die in bed of a nice quiet heart-attack? I been down by East Head most of the day, sittin on those rickety stairs and thinkin about that . . . that and a few hundred other things. First I'd think no, a bowl of oatmeal has more brains than Vera Donovan had at the end, and then I'd remember how she was about the vacuum cleaner and I'd think maybe . . . yes, maybe . . .

But it don't matter now. The only thing that matters now is that I have flopped out of the frying pan and into the fire, and I'd dearly love to drag myself clear before my ass gets burned any worse. If I still can.

I started off as Vera Donovan's housekeeper, and I ended up bein something they call a "paid companion." It didn't take me too long to figure out the difference. As Vera's housekeeper, I had to eat shit eight hours a day, five days a week. As her paid companion, I had to eat it around the clock.

She had her first stroke in the summer of 1968, while she was watchin the Democratic National Convention in Chicago on her television. That was just a little one,

and she used to blame it on Hubert Humphrey. "I finally looked at that happy asshole one too many times," she said, "and I popped a goddam blood-vessel. I should have known it was gonna happen, and it could just as easily have been Nixon."

She had a bigger one in 1975, and that time she didn't have no politicians to blame it on. Dr. Freneau told her she better quit smokin and drinkin, but he could have saved his breath—no high-steppin kitty like Vera Kiss-My-Back-Cheeks Donovan was going to listen to a plain old country doctor like Chip Freneau. "I'll bury him," she used to say, "and have a Scotch and soda sitting on his headstone."

For awhile it seemed like maybe she would do just that—he kept scoldin her, and she kept sailin along like the *Queen Mary.* Then, in 1981, she had her first whopper, and the hunky got killed in a car-wreck over on the mainland the very next year. That was when I moved in with her—October of 1982.

Did I have to? I dunno. I guess not. I had my Sociable Security, as old Hattie McLeod used to call it. It wasn't much, but the kids were long gone by then—Little Pete right off the face of the earth, poor little lost lamb—and I had managed to put a few dollars away, too. Living on the island has always been cheap, and while it ain't what it once was, it's still a whale of a lot cheaper than livin on the mainland. So I guess I didn't *have* to go live with Vera, no.

But by then her and me was used to each other. It's hard to explain to a man. I 'spect Nancy there with her pads n pens n tape-recorder understands, but I don't think she's s'posed to talk. We was used to each other in the way I s'pose two old bats can get used to hangin upside-down next to each other in the same cave, even though they're a long way from what you'd call the best of friends. And it wasn't really no big change. Hanging my Sunday clothes in the closet next to my house-dresses was really the biggest part of it, because by the fall of '82 I was there all day every day and most nights as well. The money was a little better, but not so good I'd made the downpayment on my first Cadillac, if you know what I mean. Ha!

I guess I did it mostly because there wasn't nobody else. She had a business manager down in New York, a man named Greenbush, but Greenbush wa'ant going to come up to Little Tall so she could scream down at him from her bedroom window to be sure and hang those sheets with six pins, not four, nor was he gonna move into the guest-room and change her diapers and wipe the shit off her fat old can while she accused him of stealin the dimes out of her goddam china pig and told him how she was gonna see him in jail for it. Greenbush cut the checks; I cleaned up her shit and listened to her rave on about the sheets and the dust bunnies and her goddam china pig.

And what of it? I don't expect no medal for it, not even a Purple Heart. I've wiped up a lot of shit in my time, listened to even more of it (I was married to Joe St. George for sixteen years, remember), and none of it ever gave me the rickets. I guess in the end I stuck with her because she didn't have nobody else; it was either me or the nursin home. Her kids never came to see her, and that was one thing I felt sorry for her

about. I didn't expect them to pitch in, don't get that idear, but I didn't see why they couldn't mend their old quarrel, whatever it was, and come once in awhile to spend the day or maybe a weekend with her. She was a miserable bitch, no doubt about it, but she was their *Ma.* And by then she was old. Accourse I know a lot more now than I did then, but—

What?

Yes, it's true. If I'm lyin, I'm dyin, as my grandsons like to say. You just call that fella Greenbush if you don't believe me. I expect when the news gets out—and it will, it always does—there'll be one of those soppy articles in the Bangor *Daily News* about how wonderful it all is. Well, I got news for you—it *ain't* wonderful. A friggin nightmare is what it is. No matter what happens in here, folks are gonna say I brainwarshed her into doin what she done n then killed her. I know it, Andy, n so do you. There ain't no power in heaven or on earth that can stop people from thinkin the worst when they want to.

Well, not one goddam word of it's true. I didn't force her to do nothing, and she sure didn't do what she did because she loved me, or even liked me. I suppose she *might* have done it because she thought she owed me—in her own peculiar way she could have thought she owed me plenty, and t'wouldn't have been her way to say anything. Could even be what she done was her way of thankin me . . . not for changin her shitty diapers but for bein there on all the nights when the wires came out of the corners or the dust bunnies came out from under the bed.

You don't understand that, I know, but you will. Before you open that door and walk out of this room, I promise you'll understand everything.

She had three ways of bein a bitch. I've known women who had more, but three's good for a senile old lady mostly stuck in a wheelchair or in bed. Three's *damn* good for a woman like that.

The first way was when she was a bitch because she couldn't help it. You remember what I said about the clothespins, how you had to use six of em to hang the sheets, never just four? Well, that was just one example.

There were certain ways things *had* to be done if you worked for Mrs. Kiss-My-Back-Cheeks Vera Donovan, and you didn't want to forget a single one of them. She told you how things were going to go right up front, and I'm here to tell you that's how things went. If you forgot something once, you got the rough side of her tongue. If you forgot twice, you got docked on payday. If you forgot three times, that was it—you were down the road, and no excuses listened to. That was Vera's rule, and it sat all right with me. I thought it was hard, but I thought it was fair. If you was told twice which racks she wanted the bakin put on after it came out of the oven, and not *ever* to stick it on the kitchen windowsills to cool like shanty Irish would do, and if you *still* couldn't remember, the chances were good you wasn't *never* going to remember.

Three strikes and you're out was the rule, there was absolutely no exceptions to it, and I worked with a lot of different people in that house over the years because of it. I heard it said more'n once in the old days that workin for the Donovans was like steppin into one of those revolvin doors. You might get one spin, or two, and some folks went around as many as ten times or a dozen, but you always got spat out onto the sidewalk in the end. So when I went to work for her in the first place—this was in 1949—I went like you'd go into a dragon's cave. But she wasn't as bad as people liked to make out. If you kept your ears open, you could stay. I did, and the hunky did, too. But you had to stay on your toes all the time, because she was sharp, because she always knew more of what was going on with the island folk than any of the other summer people did . . . and because she could be mean. Even back then, before all her other troubles befell her, she could be mean. It was like a hobby with her.

"What are you doing here?" she says to me on that first day. "Shouldn't you be home minding that new baby of yours and making nice big dinners for the light of your life?"

"Mrs. Cullum's happy to watch Selena four hours a day," I said. "Part-time is all I can take, ma'am."

"Part-time is all I need, as I believe my advertisement in the local excuse for a newspaper said," she comes right back—just showin me the edge of that sharp tongue of hers, not actually cuttin me with it like she would so many times later. She was knittin that day, as I remember. That woman could knit like a flash—a whole pair of socks in a single day was no problem for her, even if she started as late as ten o'clock. But she said she had to be in the mood.

"Yessum," I said. "It did."

"My name isn't Yessum," she said, putting her knit-

ting down. "It's Vera Donovan. If I hire you, you'll call me Missus Donovan—at least until we know each other well enough to make a change—and I'll call you Dolores. Is that clear?"

"Yes, Missus Donovan," I said.

"All right, we're off to a good start. Now answer my question. What are you doing here when you've got a house of your own to keep, Dolores?"

"I want to earn a little extra money for Christmas," I said. I'd already decided on my way over I'd say that if she asked. "And if I'm satisfactory until then—and if I like working for you, of course—maybe I'll stay on a little longer."

"If *you* like working for *me*," she repeats back, then rolls her eyes like it was the silliest thing she'd ever heard—how could anybody *not* like working for the great Vera Donovan? Then she repeats back, "Christmas money." She takes a pause, lookin at me the whole time, then says it again, even more sarcastic. "Kuh-*risss*-mas money!"

Like she suspected I was really there because I barely had the rice shook out of my hair and was havin marriage troubles already, and she only wanted to see me blush and drop my eyes to know for sure. So I didn't blush and I didn't drop my eyes, although I was only twenty-two and it was a near thing. Nor would I have admitted to a single soul that I *was* already havin trouble—wild hosses wouldn't have dragged it out of me. Christmas money was good enough for Vera, no matter how sarcastic she might say it, and all I'd allow to myself was that the house-money was a little tight that summer. It was only years later that I could admit

the real reason why I went up to face the dragon in her den that day: I had to find a way to put back some of the money Joe was drinking up through the week and losin in the Friday-night poker games at Fudgy's Tavern over on the mainland. In those days I still believed the love of a man for a woman and a woman for a man was stronger than the love of drinkin and hell-raisin—that love would eventually rise to the top like cream in a bottle of milk. I learned better over the next ten years. The world's a sorry schoolroom sometimes, ain't it?

"Well," Vera said, "we'll give each other a try, Dolores St. George . . . although even if you work out, I imagine you'll be pregnant again in a year or so, and that's the last I'll see of you."

The fact was I was two months pregnant right then, but wild hosses wouldn't have dragged that outta me, either. I wanted the ten dollars a week the job paid, and I got it, and you better believe me when I say I earned every red cent of it. I worked my tail off that summer, and when Labor Day rolled around, Vera ast me if I wanted to keep on after they went back to Baltimore—someone has to keep a big place like that up to snuff all the year round, you know—and I said fine.

I kep at it until a month before Joe Junior was born, and I was back at it even before he was off the titty. In the summer I left him with Arlene Cullum—Vera wouldn't have a crying baby in the house, not her—but when she and her husband were gone, I'd bring both him and Selena in with me. Selena could be mostly left alone—even at two going on three she could be

trusted most of the time. Joe Junior I carted with me on my daily rounds. He took his first steps in the master bedroom, although you can believe Vera never heard of it.

She called me a week after I delivered (I almost didn't send her a birth announcement, then decided if she thought I was lookin for a fancy present that was her problem), congratulated me on givin birth to a son, and then said what I think she really called to say—that she was holdin my place for me. I think she intended me to be flattered, and I was. It was about the highest compliment a woman like Vera can pay, and it meant a lot more to me than the twenty-five-dollar bonus check I got in the mail from her in December of that year.

She was hard but she was fair, and around that house of hers she was always the boss. Her husband wasn't there but one day in ten anyway, even in the summers when they were supposed to be livin there full-time, but when he was, you still knew who was in charge. Maybe he had two or three hundred executives who dropped their drawers every time he said shit, but Vera was boss of the shootin match on Little Tall Island, and when she told him to take his shoes off and stop trackin dirt on her nice clean carpet, he minded.

And like I say, she had her ways of doin things. Did she ever! I don't know where she got her idears, but I *do* know she was a prisoner of them. If things wasn't done a certain way, she'd get a headache or one in her gut. She spent so much of her day checkin up on things that I thought plenty of times she would have had more

peace of mind if she'd just given over and kep that house herself.

All the tubs had to be scrubbed out with Spic n Span, that was one thing. No Lestoil, no Top Job, no Mr. Clean. Just Spic n Span. If she caught you scrubbin one of the tubs with anything else, God help you.

When it came to the ironin, you had to use a special spray-bottle of starch on the collars of the shirts and the blouses, and there was a piece of gauze you were supposed to put over the collar before you sprayed. Friggin gauze didn't do a goddam thing, so far as I could ever tell, and I must have ironed at least ten thousand shirts and blouses in that house, but if she came into the laundry room and saw you was doin shirts without that little piece of netting on a collar, or at least hung over the end of the ironin board, God help you.

If you didn't remember to turn on the exhaust fan in the kitchen when you were fryin somethin, God help you.

The garbage cans in the garage, that was another thing. There was six of em. Sonny Quist came once a week to pick up the swill, and either the housekeeper or one of the maids—whoever was most handy—was supposed to bring those cans back into the garage the minute, the very *second*, he was gone. And you couldn't just drag em into the corner and leave em; they had to be lined up two and two and two along the garage's east wall, with their covers turned upside-down on top of em. If you forgot to do it just that way, God help you.

Then there was the welcome mats. There were three of em—one for the front door, one for the patio door, and one for the back door, which had one of those snooty TRADESMAN'S ENTRANCE signs on it right up until last year, when I got tired of looking at it and took it down. Once a week I had to take those welcome mats and lay em on a big rock at the end of the back yard, oh, I'm gonna say about forty yards down from the swimmin pool, and beat the dirt out of em with a broom. Really had to make the dust fly. And if you lagged off, she was apt to catch you. She didn't watch *every* time you beat the welcome mats, but lots of times she would. She'd stand on the patio with a pair of her husband's binoculars. And the thing was, when you brought the mats back to the house, you had to make sure WELCOME was pointin the right way. The right way was so people walkin up to whichever door it was could read it. Put a welcome mat back on the stoop upside-down and God help you.

There must have been four dozen different things like that. In the old days, back when I started as a day-maid, you'd hear a lot of bitching about Vera Donovan down at the general store. The Donovans entertained a lot, all through the fifties they had a lot of house-help, and usually the one bitching loudest was some little girl who'd been hired for part-time and then got fired for forgetting one of the rules three times in a row. She'd be tellin anyone who wanted to listen that Vera Donovan was a mean, sharp-tongued old bat, and crazy as a loon in the bargain. Well, maybe she was crazy and maybe she wasn't, but I can tell you one thing—if you remembered, she didn't give you the

heat. And my way of thinking is this: anyone who can remember who's sleepin with who on all those soap opera stories they show in the afternoon should be able to remember to use Spic n Span in the tubs and put the welcome mats back down facin the right way.

But the sheets, now. That was one thing you didn't *ever* want to get wrong. They had to be hung perfectly even over the lines—so the hems matched, you know—and you had to use six clothespins on each one. Never four; always six. And if you dragged one in the mud, you didn't have to worry about waitin to get something wrong three times. The lines have always been out in the side yard, which is right under her bedroom window. She'd go to that window, year in and year out, and yell at me: "*Six pins, now, Dolores! You mind me, now! Six, not four! I'm counting, and my eyes are just as good now as they ever were!*" She'd—

What, honey?

Oh bosh, Andy—let her alone. That's a fair enough question, and it's one no man would have brains enough to ask.

I'll tell you, Nancy Bannister from Kennebunk, Maine—yes, she *did* have a dryer, a nice big one, but we were forbidden to put the sheets in it unless there was five days' rain in the forecast. "The only sheet worth having on a decent person's bed is a sheet that's been dried out-of-doors," Vera'd say, "because they smell sweet. They catch a little bit of the wind that flapped them, and they hold it, and that smell sends you off to sweet dreams."

She was full of bull about a lot of things, but not about the smell of fresh air in the sheets; about that I

thought she was dead right. Anyone can smell the difference between a sheet that was tumbled in a Maytag and one that was flapped by a good south wind. But there were plenty of winter mornins when it was just ten degrees and the wind was strong and damp and comin from the east, straight in off the Atlantic. On mornins like that I would have given up that sweet smell without a peep of argument. Hangin sheets in deep cold is a kind of torture. Nobody knows what it's like unless they've done it, and once you've done it, you never ever forget it.

You take the basket out to the lines, and the steam comes risin off the top, and the first sheet is warm, and maybe you think to y'self—if you ain't never done it before, that is—"Aw, this ain't so bad." But by the time you've got that first one up, and the edges even, and those six pins on, it's stopped steaming. It's still wet, but now it's cold, too. And your fingers are wet, and *they're* cold. But you go on to the next one, and the next, and the next, and your fingers turn red, and they slow up, and your shoulders ache, and your mouth is cramped from holdin pins in it so your hands are free to keep that befrigged sheet nice and even the whole while, but most of the misery is right there in your fingers. If they'd go numb, that'd be one thing. You almost wish they would. But they just get red, and if there are enough sheets they go beyond that to a pale purple color, like the edges of some lilies. By the time you finish, your hands are really just claws. The worst thing, though, is you know what's gonna happen when you finally get back inside with that empty laundry basket and the heat hits your hands.

They start to tingle, and then they start to throb in the joints—only it's a feelin so deep it's really more like *cryin* than throbbin; I wish I could describe it to you so you'd know, Andy, but I can't. Nancy Bannister there looks like *she* knows, a little bit, anyway, but there is a world of difference between hangin out your warsh on the mainland in winter and hangin it out on the island. When your fingers start to warm up again, it feels like there's a hive of bugs in em. So you rub em all over with some kind of hand lotion and wait for the itch to go away, and you know it don't matter how much store lotion or plain old sheep-dip you rub into your hands; by the end of February the skin is still going to be cracked so bad that it'll break open and bleed if you clench a hard fist. And sometimes, even after you've gotten warm again and maybe even gone to bed, your hands will wake you up in the middle of the night, sobbin with the memory of that pain. You think I'm jokin? You can laugh if you want to, but I ain't, not a bit. You can almost hear em, like little children who can't find their mammas. It comes from deep inside, and you lie there and listen to it, knowin all the time that you'll be goin back outside again just the same, nothin can stop it, and it's all a part of woman's work no man knows about or wants to know about.

And while you were goin through that, hands numb, fingers purple, shoulders achin, snot leakin off the end of y'nose and freezin tight as a tick to your upper lip, she'd more often than not be standin or sittin there in her bedroom window, lookin out at you. Her forehead'd be furrowed and her lips drawed down and her hands workin on each other—all tensed up, she'd be,

like it was some kind of complicated hospital operation instead of just hangin sheets out to dry in the winter wind. You could see her tryin to hold herself back, to keep her big trap shut this time, but after awhile she wouldn't be able to no more and she'd throw up the window and lean out so that cold east wind streamed her hair back, and she'd howl down, "*Six pins! Remember to use six pins! Don't you let the wind blow my good sheets down to the corner of the yard! Mind me, now! You better, because I'm watching, and I'm counting!*"

By the time March came, I'd be dreamin of gettin the hatchet me n the hunky used to chop up kindling for the kitchen stove (until he died, that is; after that I had the job all to myself, lucky me) and hittin that loudmouth bitch a good lick with it right between the eyes. Sometimes I could actually see myself doin it, that's how mad she made me, but I guess I always knew there was a part of her that hated yellin down that way as much as I hated hearin it.

That was the first way she had of bein a bitch—not bein able to help it. It was really worse for her than it was for me, specially after she'd had her bad strokes. There was a lot less warshin to hang out by then, but she was just as crazy on the subject as she'd been before most of the rooms in the house were shut off and most of the guest-beds stripped and the sheets wrapped in plastic and put away in the linen closet.

What made it hard for her was that by 1985 or so, her days of surprisin folks was through—she had to depend on me just to get around. If I wa'ant there to lift her out of bed and set her in her wheelchair, in

bed she stayed. She'd porked up a lot, you see—went from a hundred and thirty or so in the early sixties to a hundred and ninety, and most of the gain was that yellowish, blubbery fat you see on some old people. It hung off her arms and legs and butt like bread-dough on a stick. Some people get thin as jerky in their sundown years, but not Vera Donovan. Dr. Freneau said it was because her kidneys weren't doin their job. I s'pose so, but I had plenty of days when I thought she put on that weight just to spite me.

The weight wasn't all, either; she was halfway to bein blind, as well. The strokes done that. What eyesight she had left came and went. Some days she could see a little bit out her left eye and pretty damned good out of the right one, but most times she said it was like lookin through a heavy gray curtain. I guess you can understand why it drove her crazy, her that was such a one to always keep her eye on everythin. A few times she even cried over it, and you want to believe that it took a lot to make a hard baby like her to cry . . . and even after the years had beat her to her knees, she was still a hard baby.

What, Frank?

Senile?

I dunno for sure, and that's the truth. I don't think so. And if she was, it sure wasn't in the ordinary way old folks go senile. And I'm not just sayin that because if it turns out she was, the judge in charge of probatin her will's apt to use it to blow his nose with. He can wipe his ass with it, for all of me; all I want's to get outta this friggin mess she's landed me in. But I still

gotta say she probably wa'ant *completely* vacant upstairs, not even at the end. A few rooms to rent, maybe, but not completely vacant.

The main reason I say so was she had days when she was almost as sharp as ever. They were usually the same days when she could see a little, and help you to sit her up in bed, or maybe even take those two steps from the bed to the wheelchair instead of having to be hoisted across like a bag of grain. I'd put her in the wheelchair so I could change her bed, and she wanted to be in it so she could go over to her window—the one that looked out on the side yard and the harbor view beyond that. She told me once that she'd go out of her mind for good if she had to lay in bed all day and all night, with nothing but the ceiling and the walls to look at, and I believed her.

She had her confused days, yes—days when she didn't know who I was, and hardly even who *she* was. On those days she was like a boat that's come loose from its moorins, except the ocean she was adrift on was time—she was apt to think it was 1947 in the mornin and 1974 in the afternoon. But she had good days, too. There were less of them as time went on and she kept havin those little strokes—shocks, the old folks call em—but she did have em. Her good days was often my bad ones, though, because she'd get up to all her old bitchery if I let her.

She'd get mean. That was the second way she had of bein a bitch. That woman could be as mean as cat-dirt when she wanted to. Even stuck in a bed most of the time, wearin diapers and rubber pants, she could be a real stinker. The messes she made on cleanin days

is as good an example of what I mean as anything. She didn't make em *every* week, but by God I'll tell you that she made em on Thursdays too often for it to be just a coincidence.

Thursdays was cleanin day at the Donovans'. It's a huge house—you don't have any idear until you're actually wanderin around inside it—but most of it's closed off. The days when there might be half a dozen girls with their hair done up in kerchiefs, polishin here and warshin windows there and dustin cobwebs outta the ceiling corners somewhere else, are twenty years or more in the past. I have walked through those gloomy rooms sometimes, lookin at the furniture swaddled up in dust-sheets, and thought of how the place used to look back in the fifties, when they had their summer parties—there was always different-colored Japanese lanterns on the lawn, how well I remember that!—and I get the funniest chill. In the end the bright colors always go out of life, have you ever noticed that? In the end things always look gray, like a dress that's been warshed too many times.

For the last four years, the open part of the house has been the kitchen, the main parlor, the dinin room, the sun-room that looks out on the pool and the patio, and four bedrooms upstairs—hers, mine, and the two guest-rooms. The guest-rooms weren't heated much in wintertime, but they were kept nice in case her children *did* come to spend some time.

Even in these last few years I always had two girls from town who helped me on cleanin days. There's always been a pretty lively turnover there, but since 1990 or so it's been Shawna Wyndham and Frank's

sister Susy. I couldn't do it without em, but I still do a lot of it m'self, and by the time the girls go home at four on Thursday afternoons, I'm 'bout dead on my feet. There's still a lot to do, though—the last of the ironin, Friday's shoppin list to write out, and Her Nibs' supper to get, accourse. No rest for the wicked, as they say.

Only before *any* of those things, like as not, there'd be some of her bitchery to sort out.

She was regular about her calls of nature most of the time. I'd slip the bedpan under her every three hours, and she'd do a tinkle for me. And on most days there was apt to be a clinker in the pan along with the pee after the noon call.

Except on Thursdays, that is.

Not *every* Thursday, but on the Thursdays when she was bright, I could count on trouble more often than not . . . and on a backache that'd keep me awake until midnight. Even Anacin-3 wouldn't ease it at the end. I've been healthy as a horse most of my life and I'm *still* healthy as a horse, but sixty-five is sixty-five. You can't shake things off the way you once could.

On Thursday, instead of gettin half a bedpan filled with pee at six in the morning, I'd get just a dribble. The same thing at nine. And at noon, instead of some pee and a clinker, there was apt to be nothing at all. I'd know then I *might* be in for it. The only times I absolutely *knew* I was in for it were the times when I hadn't gotten a clinker out of her Wednesday noon, either.

I see you tryin not to laugh, Andy, but that's all right—you let it out if you have to. It wasn't no laugh-

ing matter then, but it's over now, and what you're thinkin ain't nothin but the truth. The dirty old bag had her a shit savings account, and it was like some weeks she banked it in order to collect the interest . . . only I was the one who got all the withdrawals. I got em whether I wanted em or not.

I spent most of my Thursday afternoons runnin upstairs, tryin to catch her in time, and sometimes I even did. But whatever the state of her *eyes* might be, there was nothing wrong with her *ears*, and she knew I never let any of the town girls vacuum the Aubusson rug in the parlor. And when she heard the vacuum cleaner start up in there, she'd crank up her tired old fudge factory and that Shit Account of hers'd start payin dividends.

Then I thought up a way of catchin her. I'd yell to one of the girls that I guessed I'd vacuum the parlor next. I'd yell that even if they was both right next door in the dinin room. I'd turn on the vacuum, all right, but instead of usin it, I'd go to the foot of the stairs and stand there with one foot on the bottom step and my hand on the knob of the newel post, like one of those track fellows all hunkered down waitin for the starter to shoot off his gun and let them go.

Once or twice I went up too soon. That wa'ant no good. It was like a racer gettin disqualified for jumpin the gun. You had to get up there after she had her motor runnin too fast to shut down, but before she'd actually popped her clutch and dumped a load into those big old continence pants she wore. I got pretty good at it. You would, too, if you knew you'd end up hossin a hundred and ninety pounds of old lady around

if you timed it wrong. It was like tryin to deal with a hand grenade loaded with shit instead of high explosives.

I'd get up there and she'd be layin in that hospital bed of hers, face all red, her mouth all screwed up, her elbows diggin into the mattress and her hands balled up in fists, and she'd be goin "*Unnh! Unnnnnhhhh! UNNNNNNNNNHHHH!*" I tell you something—all she needed was a coupla rolls of flypaper danglin down from the ceilin and a Sears catalogue in her lap to look right at home.

Aw, Nancy, quit bitin the insides of y'cheeks—better to let it out n bear the shame than hold it in n bear the pain, as they say. Besides, it *does* have its funny side; shit *always* does. Ask any kid. I c'n even let it be a little funny to me now that it's over, and that's somethin, ain't it? No matter how big a jam I'm in, my time of dealin with Vera Donovan's Shit Thursdays is over.

She'd hear me come in, and mad? She'd be just as mad as a bear with one paw caught in a honey-tree. "What are *you* doing up here?" she'd ask in that hoity-toity way of talking she'd use whenever you caught her gettin up to dickens, like she was still going to Vassar or Holy Oaks or whichever one of the Seven Sisters it was her folks sent her to. "This is *cleaning day*, Dolores! You go on about your business! I didn't ring for you and I don't need you!"

She didn't scare me none. "I think you *do* need me," I'd say. "That ain't Chanel Number Five I smell comin from the direction of your butt, is it?"

Sometimes she'd even try to slap at my hands when I pulled down the sheet and the blanket. She'd be glarin

like she meant to turn me to stone if I didn't leave off and she'd have her lower lip all pooched out like a little kid who don't want to go to school. I never let any of that stop me, though. Not Patricia Claiborne's daughter Dolores. I'd get the sheet down in about three seconds, and it never took much more'n another five to drop her drawers and yank the tapes on those diapers she wore, whether she was slappin my hands or not. Most times she left off doin that after a couple of tries, anyway, because she was caught and we both knew it. Her equipment was so old that once she got it goin, things just had to run their course. I'd slide the bedpan under her just as neat as you please, and when I left to go back downstairs n *really* vacuum the parlor, she was apt to be swearin like a dock walloper—didn't sound a bit like a Vassar girl *then,* let me tell you! Because she knew that time she'd lost the game, you see, and there was nothing Vera hated worse'n that. Even in her dotage, she hated to lose somethin fierce.

Things went on that way for quite awhile, and I started to think I'd won the whole war instead of just a couple of battles. I should have known better.

There came a cleaning day—this was about a year and a half ago—when I was all set and ready to run my race upstairs and catch her again. I'd even got to like it, sort of; it made up for a lot of times in the past when I'd come off second best with her. And I figured she was plannin on a real shit tornado that time, if she could get away with it. All the signs were there, and then some. For one thing, she wasn't just havin a bright *day,* she'd been havin a bright *week*—she'd even asked me that Monday to put the board across the arms of

her chair so she could have a few games of Big Clock solitaire, just like in the old days. And as far as her bowels went, she was havin one hell of a dry spell; she hadn't dropped nothing in the collection plate since the weekend. I figured that particular Thursday she was plannin on givin me her goddam Christmas Club as well as her savins account.

After I took the bedpan out from under her that cleaning day noon and saw it was as dry as a bone, I says to her, "Don't you think you could do something if you tried a little bit harder, Vera?"

"Oh Dolores," she says back, looking up at me with her filmy blue eyes just as innocent as Mary's little lamb, "I've already tried as hard as I can—I tried so hard it hurt me. I guess I am just constipated."

I agreed with her right off. "I guess you are, and if it doesn't clear up soon, dear, I'll just have to feed you a whole box of Ex-Lax to dynamite you loose."

"Oh, I think it'll take care of itself in time," she said, and give me one of her smiles. She didn't have any teeth by then, accourse, and she couldn't wear her lower plate unless she was sittin up in her chair, in case she might cough and pull it down her throat and choke on it. When she smiled, her face looked like an old piece of tree-trunk with a punky knothole in it. "You know me, Dolores—I believe in letting nature take her course."

"I know you, all right," I kind of muttered, turnin away.

"What did you say, dear?" she asks back, so sweet you'd've thought sugar wouldn't melt in her mouth.

"I said I can't just stand around here waitin for you

to go number two," I said. "I got housework. It's cleaning day, you know."

"Oh, *is* it?" she says back, just as if she hadn't known what day it was from the first second she woke up that morning. "Then you go on, Dolores. If I feel the need to move my bowels, I'll call you."

I bet you will, I was thinkin, about five minutes after it happens. But I didn't say it; I just went on back downstairs.

I got the vacuum cleaner out of the kitchen closet, took it into the parlor, and plugged it in. I didn't start it up right away, though; I spent a few minutes dusting first. I had gotten so I could depend on my instincts by then, and I was waiting for somethin inside to tell me the time was right.

When that thing spoke up and said it was, I hollered to Susy and Shawna that I was going to vacuum the parlor. I yelled loud enough so I imagine half the people down in the village heard me right along with the Queen Mother upstairs. I started the Kirby, then went to the foot of the stairs. I didn't give it long that day; thirty or forty seconds was all. I figured she *had* to be hangin on by a thread. So up I went, two stairs at a time, and what do you think?

Nothin!

Not . . . one . . . thing.

Except.

Except the way she was *lookin* at me, that was. Just as calm and as sweet as you please.

"Did you forget somethin, Dolores?" she coos.

"Ayuh," I says back, "I forgot to quit this job five years ago. Let's just stop it, Vera."

"Stop *what,* dear?" she asks, kinda flutterin her eyelashes, like she didn't have the slightest idear what I could be talkin about.

"Let's quit evens, is what I mean. Just tell me straight out—do you need the bedpan or not?"

"I don't," she says in her best, most totally honest voice. "I *told* you that!" And just smiled at me. She didn't say a word, but she didn't have to. Her face did all the talkin that needed to be done. I got you, Dolores, it was sayin. I got you good.

But I wasn't done. I *knew* she was holdin onto one gut-buster of a b.m., and I knew there'd be hell to pay if she got a good start before I could get the bedpan under her. So I went downstairs and stood by that vacuum, and I waited five minutes, and then I ran up *again.* Only that time she didn't smile at me when I came in. That time she was lyin on her side, fast asleep . . . or that was what I thought. I really did. She fooled me good and proper, and you know what they say—fool me once, shame on you; fool me twice, shame on me.

When I went back down the second time, I really *did* vacuum the parlor. When the job was done, I put the Kirby away and went back to check on her. She was sittin up in bed, wide awake, covers thrown back, her rubber pants pushed down to her big old flabby knees and her diapers undone. Had she made a mess? Great God! The bed was full of shit, she was covered with shit, there was shit on the rug, on the wheelchair, on the walls. There was even shit on the curtains. It looked like she musta taken up a handful and *flang* it,

the way kids'll fling mud at each other when they're swimmin in a cowpond.

Was I mad! Mad enough to *spit!*

"Oh, Vera! Oh, you dirty BITCH!" I screamed at her. I never killed her, Andy, but if I was gonna, I would've done it that day, when I saw that mess and smelled that room. I wanted to kill her, all right; no use lyin about *that.* And she just looked at me with that foozled expression she got when her mind was playing tricks on her . . . but I could see the devil dancin in her eyes, and I knew well enough who the trick had been played on that time. Fool me twice, shame on me.

"Who's that?" she asked. "Brenda, is that you, dear? Have the cows got out again?"

"You know there ain't been a cow within three mile of here since 1955!" I hollered. I came across the room, takin great big strides, and that was a mistake, because one of my loafers come down on a turd and I damn near went spang on my back. If I had done, I guess I really might have killed her; I wouldn't have been able to stop myself. Right then I was ready to plow fire and reap brimstone.

"I *dooon't,*" she says, tryin to sound like the poor old pitiful lady she really was on a lot of days. "I *dooo-ooon't!* I can't *see,* and my stomach is *so* upset. I think I'm going to be whoopsy. Is it you, Dolores?"

"Coss it's me, you old bat!" I said, still hollerin at the top of my lungs. "I could just *kill* you!"

I imagine by then Susy Proulx and Shawna Wyndham were standin at the foot of the stairs, gettin an earful, and I imagine you've already talked to em and that

they've got me halfway to hung. No need to tell me one way or the other, Andy; awful open, your face is.

Vera seen she wasn't fooling me a bit, at least not anymore, so she gave up tryin to make me believe she'd gone into one of her bad times and got mad herself in self-defense. I think maybe I scared her a little, too. Lookin back on it, I scared *myself*—but Andy, if you'd seen that room! It looked like dinner-time in hell.

"I guess you'll do it, too!" she yelled back at me. "Someday you really *will*, you ugly, bad-natured old harridan! You'll kill me just like you killed your husband!"

"No, ma'am," I said. "Not exactly. When I get ready to settle *your* hash, I won't bother makin it look like an accident—I'll just shove you out the window, and there'll be one less smelly bitch in the world."

I grabbed her around the middle and h'isted her up like I was Superwoman. I felt it in my back that night, I can tell you, and by the next morning I could hardly walk, I was in such pain. I went to that chiropractor in Machias and he did something to it that made it feel a little better, but it ain't never really been right since that day. Right then I didn't feel a thing, though. I pulled her out of that bed of hers like I was a pissed-off little girl and she was the Raggedy Ann doll I was gonna take it out on. She started to tremble all over, and just knowing that she really *was* scared helped me catch hold of my temper again, but I'd be a dirty liar if I didn't say I was glad she was scared.

"*Ooooouuu!*" she screams. "*Ooouuuu, doooon't! Don't take me over to the window! Don't you throw me out, don't*

you dare! Put me down! You're hurrrting me, Dolores! OOOUUUUU PUT ME DOOOWWWWN!"

"Oh quitcha yappin," I says, and drops her into her wheelchair hard enough to rattle her teeth . . . if she'd had any teeth to rattle, that is. "Lookit the mess you made. And don't try to tell me you can't see it, either, because I know you can. Just look!"

"I'm sorry, Dolores," she says. She started to blubber, but I saw that mean little light dancing way down in her eyes. I saw it the way you can sometimes see fish in clear water when you get up on your knees in a boat and look over the side. "I'm sorry, I didn't mean to make a mess, I was just trying to help." That's what she *always* said when she shit the bed and then squooshed around in it a little . . . although that day was the first time she ever decided to fingerpaint with it as well. *I was just tryin to help, Dolores*—Jesus wept.

"Sit there and shut up," I said. "If you really don't want a fast ride over to that window and an even faster one down to the rock garden, you best mind what I say." And those girls down there at the foot of the stairs, I have no doubt at all, listenin to every word we was sayin. But right then I was too goddam mad to think about anythin like that.

She had enough sense to shut up like I told her, but she looked satisfied, and why not? She'd done what she set out to do—this time it was her who'd won the battle, and made it clear as windowglass that the war wasn't over, not by a long chalk. I went to work, cleaning and settin the place to rights again. It took the best part of two hours, and by the time I was done, my back was singin "Ave Maria."

I told you about the sheets, how that was, and I could see by your faces that you understood some of that. It's harder to understand about her messes. I mean, shit don't cross my eyes. I been wipin it up all my life and the sight of it *never* crossed my eyes. It don't smell like a flower-garden, accourse, and you have to be careful of it because it carries disease just like snot and spit and spilled blood, but it warshes off, you know. Anyone who's ever had a baby knows that shit warshes off. So that wasn't what made it so bad.

I think it was that she was so *mean* about it. So *sly* about it. She bided her time, and when she got a chance, she made the worst mess she could, and she did it just as *fast* as she could, because she knew I wouldn't give her long. She did that nasty thing on purpose, do you see what I'm gettin at? As far as her fogged-in brain would let her, she *planned it out*, and that weighed on my heart and darkened my outlook while I was cleanin up after her. While I was strippin the bed; while I was takin the shitty mattress pad and the shitty sheets and the shitty pillowslips down to the laundry chute; while I was scrubbin the floor, and the walls, and the windowpanes; while I was takin down the curtains and puttin up fresh ones; while I was makin her bed again; while I was grittin my teeth n tryin to keep my back locked in place while I cleaned her up n got a fresh nightgown on her n then hossed her outta the chair and back into bed again (and her not helpin a bit but just lollin there in my arms, dead weight, although I know damn well that was one of the days when she *could* have helped, if she'd wanted to); while I was warshin the floor; while I was warshin off her goddam wheelchair, and really havin t'scrub by then because the stuff was dried on—while I was doin all that, my heart was low and my outlook was darkened. She knew it, too.

She knew it and it made her happy.

When I went home that night I took some Anacin-3 for my aching back and then I went to bed and I curled up in a little ball even though that hurt my back, too, and I cried and cried and cried. It seemed like I couldn't stop. Never—at least since the old business with Joe—have I felt so downhearted and hopeless. Or so friggin *old.*

That was the second way she had of bein a bitch—by bein mean.

What say, Frank? Did she do it again?

You're damned tooting. She did it again the next week, and the week after that. It wasn't as bad as that first adventure either time, partly because she wasn't able to save up such a dividend, but mostly because I was prepared for it. I went to bed crying again after the second time it happened, though, and as I lay there in bed feeling that misery way down low in my back, I made up my mind to quit. I didn't know what'd happen to her or who would take care of her, but right then I didn't care a fiddlyfuck. As far as I was concerned, she could starve to death layin in her own shitty bed.

I was still crying when I fell off to sleep, because the idear of quittin—of her gettin the best of me—made me feel worse'n ever, but when I woke up, I felt good. I guess it's true how a person's mind doesn't go to sleep even if a person thinks it does; it just goes on thinkin,

and sometimes it does an even better job when the person in charge isn't there to frig it up with the usual run of chatter that goes on in a body's head—chores to do, what to have for lunch, what to watch on TV, things like that. It must be true, because the *reason* I felt so good was that I woke up knowin how she was foolin me. The only reason I hadn't seen it before was because I was apt to underestimate her—ayuh, even me, and I knew how sly she could be from time to time. And once I understood the trick, I knew what to do about it.

It hurt me to know I'd have to trust one of the Thursday girls to vacuum the Aubusson—and the idear of Shawna Wyndham doin it gave me what my grampa used to call the shiverin hits. You know how gormy she is, Andy—all the Wyndhams are gormy, accourse, but she's got the rest of em beat seven ways to downtown. It's like she grows bumps right out of her body to knock things over with when she goes by em. It ain't her fault, it's somethin in the blood, but I couldn't bear thinkin of Shawna chargin around in the parlor, with all of Vera's carnival glass and Tiffany just beggin to be knocked over.

Still, I had to do *somethin*—fool me twice, shame on me—and luckily there was Susy to fall back on. She wa'ant no ballerina, but it was her vacuumed the Aubusson for the next year, and she never broke a thing. She's a good girl, Frank, and I can't tell you how glad I was to get that weddin announcement from her, even if the fella was from away. How are they doin? What do you hear?

Well, that's fine. *Fine.* I'm glad for her. I don't s'pose

she's got a bun in the oven yet, does she? These days it seems like folks wait until they're almost ready for the old folks' home before they—

Yes, Andy, I *will!* I just wish you'd remember it's my *life* I'm talkin about here—my goddam *life!* So why don't you just flop back in that big old chair of yours and put your feet up and relax? If you keep pushin that way, you're gonna give y'self a rupture.

Anyway, Frank, you give her my best, and tell her she just about saved Dolores Claiborne's life in the summer of '91. You c'n give her the inside story about the Thursday shitstorms n how I stopped em. I never told em exactly what was goin on; all they knew for sure was that I was buttin heads with Her Royal Majesty. I see now I was *ashamed* to tell em what was goin on. I guess I don't like gettin beat any more than Vera did.

It was the sound of the vacuum, you see. *That* was what I realized when I woke up that mornin. I told you there was nothin wrong with her *ears,* and it was the sound of the vacuum that told her if I was really doin the parlor or standin at the foot of the stairs, on my mark. When a vacuum cleaner is sittin in one spot, it only makes one sound, you see. Just *zoooooooo*, like that. But when you're vacuumin a rug, it makes two sounds, and they go up and down in waves. *WHOOP*, that's when you push it out. And *zoop*, that's when you pull it back to you for another stroke. *WHOOP-zoop, WHOOP-zoop, WHOOP-zoop.*

Quit scratchin your head, you two, and look at the smile Nancy's wearin. All a body'd have to do to know which of you has spent some time runnin a vacuum

cleaner is look at your faces. If you really feel like it's that important, Andy, try it for yourself. You'll hear it right off, though I imagine Maria'd just about drop dead if she came in and saw you vacuumin the livin-room rug.

What I realized that mornin was that she'd stopped just listenin for when the vacuum cleaner started runnin, because she'd realized that wasn't good enough anymore. She was listenin to see if the sound went up and down like it does when a vacuum's actually workin. She wouldn't pull her dirty little trick until she heard that *WHOOP-zoop* wave.

I was crazy to try out my new idear, but I couldn't right away, because she went into one of her bad times right about then, and for quite awhile she just did her business in the bedpan or peed a little in her diapers if she had to. And I started to get scared that this would be the time she wouldn't come back out of it. I know that sounds funny, since she was so much easier to mind when she was confused in her thinkin, but when a person gets a good idear like that, they kinda want to take it for a test-drive. And you know, I felt *somethin* for that bitch besides wanting to throttle her. After knowin her over forty years, it'd be goddam strange if I didn't. She knitted me an afghan once, you know—this was long before she got really bad, but it's still on my bed, and it's some warm on those February nights when the wind plays up nasty.

Then, about a month or a month and a half after I woke up with my idear, she started to come around again. She'd watch *Jeopardy* on the little bedroom TV

and rag the contestants if they didn't know who was President durin the Spanish-American War or who played Melanie in *Gone With the Wind.* She started all her old globber about how her kids might come n visit her before Labor Day. And, accourse, she pestered to be put in her chair so she could watch me hang the sheets and make sure I used six pins and not just four.

Then there come a Thursday when I pulled the bedpan out from under her at noon dry as a bone and empty as a car salesman's promises. I can't tell you how pleased I was to see that empty bedpan. Here we go, you sly old fox, I thought. Now ain't we gonna see. I went downstairs and called Susy Proulx into the parlor.

"I want *you* to vacuum in here today, Susy," I told her.

"Okay, Missus Claiborne," she said. That's what both of them called me, Andy—what most people on the island call me, s'far's that goes. I never made an issue of it at church or anywhere else, but that's how it is. It's like they think I was married to a fella named Claiborne at some point in my checkered past . . . or maybe I just want to believe most of em don't remember Joe, although I guess there's plenty who do. It don't matter too much, one way or the other, in the end; I guess I am entitled to believe what I want to believe. I was the one married to the bastard, after all.

"I don't mind," she goes on, "but why are you whisperin?"

"Never mind," I said, "just keep your own voice down. And don't you break anything in here, Susan Emma Proulx—don't you dare."

Well, she blushed just as red as the side of the volunteer fire truck; it was actually sorta comical. "How'd you know my middle name was Emma?"

"None of your beeswax," I says. "I've spent donkey's years on Little Tall, and there's no end to the things I know, and the people I know em about. You just be careful of your elbows around the furniture and Missus God's carnival glass vases, especially when you're backin up, and you won't have a thing to worry about."

"I'll be extra careful," she said.

I turned the Kirby on for her, and then I stepped into the hall, cupped my hands around my mouth, and hollered: "Susy! Shawna! I'm gonna vacuum the parlor now!"

Susy was standin right there, accourse, and I tell you that girl's entire *face* was a question mark. I just kinda flapped my hand at her, tellin her to go on about her business and never mind me. Which she did.

I tiptoed over to the foot of the stairs n stood in my old place. I know it's silly, but I ain't been so excited since my Dad took me huntin for the first time when I was twelve. It was the same kind of feelin, too, with your heart beatin hard and kinda *flat* in your chest and neck. The woman had dozens of valuable antiques as well as all that expensive glass in the parlor, but I never spared a thought to Susy Proulx in there, whirlin and twirlin amongst them like a dervish. Do you believe it?

I made myself stay where I was as long as I could, about a minute and a half, I think. Then I dashed. And when I popped into her room, there she was, face red, eyes all squinched down into slits, fists balled up, goin

"*Unhh! Unhhhhh! UNHHHHH!*" Her eyes flew open in a hurry when she heard the bedroom door bang open, though. Oh, I wish I'd had a camera—it was priceless.

"Dolores, you get right back out of here!" she kinda squeaks. "I'm tryin to have a nap, and I can't do it if you're going to come busting in here like a bull with a hard-on every twenty minutes!"

"Well," I said, "I'll go, but first I think I'll put this old fanny-pan under you. From the smell, I'd say a little scare was about all you needed to take care of your constipation problem."

She slapped at my hands and cussed me—she could cuss somethin fierce when she wanted to, and she wanted to every time somebody crossed her—but I didn't pay much attention. I got the bedpan under her slick as a whistle, and, like they say, everythin came out all right. When it was done, I looked at her and she looked at me and neither one of us had to say a thing. We knew each other of old, you see.

There, you nasty old quim, I was sayin with my face. I've caught up with you again, and how do you like it?

Not much, Dolores, she was sayin with hers, but that's all right; just because you've *got* caught up doesn't mean you'll *stay* caught up.

I did, though—that time I did. There were a few more little messes, but never again anythin like the time I told you about, when there was even shit on the curtains. That was really her last hurrah. After that, the times when her mind was clear got fewer and fewer, and when they came, they were short. It saved my achin back, but it made me sad, too. She was a pain, but she

was one I'd gotten used to, if you see what I mean.

Could I have another glass of water, Frank?

Thank you. Talkin's thirsty work. And if you decide to let that bottle of Gentleman Jim Beam out of your desk for a little fresh air, Andy, *I'll* never tell.

No? Well, that's about what I expected from the likes of you.

Now—where was I?

Oh, I know. About how she was. Well, the third way she had of bein a bitch was the worst. She was a bitch because she was a sad old lady who had nothin to do but die in an upstairs bedroom on an island far from the places and the people she'd known most of her life. That was bad enough, but she was losin her mind while she did it . . . and there was part of her that knew the rest of her was like an undercut riverbank gettin ready to slide down into the stream.

She was lonely, you see, and that I didn't understand—I never understood why she threw over her whole life to come out to the island in the first place. At least not until yesterday. But she was scared, too, and I could understand that just fine. Even so, she had a horrible, scary kind of strength, like a dyin queen that won't let go of her crown even at the end; it's like God Himself has got to pry it loose a finger at a time.

She had her good days and her bad ones—I told you that. What I call her fits always happened in between, when she was changin from a few days of bein bright to a week or two of bein fogged in, or from a week or two of bein fogged in to a time of bein bright again. When she was changin, it was like she was

nowhere . . . and part of her knew that, too. That was the time when she'd have her hallucinations.

If they *were* all hallucinations. I'm not so sure about that as I used to be. Maybe I'll tell you that part and maybe I won't—I'll just have to see how I feel when the time comes.

I guess they didn't all come on Sunday afternoons or in the middle of the night; I guess it's just that I remember those ones the best because the house was so quiet and it would scare me so when she started screaming. It was like havin somebody throw a bucket of ice-cold water over you on a hot summer's day; there never was a time I didn't think my heart would stop when her screams began, and there never was a time I didn't think I'd come into her room and find her dyin. The things she was ascairt of never made sense, though. I mean, I knew she was scared, and I had a pretty good idear what she was scared *of*, but never *why.*

"The wires!" she'd be screamin sometimes when I went in. She'd be all scrunched up in bed, her hands clutched together between her boobs, her punky old mouth drawn up and tremblin; she'd be as pale as a ghost, and the tears'd be runnin down the wrinkles under her eyes. "The *wires*, Dolores, stop the *wires!*" And she'd always point at the same place . . . the baseboard in the far corner.

Wasn't nothing there, accourse, except there was to *her.* She seen all these wires comin out of the wall and scratchin across the floor toward her bed—at least that's what I *think* she seen. What I'd do was run downstairs and get one of the butcher-knives off the kitchen

rack, and then come back up with it. I'd kneel down in the corner—or closer to the bed if she acted like they'd already progressed a fairish way—and pretend to chop them off. I'd do that, bringin the blade down light and easy on the floor so I wouldn't scar that good maple, until she stopped cryin.

Then I'd go over to her and wipe the tears off her face with my apron or one of the Kleenex she always kept stuffed under her pillow, and I'd kiss her a time or two and say, "There, dear—they're gone. I chopped off every one of those pesky wires. See for yourself."

She'd look (although at these times I'm tellin you about she couldn't really see nothing), and she'd cry some more, like as not, and then she'd hug me and say, "Thank you, Dolores. I thought this time they were going to get me for sure."

Or sometimes she'd call me Brenda when she thanked me—she was the housekeeper the Donovans had in their Baltimore place. Other times she'd call me Clarice, who was her sister and died in 1958.

Some days I'd get up there to her room and she'd be half off the bed, screamin that there was a snake inside her pillow. Other times she'd be settin up with the blankets over her head, hollerin that the windows were magnifyin the sun and it was gonna burn her up. Sometimes she'd swear she could already feel her hair frizzin. Didn't matter if it was rainin, or foggier'n a drunk's head outside; she was bound and determined the sun was gonna fry her alive, so I'd pull down all the shades and then hold her until she stopped cryin. Sometimes I held her longer, because even after she'd

gotten quiet I could feel her tremblin like a puppy that's been mistreated by mean kids. She'd ask me over and over again to look at her skin and tell her if it had blistered anywhere. I'd tell her over and over again that it hadn't, and after a little of that she'd sometimes go to sleep. Other times she wouldn't—she'd just fall into a stupor, mutterin to people who weren't there. Sometimes she'd talk French, and I don't mean that *parley-voo* island French, either. She and her husband loved Paris and went there every chance they got, sometimes with the kids and sometimes by themselves. Sometimes she talked about it when she was feelin perky—the cafés, the nightclubs, the galleries, and the boats on the Seine—and I loved to listen. She had a way with words, Vera did, and when she really talked a thing up, you could almost see it.

But the worst thing—what she was scared of most of all—were nothing but dust bunnies. You know what I mean: those little balls of dust that collect under beds and behind doors and in corners. Look sort of like milkweed pods, they do. I knew it was them even when she couldn't say it, and most times I could get her calmed down again, but why she was so scared of a bunch of ghost-turds—what she really thought they were—that I don't know, although I once got an idear. Don't laugh, but it come to me in a dream.

Luckily, the business of the dust bunnies didn't come up so often as the sun burnin her skin or the wires in the corner, but when that *was* it, I knew I was in for a bad time. I knew it was dust bunnies even if it was the middle of the night and I was in my room, fast

asleep with the door closed, when she started screamin. When she got a bee in her bonnet about the other things—

What, honey?

Oh, wasn't I?

No, you don't need to move your cute little recorder any closer; if you want me to talk up, I will. Most generally I'm the bawliest bitch you ever run across —Joe used to say he wished for cotton to stick in his ears every time I was in the house. But the way she was about the dust bunnies gave me the creeps, and if my voice dropped I guess that just proves they still do. Even with her dead, they still do. Sometimes I used to scold her about it. "Why do you want to get up to such foolishness, Vera?" I'd say. But it wa'ant foolishness. Not to Vera, at least. I thought more'n once that I knew how she'd finally punch out—she'd scare herself to death over those friggin dust bunnies. And that ain't so far from the truth, either, now that I think about it.

What I started to say was that when she got a bee in her bonnet about the other things—the snake in the pillowslip, the sun, the wires—she'd scream. When it was the dust bunnies, she'd *shriek.* Wasn't even words in it most times. Just shriekin so long and loud it put ice-cubes in your heart.

I'd run in there and she'd be yankin at her hair or harrowin her face with her fingernails and lookin like a witch. Her eyes'd be so big they almost looked like softboiled eggs, and they were always starin into one corner or the other.

Sometimes she was able to say "*Dust bunnies, Dolores! Oh my God, dust bunnies!*" Other times she could

only cry and gag. She'd clap her hands over her eyes for a second or two, but then she'd take em back down. It was like she couldn't bear to look, but couldn't bear *not* to look, either. And she'd start goin at her face with her fingernails again. I kep em clipped just as short as I could, but she still drew blood lots of times, and I wondered every time it happened how her heart could stand the plain terror of it, as old and fat's she was.

One time she fell right out of bed and just lay there with one leg twisted under her. Scared the bejesus out of me, it did. I ran in and there she was on the floor, beatin her fists on the boards like a kid doin a tantrum and screamin fit to raise the roof. That was the only time in all the years I did for her that I called Dr. Freneau in the middle of the night. He came over from Jonesport in Collie Violette's speedboat. I called him because I thought her leg was broken, *had* to be, the way it was bent under her, and she'd almost surely die of the shock. But it wasn't—I don't know *how* it wasn't, but Freneau said it was just sprained—and the next day she slipped into one of her bright periods again and didn't remember a thing of it. I asked her about the dust bunnies a couple of times when she had the world more or less in focus, and she looked at me like I was crazy. Didn't have the slightest idear what I was talkin about.

After it happened a few times, I knew what to do. As soon as I heard her shriekin that way, I was up from bed and out my door—my bedroom's only two doors down from hers, you know, with the linen closet in between. I kep a broom propped in the hall with the dustpan poked onto the end of the handle ever since

she had her first hissy over the dust bunnies. I'd go peltin into her room, wavin the broom like I was tryin to flag down a goddam mail-train, screamin myself (it was the only way I could make myself heard).

"I'll get em, Vera!" I'd shout. *"I'll get em! Just hold the friggin phone!"*

And I'd sweep at whatever corner she was starin into, and then I'd do the other one for good measure. Sometimes she'd calm down after that, but more often she'd start hollerin that there were more under the bed. So I'd get down on my hands n knees and make like I was sweepin under there, too. Once the stupid, scared, pitiful old dub almost fell right outta bed on top of me, tryin to lean over and look for herself. She prob'ly woulda squashed me like a fly. What a comedy *that* woulda been!

Once I'd swept everyplace that had her scared, I'd show her my empty dustpan and say, "There, dear—see? I got every one of those prickish things."

She'd look into the dustpan first, and then she'd look up at me, tremblin all over, her eyes so drowned in her own tears that they swam like rocks when you look down and see em in a stream, and she'd whisper, "Oh, Dolores, they're so *gray!* So *nasty!* Take them away. Please take them away!"

I'd put the broom and the empty dustpan back outside my door, handy for action next time, and then I'd go back in to soothe her as best I could. To soothe myself, as well. And if you think I didn't need a little soothin, *you* try wakin up all alone in a big old museum like that in the middle of the night, with the wind screamin outside and an old crazy woman screamin

inside. My heart'd be goin like a locomotive and I couldn't hardly get my breath . . . but I couldn't let her see how I was, or she'd have started to doubt me, and wherever would we have gone from there?

What I'd do most times after those set-to's was brush her hair—it was the thing that seemed to calm her down the quickest. She'd moan n cry at first, and sometimes she'd reach out her arms and hug me, pushin her face against my belly. I remember how hot her cheeks and forehead always were after she threw one of her dust bunny wingdings, and how sometimes she'd wet my nightie right through with her tears. Poor old woman! I don't guess any of us here know what it is to be that old, and to have devils after you you can't explain, even to yourself.

Sometimes not even half an hour with the hairbrush would do the trick. She'd keep lookin past me into the corner, and every so often she'd catch her breath n whimper. Or she'd flap her hand at the dark under the bed and then kinda snatch it back, like she expected somethin under there to try n bite it. Once or twice even *I* thought I saw somethin movin under there, and I had to clamp my mouth shut to keep from screamin myself. All I saw was just the movin shadow of her own hand, accourse, *I* know that, but it shows what a state she got me in, don't it? Ayuh, even me, and I'm usually just as hardheaded as I am loudmouthed.

On those times when nothin else'd do, I'd get into bed with her. Her arms would creep around me and hold onto my sides and she'd lay the side of her head down on what's left of my bosom, and I'd put *my* arms around *her* and just hold her until she drifted off. Then

I'd creep out of bed, real slow and easy, so as not to wake her up, and go back to my own room. There was a few times I didn't even do that. Those times—they always came when she woke me up in the middle of the night with her yowlin—I fell asleep with her.

It was on one of those nights that I dreamed about the dust bunnies. Only in the dream I wasn't me. I was *her,* stuck in that hospital bed, so fat I couldn't even hardly turn over without help, and my cooze burnin way down deep from the urinary infection that wouldn't never really go away on account of how she was always damp down there, and had no real resistance to anything. The welcome mat was out for any bug or germ that came along, you might say, and it was always turned around the right way.

I looked over in the corner, and what I saw was this thing that looked like a head made out of dust. Its eyes were all rolled up and its mouth was open and full of long snaggly dust-teeth. It started comin toward the bed, but slow, and when it rolled around to the face side again the eyes were lookin right at me and I saw it was Michael Donovan, Vera's husband. The second time the face come around, though, it was *my* husband. It was Joe St. George, with a mean grin on his face and a lot of long dust-teeth all snappin. The third time it rolled around it wasn't nobody I knew, but it was *alive*, it was *hungry*, and it meant to roll all the way over to where I was so it could eat *me.*

I woke myself up with such a godawful jerk that I almost fell out of bed myself. It was early mornin, with the first sun layin across the floor in a stripe. Vera was still sleepin. She'd drooled all over my arm, but at first

I didn't even have the strength to wipe it off. I just laid there trembling, all covered with sweat, tryin to make myself believe I was really awake and things was really all right—the way you do, y'know, after a really bad nightmare. And for a second there I could still see that dust-head with its big empty eyes and long dusty teeth layin on the floor beside the bed. That's how bad the dream was. Then it was gone; the floor and the corners of the room were as clean and empty as always. But I've always wondered since then if maybe she didn't *send* me that dream, if I didn't see a little of what *she* saw those times when she screamed. Maybe I picked up a little of her fear and made it my own. Do you think things like that ever happen in real life, or only in those cheap newspapers they sell down to the grocery? I dunno . . . but I know that dream scared the bejesus out of me.

Well, never mind. Suffice it to say that screamin her friggin head off on Sunday afternoons and in the middle of the night was the third way she had of bein a bitch. But it was a sad, sad thing, all the same. *All* her bitchiness was sad at the bottom, although that didn't stop me from sometimes wantin to spin her head around like a spool on a spindle, and I think anybody but Saint Joan of Friggin Arc woulda felt the same. I guess when Susy and Shawna heard me yellin that day that I'd like to kill her . . . or when other people heard me . . . or heard us yellin mean things at each other . . . well, they must have thought I'd hike up my skirts and tapdance on her grave when she finally give over. And I imagine you've heard from some of em yesterday and today, haven't you, Andy? No need to answer; all the answer

I need's right there on your face. It's a regular billboard. Besides, I know how people love to talk. They talked about me n Vera, and there was a country-fair amount of globber about me n Joe, too—some before he died and even more after. Out here in the boondocks about the most int'restin thing a person can do is die sudden, did you ever notice that?

So here we are at Joe.

I been dreadin this part, and I guess there's no use lyin about it. I already told you I killed him, so that's over with, but the hard part is still all ahead: how . . . and why . . . and when it had to be.

I been thinkin about Joe a lot today, Andy—more about him than about Vera, truth to tell. I kep tryin to remember just why I married him in the first place, for one thing, and at first I couldn't do it. After awhile I got into a kind of panic about it, like Vera when she'd get the idear there was a snake inside her pillowslip. Then I realized what the trouble was—I was lookin for the love part, like I was one of those foolish little girls Vera used to hire in June and then fire before the summer was halfway done because they couldn't keep to her rules. I was lookin for the love part, and there was precious little of that even back in 1945, when I was eighteen and he was nineteen and the world was new.

You know the only thing that come to me while I was out there on the steps today, freezin my tookus off and tryin to remember about the love part? He had a nice forehead. I sat near him in study-hall back when we was in high school together—during World War II, that was—and I remember his forehead, how smooth it looked, without a single pimple on it. There were some on his cheeks and chin, and he was prone to blackheads on the sides of his nose, but his forehead looked as smooth as cream. I remember wantin to touch it . . . *dreamin* about touchin it, to tell the truth; wantin to see if it was as smooth as it looked. And when he asked me to the Junior-Senior Prom, I said yes, and I got my chance to touch his forehead, and it was every bit as smooth as it looked, with his hair goin back from it in these nice smooth waves. Me strokin his hair and his smooth forehead in the dark while the band inside the ballroom of The Samoset Inn played "Moonlight Cocktail" . . . After a few hours of sittin on those damned rickety steps and shiverin, *that* came back to me, at least, so you see there was a *little* something there, after all. Accourse I found m'self touchin a lot more than just his forehead before too many more weeks had passed, and that was where I made my mistake.

Now let's get one thing straight—I ain't tryin to say I ended up spendin the best years of my life with that old rumpot just because I liked the look of his forehead in period seven study-hall when the light came slantin in on it. Shit, no. But I *am* tryin to tell you that's all the love part I was able to remember today, and that makes me feel bad. Sittin out on the stairs today by the East Head, thinkin over those old times . . . that was damned hard work. It was the first time I saw that I might have sold myself cheap, and maybe I did it because I thought cheap was the best the likes of me could expect to get for herself. I *know* it was the first time I dared to think that I deserved to be loved more'n

Joe St. George could love anybody (except himself, maybe). You mightn't think a hard-talking old bitch like me believes in love, but the truth is it's just about the only thing I *do* believe in.

It didn't have much to do with why I married him, though—I got to tell you that straight out. I had six weeks' worth of baby girl in my belly when I told him I did n I would, until death do us part. And that was the smartest part of it . . . sad but true. The rest of it was all the usual stupid reasons, and one thing I've learned in my life is that stupid reasons make stupid marriages.

I was tired of fightin with my mother.

I was tired of bein scolded by my father.

All my friends was doin it, they was gettin homes of their own, and I wanted to be a grownup like them; I was tired of bein a silly little girl.

He said he wanted me, and I believed him.

He said he loved me, and I believed that, too . . . and after he'd said it n asked me if I felt the same for him, it only seemed polite to say I did.

I was scared of what would happen to me if I didn't—where I'd have to go, what I'd have to do, who'd look after my baby while I was doin it.

All that's gonna look pretty silly if you ever write it up, Nancy, but the silliest thing is I know a dozen women who were girls I went to school with who got married for those same reasons, and most of them are still married, and a good many of em are only holdin on, hopin to outlive the old man so they can bury him and then shake his beer-farts out of the sheets forever.

By 1952 or so I'd pretty well forgotten his forehead,

and by 1956 I didn't have much use for the rest of him either, and I guess I'd started hatin him by the time Kennedy took over from Ike, but I never had a thought of killing him until later. I thought I'd stay with him because my kids needed a father, if for no other reason. Ain't that a laugh? But it's the truth. I swear it is. And I swear somethin else as well: if God gave me a second chance, I'd kill him again, even if it meant hellfire and damnation forever . . . which it probably does.

I guess everybody on Little Tall who ain't a johnny-come-lately knows I killed him, and most of em prob'ly think they know why—because of the way he had of usin his hands on me. But it wasn't his hands on *me* that brought him to grief, and the simple truth is that, no matter what people on the island might have thought at the time, he never hit me a single lick during the last three years of our marriage. I cured him of *that* foolishness in late 1960 or early '61.

Up until then, he hit me quite a lot, yes. I can't deny it. And I stood for it—I can't deny that, either. The first time was the second night of the marriage. We'd gone down to Boston for the weekend—that was our honeymoon—and stayed at the Parker House. Hardly went out the whole time. We was just a couple of country mice, you know, and afraid we'd get lost. Joe said he was damned if he was gonna spend the twenty-five dollars my folks'd given us for mad-money on a taxi ride just because he couldn't find his way back to the hotel. Gorry, wa'ant that man dumb! Of course I was, too . . . but one thing Joe had that I didn't (and I'm glad of it, too) was that everlastin suspicious nature of his. He had the idear the whole human race was out

to do him dirty, Joe did, and I've thought plenty of times that when he did get drunk, maybe it was because it was the only way he could go to sleep without leavin one eye open.

Well, that ain't neither here nor there. What I set out to tell you was that we went down to the dinin room that Sat'dy night, had a good dinner, and then went back up to our room again. Joe was listin considerably to starboard on the walk down the hall, I remember—he'd had four or five beers with his dinner to go with the nine or ten he'd took on over the course of the afternoon. Once we were inside the room, he stood there lookin at me so long I asked him if he saw anythin green.

"No," he says, "but I seen a man down there in that restaurant lookin up your dress, Dolores. His eyes were just about hangin out on springs. And you *knew* he was lookin, didn't you?"

I almost told him Gary Cooper coulda been sittin in the corner with Rita Hayworth and I wouldn't have known it, and then thought, Why bother? It didn't do any good to argue with Joe when he'd been drinkin; I didn't go into that marriage with my eyes entirely shut, and I'm not gonna try to kid you that I did.

"If there was a man lookin up my dress, why didn't you go over and tell him to shut his eyes, Joe?" I asked. It was only a joke—maybe I was tryin to turn him aside, I really don't remember—but he didn't take it as a joke. That I *do* remember. Joe wasn't a man to take a joke; in fact, I'd have to say he had almost no sense of humor at all. That was something I *didn't* know goin into it with him; I thought back then that a sense

of humor was like a nose, or a pair of ears—that some worked better than others, but everybody had one.

He grabbed me, and turned me over his knee, and paddled me with his shoe. "For the rest of your life, nobody's gonna have any idear what color underwear you've got on but me, Dolores," he said. "Do you hear that? Nobody but me."

I actually thought it was a kind of love-play, him pretendin to be jealous to flatter me—that's what a little ninny *I* was. It was jealousy, all right, but love had nothing to do with it. It was more like the way a dog will put a paw over his bone and growl if you come too near it. I didn't know that then, so I put up with it. Later on I put up with it because I thought a man hittin his wife from time to time was only another part of bein married—not a nice part, but then, cleanin toilets ain't a nice part of bein married, either, but most women have done their fair share of it after the bridal dress and veil have been packed away in the attic. Ain't they, Nancy?

My own Dad used his hands on my Mum from time to time, and I suppose that was where I got the idear that it was all right—just somethin to be put up with. I loved my Dad dearly, and him and her loved each other dearly, but he could be a handsy kind of man when he had a hair layin just right across his ass.

I remember one time, I must have been, oh I'm gonna say nine years old, when Dad came in from hayin George Richards's field over on the West End, and Mum didn't have his dinner on. I can't remember anymore why she didn't, but I remember real well what happened when he came in. He was wearin only his

biballs (he'd taken his workboots and socks off out on the stoop because they were full of chaff), and his face and shoulders was burned bright red. His hair was sweated against his temples, and there was a piece of hay stuck to his forehead right in the middle of the lines that waved across his brow. He looked hot and tired and ready to be pissed off.

He went into the kitchen and there wasn't nothing on the table but a glass pitcher with flowers in it. He turns to Mum and says, "Where's my supper, dummy?" She opened her mouth, but before she could say anythin, he put his hand over her face and pushed her down in the corner. I was standin in the kitchen entry and seen it all. He come walkin toward me with his head lowered and his hair kinda hangin in his eyes—whenever I see a man walkin home that way, tired out from his day of work and his dinner-bucket in his hand, it makes me think of my Dad—and I was some scared. I wanted to get out of his way because I felt he would push me down, too, but my legs was too heavy to move. He never, though. He just took hold of me with his big warm hard hands and set me aside and went out back. He sat down on the choppin block with his hands in his lap and his head hung down like he was lookin at them. He scared the chickens away at first, but they come back after awhile and started peckin all around his shoes. I thought he'd kick out at em, make the feathers fly, but he never done that, either.

After awhile I looked around at my Mum. She was still sittin in the corner. She'd put a dishtowel over her face and was cryin underneath it. Her arms were crossed over her bosom. That's what I remember best

of all, though I don't know why—how her arms were crossed over her bosom like that. I went over and hugged her and she felt my arms around her middle and hugged me back. Then she took the dishtowel off her face and used it to wipe her eyes and told me to go out back and ask Daddy if he wanted a glass of cold lemonade or a bottle of beer.

"Be sure to tell him there's only two bottles of beer," she said. "If he wants more'n that, he better go to the store or not get started at all."

I went out and told him and he said he didn't want no beer but a glass of lemonade would hit the spot. I ran to fetch it. Mum was gettin his supper. Her face was still kinda swole from cryin, but she was hummin a tune, and that night they bounced the bedsprings just like they did most nights. Nothing else was ever said or made of it. That sort of thing was called home correction in those days, it was part of a man's job, and if I thought of it afterward at all, I only thought that my Mum must have needed some or Dad never would have done what he did.

There was a few other times I saw him correct her, but that's the one I remember best. I never saw him hit her with his fist, like Joe sometimes hit me, but once he stropped her across the legs with a piece of wet canvas sailcloth, and that must have hurt like a bastard. I know it left red marks that didn't go away all afternoon.

No one calls it home correction anymore—the term has passed right out of conversation, so far as I can tell, and good riddance—but I grew up with the idear that when women and children step off the straight n nar-

row, it's a man's job to herd them back onto it. I ain't tryin to tell you that just because I grew up with the idear, I thought it was right, though—I won't let myself slip off that easy. I knew that a man usin his hands on a woman didn't have much to do with correction . . . but I let Joe go on doin it to me for a long time, just the same. I guess I was just too tired from keeping house, cleanin for the summer people, raisin m'family, and tryin to clean up Joe's messes with the neighbors to think much about it.

Bein married to Joe . . . aw, shit! What's *any* marriage like? I guess they are all different ways, but there ain't one of em that's what it looks like from the outside, I c'n tell you that. What people see of a married life and what actually goes on inside it are usually not much more than kissin cousins. Sometimes that's awful, and sometimes it's funny, but usually it's like all the other parts of life—both things at the same time.

What people *think* is that Joe was an alcoholic who used to beat me—and probably the kids, too—when he was drunk. They think he finally did it once too often and I punched his ticket for it. It's true that Joe drank, and that he sometimes went to the A.A. meetins over in Jonesport, but he was no more an alcoholic than I am. He'd throw a drunk every four or five months, mostly with trash like Rick Thibodeau or Stevie Brooks—those men really *were* alcoholics—but then he'd leave it alone except for a nip or two when he come in at night. No more than that, because when he had a bottle he liked to make it last. The real alkies I've known in my time, none of em was int'rested in makin a bottle of *anythin* last—not Jim Beam, not Old

Duke, not even derail, which is antifreeze strained through cotton battin. A real drunk is only int'rested in two things: puttin paid to the jug in the hand, and huntin for the one still in the bush.

No, he wasn't an alcoholic, but he didn't mind if people thought he'd *been* one. It helped him get work, especially in the summer. I guess the way people think about Alcoholics Anonymous has changed over the years—I know they talk about it a lot more than they used to—but one thing that hasn't changed is the way people will try to help somebody who claims he's already gone to work helpin himself. Joe spent one whole year not drinkin—or at least not talkin about it when he did—and they had a party for him over in Jonesport. Gave him a cake and a medallion, they did. So when he went for a job one of the summer people needed done, the first thing he'd tell em was that he was a recoverin alcoholic. "If you don't want to hire me because of that, I won't have any hard feelins," he'd say, "but I have to get it off my chest. I been goin to A.A. meetins for over a year now, and they tell us we can't stay sober if we can't be honest."

And then he'd pull out his gold one-year medallion and show it to em, all the while lookin like he hadn't had nothin to eat but humble pie for a month of Sundays. I guess one or two of em just about cried when Joe told em about how he was workin it a day at a time and takin it easy and lettin go and lettin God whenever the urge for a drink hit him . . . which it did about every fifteen minutes, accordin to him. They'd usually fall all over themselves takin him on, and at fifty cents or even a dollar an hour more than they'd intended to

pay, like as not. You'd have thought the gimmick would have fallen flat after Labor Day, but it worked amazin well even here on the island, where people saw him every day and should have known better.

The truth is most of the times Joe hit me, he was cold sober. When he had a skinful, he didn't much mind me at all, one way or the other. Then, in '60 or '61, he come in one night after helpin Charlie Dispenzieri get his boat out of the water, and when he bent over to get a Coke out of the fridge, I seen his britches were split right up the back. I laughed. I couldn't help myself. He didn't say nothin, but when I went over to the stove to check on the cabbage—I was makin a boiled dinner that night, I remember like it was yesterday—he got a chunk of rock maple out of the woodbox and whacked me in the small of the back with it. Oh, that hurt. You know what I mean if anyone's ever hit you in the kidneys. It makes them feel small and hot and so *heavy,* like they're gonna bust loose from whatever holds them where they're supposed to be and they'll just sink, like lead shot in a bucket.

I hobbled as far as the table and sat in one of the chairs. I woulda fallen on the floor if that chair'd been any further away. I just sat there, waitin to see if the pain was gonna pass. I didn't cry, exactly, because I didn't want to scare the kids, but the tears went rollin down my face just the same. I couldn't stop them. They were tears of pain, the kind you can't hold back for anybody or anythin.

"Don't you ever laugh at me, you bitch," Joe says. He slang the stovelength he hit me with back into the

woodbox, then sat down to read the *American.* "You ought to have known better'n that ten year ago."

It was twenty minutes before I could get outta that chair. I had to call Selena to turn down the heat under the veg and the meat, even though the stove wasn't but four steps away from where I was sittin.

"Why didn't you do it, Mommy?" she asked me. "I was watchin cartoons with Joey."

"I'm restin," I told her.

"That's right," Joe says from behind his paper, "she ran her mouth until she got all tuckered out." And he laughed. That did it; that one laugh was all it took. I decided right then he wasn't never going to hit me again, unless he wanted to pay a dear price for it.

We had supper just like usual, and watched the TV just like usual afterward, me and the big kids on the sofa and Little Pete on his father's lap in the big easy-chair. Pete dozed off there, same as he almost always did, around seven-thirty, and Joe carried him to bed. I sent Joe Junior an hour later, and Selena went at nine. I usually turned in around ten and Joe'd sit up until maybe midnight, dozin in and out, watchin a little TV, readin parts of the paper he'd missed the first time, and pickin his nose. So you see, Frank, you're not so bad; some people never lose the habit, even when they grow up.

That night I didn't go to bed when I usually did. I sat up with Joe instead. My back felt a little better. Good enough to do what I had to do, anyway. Maybe I was nervous about it, but if I was, I don't recall. I was mostly waitin for him to doze off, and finally he did.

I got up, went into the kitchen, and got the little cream-pitcher off the table. I didn't go out lookin for that special; it was only there because it was Joe Junior's night to clean off the table and he'd forgotten to put it in the refrigerator. Joe Junior always forgot something—to put away the cream-pitcher, to put the glass top on the butter dish, to fold the bread-wrapper under so the first slice wouldn't get all hard overnight—and now when I see him on the TV news, makin a speech or givin an interview, that's what I'm most apt to think about . . . and I wonder what the Democrats would think if they knew the Majority Leader of the Maine State Senate couldn't never manage to get the kitchen table completely cleared off when he was eleven. I'm proud of him, though, and don't you ever, ever think any different. I'm proud of him even if he *is* a goddam Democrat.

Anyway, he sure managed to forget the right thing that night; it was little but it was heavy, and it felt just right in my hand. I went over to the woodbox and got the short-handled hatchet we kep on the shelf just above it. Then I walked back into the livin room where he was dozin. I had the pitcher cupped in my right hand, and I just brought it down and around and smacked it against the side of his face. It broke into about a thousand pieces.

He sat up pretty pert when I done that, Andy. And you shoulda heard him. Loud? Father God and Sonny Jesus! Sounded like a bull with his pizzle caught in the garden gate. His eyes come wide open and he clapped his hand to his ear, which was already bleedin. There

was little dots of clotted cream on his cheek and in that scraggle down the side of his face he called a sideburn.

"Guess what, Joe?" I says. "I ain't feelin tired anymore."

I heard Selena jump outta bed, but I didn't dare look around. I could have been in hot water if I'd done that—when he wanted to, he could be sneaky-fast. I'd been holdin the hatchet in my left hand, down to my side with my apron almost coverin it. And when Joe started to get up outta his chair, I brought it out and showed it to him. "If you don't want this in your head, Joe, you better sit down again," I said.

For a second I thought he was gonna get up anyway. If he had, that would have been the end of him right then, because I wasn't kiddin. He seen it, too, and froze with his butt about five inches off the seat.

"Mommy?" Selena called from the doorway of her room.

"You go on back to bed, honey," I says, not takin my eyes off Joe for a single second. "Your father n I're havin a little discussion here."

"Is everything all right?"

"Ayuh," I says. "Isn't it, Joe?"

"Uh-huh," he says. "Right as rain."

I heard her take a few steps back, but I didn't hear the door of her room close for a little while—ten, maybe fifteen seconds—and I knew she was standin there and lookin at us. Joe stayed just like he was, with one hand on the arm of his chair and his butt hiked up offa the seat. Then we heard her door close, and that seemed to make Joe realize how foolish he must

look, half in his seat and half out of it, with his other hand clapped over his ear and little clots of cream dribblin down the side of his face.

He sat all the way down and took his hand away. Both it and his ear were full of blood, but his hand wasn't swellin up and his ear was. "Oh bitch, ain't you gonna get a payback," he says.

"Am I?" I told him. "Well then, you better remember this, Joe St. George: what you pay out to me, you are gonna get back double."

He was grinnin at me like he couldn't believe what he was hearin. "Why, I guess I'll just have to kill you, then, won't I?"

I handed over the hatchet to him almost before the words were out of his mouth. It hadn't been in my mind to do it, but as soon as I seen him holdin it, I knew it was the only thing I *coulda* done.

"Go on," I says. "Just make the first one count so's I don't have to suffer."

He looked from me to the hatchet and then back to me again. The look of surprise on his face would have been comical if the business hadn't been so serious.

"Then, once it's done, you better heat up that boiled dinner and help yourself to some more of it," I told him. "Eat til you bust, because you'll be goin to jail and I ain't heard they serve anything good and home-cooked in jail. You'll be over in Belfast to start with, I guess. I bet they got one of those orange suits just your size."

"Shut up, you cunt," he says.

I wouldn't, though. "After that you'll most likely be in Shawshank, and I *know* they don't bring your meals

hot to the table there. They don't let you out Friday nights to play poker with your beerjoint buddies, either. All I ask is that you do it quick and don't let the kids see the mess once it's over."

Then I closed my eyes. I was pretty sure he wouldn't do it, but bein pretty sure don't squeeze much water when it's your life on the line. That's one thing I found out that night. I stood there with my eyes shut, seein nothin but dark and wonderin what it'd feel like, havin that hatchet come carvin through my nose n lips n teeth. I remember thinkin I'd most likely taste the wood-splinters on the blade before I died, and I remember bein glad I'd had it on the grindstone only two or three days before. If he was gonna kill me, I didn't want it to be with a dull hatchet.

Seemed like I stood there like that for about ten years. Then he said, kinda gruff and pissed off, "Are you gonna get ready for bed or just stand there like Helen Keller havin a wet-dream?"

I opened my eyes and saw he'd put the hatchet under his chair—I could just see the end of the handle stickin out from under the flounce. His newspaper was layin on top of his feet in a kind of tent. He bent over, picked it up, and shook it out—tryin to behave like it hadn't happened, none of it—but there was blood pourin down his cheek from his ear and his hands were tremblin just enough to make the pages of the paper rattle a tiny bit. He'd left his fingerprints in red on the front n back pages, too, and I made up my mind to burn the damned thing before he went to bed so the kids wouldn't see it and wonder what happened.

"I'll be gettin into my nightgown soon enough, but

we're gonna have an understandin on this first, Joe."

He looks up and says, all tight-lipped, "You don't want to get too fresh, Dolores. That'd be a bad, *bad* mistake. You don't want to tease me."

"I ain't teasin," I says. "Your days of hittin me are over, that's all I want to say. If you ever do it again, one of us is goin to the hospital. Or to the morgue."

He looked at me for a long, long time, Andy, and I looked back at him. The hatchet was out of his hand and under the chair, but that didn't matter; I knew that if I dropped my eyes before he did, the punches in the neck and the hits in the back wouldn't never end. But at long last he looked down at his newspaper again and kinda muttered, "Make yourself useful, woman. Bring me a towel for my head, if you can't do nothin else. I'm bleedin all over my goddam shirt."

That was the last time he ever hit me. He was a coward at heart, you see, although I never said the word out loud to him—not then and not ever. Doin that's about the most dangerous thing a person can do, I think, because a coward is more afraid of bein discovered than he is of anything else, even dyin.

Of course I knew he had a yellow streak in him; I never would have dared hit him upside the head with that cream-pitcher in the first place I hadn't felt I had a pretty good chance of comin out on top. Besides, I realized somethin as I sat in that chair after he hit me, waitin for my kidneys to stop achin: if I didn't stand up to him then, I probably wouldn't *ever* stand up to him. So I did.

You know, taking the cream-pitcher to Joe was really the easy part. Before I could do it, I had to once n for all rise above the memory of my Dad pushin my Mum down, and of him stroppin the backs of her legs with that length of wet sailcloth. Gettin over those memories was hard, because I dearly loved them both, but in the end I was able to do it . . . prob'ly because I *had* to do it. And I'm thankful I did, if only because Selena ain't never going to have to remember her mother sittin in the corner and bawlin with a dishtowel over her face. My Mum took it when her husband dished it up, but I ain't goin to sit in judgement of either of em. Maybe she had to take it, and maybe he had to dish it up, or be belittled by the men he had to live n work with every day. Times were different back then—most people don't realize *how* different—but that didn't mean I had to take it from Joe just because I'd been enough of a goose to marry him in the first place. There ain't no home correction in a man beating a woman with his fists or a stovelength outta the woodbox, and in the end I decided I wasn't going to take it from the likes of Joe St. George, or from the likes of any man.

There were times when he raised his hand to me, but then he'd think better of it. Sometimes when the hand was up, *wantin* to hit but not quite *darin* to hit, I'd see in his eyes that he was rememberin the cream-pitcher . . . maybe the hatchet, too. And then he'd make like he only raised that hand because his head needed scratchin, or his forehead wipin. That was one lesson he got the first time. Maybe the only one.

There was somethin else come out of the night he hit me with the stovelength and I hit him with the cream-pitcher. I don't like to bring it up—I'm one of those old-fashioned folks that believes what goes on

behind the bedroom door should stay there—but I guess I better, because it's prob'ly part of why things turned out as they did.

Although we were married and livin under the same roof together for the next two years—and it might have been closer to three, I really can't remember—he only tried to take his privilege with me a few times after that. He—

What, Andy?

Accourse I mean he was impotent! What else would I be talkin about, his right to wear my underwear if the urge took him? I never denied him; he just quit bein able to do it. He wasn't what you'd call an every-night sort of man, not even back at the start, and he wasn't one to draw it out, either—it was always pretty much wham, bam, and thank you, ma'am. Still n all, he'd stayed int'rested enough to climb on top once or twice a week . . . until I hit him with the creamer, that is.

Part of it was probably the booze—he was drinkin a lot more durin those last years—but I don't think that was *all* of it. I remember him rollin offa me one night after about twenty minutes of useless puffin and blowin, and his little thing still just hangin there, limp as a noodle. I dunno how long after the night I just told you about this would have been, but I know it was after because I remember layin there with my kidneys throbbin and thinkin I'd get up pretty soon and take some aspirin to quiet them down.

"There," he says, almost cryin, "I hope you're satisfied, Dolores. Are you?"

I didn't say nothing. Sometimes anything a woman says to a man is bound to be the wrong thing.

"*Are* you?" he says. "*Are* you satisfied, Dolores?"

I didn't say nothing still, just laid there and looked up at the ceilin and listened to the wind outside. It was from the east that night, and I could hear the ocean in it. That's a sound I've always loved. It soothes me.

He turned over and I could smell his beer-breath on my face, rank and sour. "Turnin out the light used to help," he says, "but it don't no more. I can see your ugly face even in the dark." He reached out, grabbed my boob, and kinda shook it. "And this," he says. "All floppy and flat as a pancake. Your cunt's even worse. Christ, you ain't thirty-five yet and fuckin you's like fuckin a mudpuddle."

I thought of sayin "If it *was* a mudpuddle you could stick it in soft, Joe, and wouldn't *that* relieve your mind," but I kep my mouth shut. Patricia Claiborne didn't raise any fools, like I told you.

There was some more quiet, I'd 'bout decided he'd said enough mean things to finally send him off to sleep and I was thinkin about slippin out to get my aspirin when he spoke up again . . . and that time, I'm pretty sure he *was* cryin.

"I wish I'd never seen your face," he says, and then he says, "Why didn't you just use that friggin hatchet to whack it off, Dolores? It would have come to the same."

So you see, I wasn't the only one that thought gettin hit with the cream-pitcher—and bein told things was gonna change around the house—might have had some-

thin to do with his problem. I still didn't say nothing, though, just waited to see if he was gonna go to sleep or try to use his hands on me again. He was layin there naked, and I knew the very first place I was gonna go for if he did try. Pretty soon I heard him snorin. I don't know if that was the very last time he tried to be a man with me, but if it wasn't, it was close.

None of his friends got so much as a whiff of these goins-ons, accourse—he sure as hell wasn't gonna tell em his wife'd whopped the bejesus out of him with a creamer and his weasel wouldn't stick its head up anymore, was he? Not him! So when the others'd talk big about how they was handlin their wives, he'd talk big right along with em, sayin how he laid one on me for gettin fresh with my mouth, or maybe for buyin a dress over in Jonesport without askin him first if it was all right to take money out of the cookie jar.

How do I know? Why, because there are times when I can keep my ears open instead of my mouth. I know that's hard to believe, listenin to me tonight, but it's true.

I remember one time when I was workin part-time for the Marshalls—remember John Marshall, Andy, how he was always talkin about buildin a bridge over to the mainland?—and the doorbell rang. I was all alone in the house, and I was hurryin to answer the door and I slipped on a throw-rug and fell hard against the corner of the mantel. It left a great big bruise on my arm, just above the elbow.

About three days later, just when that bruise was goin from dark brown to a kind of yellow-green like they do, I ran into Yvette Anderson in the village. She

was comin out of the grocery and I was goin in. She looked at the bruise on my arm, and when she spoke to me, her voice was just *drippin* with sympathy. Only a woman who's just seen something that makes her happier'n a pig in shit can drip that way. "Ain't men *awful*, Dolores?" she says.

"Well, sometimes they are and sometimes they aren't," I says back. I didn't have the slightest idear what she was talkin about—what I was mostly concerned with was gettin some of the pork chops that were on special that day before they were all gone.

She pats me kinda gentle on the arm—the one that wasn't bruised—and says, "You be strong, now. All things work for the best. I've been through it and I know. I'll pray for you, Dolores." She said that last like she'd just told me she was gonna give me a million dollars and then went on her way upstreet. I went into the market, still mystified. I would have thought she'd lost her mind, except anyone who's ever passed the time of day with Yvette knows she ain't got a whole hell of a lot to lose.

I had my shoppin half done when it hit me. I stood there watchin Skippy Porter weigh my chops, my marketbasket over my arm and my head thrown back, laughin from way down deep inside my belly, the way you do when you know you can't do nothing but let her rip. Skippy looked around at me and says, "You all right, Missus Claiborne?"

"I'm fine," I says. "I just thought of somethin funny." And off I went again.

"I guess you did," Skippy says, and then he went back to his scales. God bless the Porters, Andy; as long as they stay, there'll be at least one family on the island knows how to mind its business. Meantime, I just went on laughin. A few other people looked at me like I'd gone nuts, but I didn't care. Sometimes life is so goddam funny you just *have* to laugh.

Yvette's married to Tommy Anderson, accourse, and Tommy was one of Joe's beer-and-poker buddies in the late fifties and early sixties. There'd been a bunch of them out at our place a day or two after I bruised my arm, tryin to get Joe's latest bargain, an old Ford pick-em-up, runnin. It was my day off, and I brought em all out a pitcher of iced tea, mostly in hopes of keepin em off the suds at least until the sun went down.

Tommy must have seen the bruise when I was pourin the tea. Maybe he asked Joe what happened after I left, or maybe he just remarked on it. Either way, Joe St. George wasn't a fella to let opportunity pass him by—not one like that, at least. Thinkin it over on my way home from the market, the only thing I was curious about was what Joe told Tommy and the others I'd done—forgot to put his bedroom slippers under the stove so they'd be warm when he stepped into em, maybe, or cooked the beans too mushy on Sat'dy night. Whatever it was, Tommy went home and told Yvette that Joe St. George had needed to give his wife a little home correction. And all I'd ever done was bang off the corner of the Marshalls' mantelpiece runnin to see who was at the door!

That's what I mean when I say there's two sides to a marriage—the outside and the inside. People on the island saw me and Joe like they saw most other couples our age: not too happy, not too sad, mostly just goin

along like two hosses pullin a wagon . . . they may not notice each other like they once did, and they may not get along with each other as well as they once did when they *do* notice each other, but they're harnessed side by side n goin down the road as well's they can just the same, not bitin each other, or lollygaggin, or doin any of the other things that draw the whip.

But people aren't hosses, n marriage ain't much like pullin a wagon, even though I know it sometimes looks that way on the outside. The folks on the island didn't know about the cream-pitcher, or how Joe cried in the dark and said he wished he'd never seen my ugly face. Nor was that the worst of it. The worst didn't start until a year or so after we finished our doins in bed. It's funny, ain't it, how folks can look right at a thing and draw a completely wrong conclusion about why it happened. But it's natural enough, as long as you remember that the inside and outside of a marriage aren't usually much alike. What I'm gonna tell you now was on the inside of ours, and until today I always thought it would stay there.

Lookin back, I think the trouble must have really started in '62. Selena'd just started high school over on the mainland. She had come on real pretty, and I remember that summer after her freshman year she got along with her Dad better than she had for the last couple of years. I'd been dreadin her teenage years, foreseein a lot of squabbles between the two of em as she grew up and started questionin his idears and what he saw as his rights over her more and more.

Instead, there was that little time of peace and quiet and good feelins between them, when she'd go out and watch him work on his old clunkers behind the house, or sit beside him on the couch while we were watchin TV at night (Little Pete didn't think much of *that* arrangement, I can tell you) and ask him questions about his day durin the commercials. He'd answer her in a calm, thoughtful way I wasn't used to . . . but I sort of remembered. From high school I remembered it, back when I was first gettin to know him and he was decidin that yes, he wanted to court me.

At the same time this was happenin, she drew a distance away from me. Oh, she'd still do the chores I set her, and sometimes she'd talk about her day at school . . . but only if I went to work and pulled it out of her. There was a coldness that hadn't been there before, and it was only later on that I began to see how everything fit together, and how it all went back to the night she'd come out of her bedroom and seen us there, her Dad with his hand clapped to his ear and blood runnin through the fingers, her Mom standin over him with a hatchet.

He was never a man to let certain kinds of opportunity pass him by, I told you, and this was just more of the same. He'd told Tommy Anderson one kind of story; the one he told his daughter was in a different pew but the same church. I don't think there was anything in his mind at first but spite; he knew how much I loved Selena, and he must have thought tellin her how mean and bad-tempered I was—maybe even how *dangerous* I was—would be a fine piece of revenge. He tried to turn her against me, and while he never really succeeded at that, he did manage to get closer to her than he'd been since she was a little girl. Why not? She was always tender-hearted, Selena was, and I never ran up against a man as good at the poor-me's as Joe was.

He got inside her life, and once he was in there, he must have finally noticed just how pretty she was getting, and decided he wanted somethin more from her than just to have her listen when he talked or hand him the next tool when he was head-down in the engine compartment of some old junk truck. And all the time this was goin on and the changes were happenin, I was runnin around, workin about four different jobs, and tryin to stay far enough ahead of the bills to sock away a little each week for the kids' college educations. I never saw a thing until it was almost too late.

She was a lively, chatty girl, my Selena, and she was always eager to please. When you wanted her to fetch somethin, she didn't walk; she went on the run. As she got older, she'd put supper on the table when I was workin out, and I never had to ask her. She burned some at first and Joe'd carp at her or make fun of her—he sent her cryin into her room more'n once—but he quit doin that around the time I'm tellin you about. Back then, in the spring and summer of 1962, he acted like every pie she made was pure ambrosia even if the crust was like cement, and he'd rave over her meatloaf like it was French cuisine. She was happy with his praise—accourse she was, anyone would have been—but she didn't get all puffed up with it. She wasn't that kind of girl. Tell you one thing, though: when Selena finally left home, she was a better cook on her worst day than I ever was on my best.

When it came to helpin out around the house, a mother never had a better daughter . . . especially a

mother who had to spend most of her time cleanin up other people's messes. Selena never forgot to make sure Joe Junior and Little Pete had their school lunches when they went out the door in the mornin, and she covered their books for em at the start of every year. Joe Junior at least could have done *that* chore for himself, but she never gave him the chance.

She was an honor roll student her freshman year, but she never lost interest in what was goin on around her at home, the way some smart kids do at that age. Most kids of thirteen or fourteen decide anyone over thirty's an old fogey, and they're apt to be out the door about two minutes after the fogies come through it. Not Selena, though. She'd get em coffee or help with the dishes or whatever, then sit down in the chair by the Franklin stove and listen to the grownups talk. Whether it was me with one or two of my friends or Joe with three or four of his, she'd listen. She would have stayed even when he and his friends played poker, if I'd let her. I wouldn't, though, because they talked so foul. That child nibbled conversation the way a mouse'll nibble a cheese-rind, and what she couldn't eat, she stored away.

Then she changed. I don't know just when that change started, but I first saw it not too long after she'd started her sophomore year. Toward the end of September, I'm gonna say.

The first thing I noticed was that she wasn't comin home on the early ferry like she had at the end of most school-days the year before, although that had worked out real well for her—she was able to get her homework finished in her room before the boys showed up,

then do a little cleanin or start supper. Instead of the two o'clock, she was takin the one that leaves the mainland at four-forty-five.

When I asked her about it, she said she'd just decided she liked doin her homework in the study-hall after school, that was all, and gave me a funny little sidelong look that said she didn't want to talk about it anymore. I thought I saw shame in that look, and maybe a lie, as well. Those things worried me, but I made up my mind I wasn't going to push on with it no further unless I found out for sure something was wrong. Talking to her was hard, you see. I'd felt the distance that had come between us, and I had a pretty good idear what it all traced back to: Joe half outta his chair, bleedin, and me standin over him with the hatchet. And for the first time I realized that he'd prob'ly been talkin to her about that, and other things. Puttin his own spin on em, so to speak.

I thought if I chaffed Selena too hard on why she was stayin late at school, my trouble with her might get worse. Every way I thought of askin her more questions came out soundin like *What have you been up to, Selena,* and if it sounded that way to me, a thirty-five-year-old woman, how was it gonna sound to a girl not quite fifteen? It's so hard to talk to kids when they're that age; you have to walk around em on tiptoe, the way you would a jar of nitroglycerine sittin on the floor.

Well, they have a thing called Parents Night not long after school lets in, and I took special pains to get to it. I didn't do as much pussyfootin around with Selena's home-room teacher as I had with Selena herself; I just stepped right up n asked her if she knew any particular

reason why Selena was stayin for the late ferry this year. The home-room teacher said she didn't know, but she guessed it was just so Selena could get her homework done. Well, I thought but didn't say, she was gettin her homework done just fine at the little desk in her room last year, so what's changed? I *might* have said it if I thought that teacher had any answers for me, but it was pretty clear she didn't. Hell, she was probably scat-gone herself the minute the last bell of the day rung.

None of the other teachers were any help, either. I listened to them praise Selena to the skies, which wa'ant hard work for me to do at all, and then I went back home again, feelin no further ahead than I'd been on my way over from the island.

I got a window-seat inside the cabin of the ferry, and watched a boy n girl not much older'n Selena standin outside by the rail, holdin hands and watchin the moon rise over the ocean. He turned to her and said somethin that made her laugh up at him. You're a fool if you miss a chance like that, sonny-boy, I thought, but he didn't miss it—just leaned toward her, took her other hand, and kissed her as nice as you please. Gorry, ain't you foolish, I said to myself as I watched em. Either that or too old to remember what it's like to be fifteen, with every nerve in your body blastin off like a Roman candle all of the day and most of the night. Selena's met a boy, that's all. She's met a boy and they are probably doin their studies together in that room after school. Studyin each other more'n their books, most likely. I was some relieved, I can tell you.

I thought about it over the next few days—one thing

about warshin sheets and ironin shirts and vacuumin rugs, you always have lots of time to think—and the more I thought, the less relieved I was. She hadn't been *talkin* about any boy, for one thing, and it wasn't ever Selena's way to be quiet about what was goin on in her life. She wasn't as open and friendly with me as she'd been before, no, but it wasn't like there was a wall of silence between us, either. Besides, I'd always thought that if Selena fell in love, she'd probably take out an ad in the paper.

The *big* thing—the *scary* thing—was the way her eyes looked to me. I've always noticed that when a girl's crazy about some boy, her eyes are apt to get so bright it's like someone turned on a flashlight behind there. When I looked for that light in Selena's eyes, it wasn't there . . . but that wasn't the bad part. The light that'd been there before had gone out of em, too—*that* was the bad part. Lookin into her eyes was like lookin at the windows of a house where the people have left without rememberin to pull down the shades.

Seein that was what finally opened *my* eyes, and I began to notice all sorts of things I should have seen earlier—*would* have seen earlier, I think, if I hadn't been workin so hard, and if I hadn't been so convinced Selena was mad at me for hurtin her Dad that time.

The first thing I saw was that it wasn't just me anymore—she'd drawn away from Joe, too. She'd stopped goin out to talk to him when he was workin on one of his old junks or somebody's outboard motor, and she'd quit sittin beside him on the couch at night to watch TV. If she stayed in the living room, she'd sit in the rocker way over by the stove with a piece of

knittin in her lap. Most nights she didn't stay, though. She'd go in her room and shut the door. Joe didn't seem to mind, or even to notice. He just went back to his easy-chair, holdin Little Pete on his lap until it was time for Pete to go to bed.

Her hair was another thing—she didn't warsh it every day like she used to. Sometimes it looked almost greasy enough to fry eggs in, and that wasn't like Selena. Her complexion was always so pretty—that nice peaches n cream skin she prob'ly got from Joe's side of the family tree—but that October pimples sprang up on her face like dandelions on the town common after Memorial Day. Her color was off, and her appetite, too.

She still went to see her two best friends, Tanya Caron and Laurie Langill, once in awhile, but not anywhere near as much as she had in junior high. That made me realize neither Tanya nor Laurie had been over to our house since school let back in . . . and maybe not durin the last month of the summer vacation, neither. That scared me, Andy, and it made me lean in for an even closer look at my good girl. What I saw scared me even more.

The way she'd changed her clothes, for instance. Not just one sweater for another, or a skirt for a dress; she'd changed her whole *style* of dressin, and all the changes were bad. You couldn't see her shape anymore, for one thing. Instead of wearin skirts or dresses to school, she was mostly wearin A-line jumpers, and they was all too big for her. They made her look fat, and she wasn't.

At home she'd wear big baggy sweaters that came

halfway to her knees, and I never saw her out of her jeans and workboots. She'd put some ugly rag of a scarf around her head whenever she went out, somethin so big it'd overhang her brow and make her eyes look like two animals peerin out of a cave. She looked like a tomboy, but I thought she'd put paid to that when she said so-long to twelve. And one night, when I forgot to knock on her door before I went into her room, she just about broke her legs gettin her robe offa the closet door, and she was wearin a slip—it wasn't like she was bollicky bareass or nothin.

But the worst thing was that she didn't talk much anymore. Not just to me; considerin the terms we were on, I coulda understood that. She pretty much quit talkin to *everybody,* though. She'd sit at the supper-table with her head down and the long bangs she'd grown hangin in her eyes, and when I tried to make conversation with her, ask her how her day had gone at school and things like that, all I'd get back was "Umkay" and "Guesso" instead of the blue streak she used to talk. Joe Junior tried, too, and run up against the same stone wall. Once or twice he looked at me, kinda puzzled. I just shrugged. And as soon as the meal was over and the dishes was warshed, out the door or up to her room she'd go.

And, God help me, the first thing I thought of after I decided it wasn't a boy was marijuana . . . and don't you give me that look, Andy, like I don't know what I'm talkin about. It was called reefer or maryjane instead of pot in those days, but it was the same stuff and there was plenty of people from the island willin to move it around if the price of lobsters went down . . .

or even if it didn't. A lot of reefer came in through the coastal islands back then, just like it does now, and some of it stayed. There was no cocaine, which was a blessing, but if you wanted to smoke pot, you could always find some. Marky Benoit had been arrested by the Coast Guard just that summer—they found four bales of the stuff in the hold of the *Maggie's Delight.* Prob'ly that's what put the idear in my head, but even now, after all these years, I wonder how I ever managed to make somethin so complicated outta what was really so simple. There was the real problem, sittin right across the table from me every night, usually needin a bath and a shave, and there *I* was, lookin right back at him—Joe St. George, Little Tall Island's biggest jack of all trades and master of none—and wonderin if my good girl was maybe out behind the high-school woodshop in the afternoons, smokin joy-sticks. And I'm the one who likes to say her mother didn't raise no fools. Gorry!

I started thinkin about goin into her room and lookin through her closet and bureau drawers, but then I got disgusted with myself. I may be a lot of things, Andy, but I hope I ain't never been a sneak. Still, even havin the idear made me see that I'd spent way too much time just creepin around the edges of whatever was goin on, hopin the problem would solve itself or that Selena would come to me on her own.

There came a day—not long before Halloween, because Little Pete'd put up a paper witch in the entry window, I remember—when I was supposed to go down to the Strayhorn place after lunch. Me and Lisa McCandless were going to turn those fancy Persian rugs downstairs—you're supposed to do that every six months so they won't fade, or so they'll fade even, or some damned thing. I put my coat on and got it buttoned and was halfway to the door when I thought, What are you doin with this heavy fall coat on, you foolish thing? It's sixty-five degrees out there, at least, real Indian Summer weather. And this other voice come back and said, It won't be sixty-five out on the reach; it'll be more like fifty out there. Damp, too. And that's how I come to know I wasn't goin anywhere near the Strayhorn place that afternoon. I was gonna take the ferry across to Jonesport instead, and have it out with my daughter. I called Lisa, told her we'd have to do the rugs another day, and left for the ferry landin. I was just in time to catch the two-fifteen. If I'd missed it, I might've missed *her,* and who knows how different things might have turned out then?

I was the first one off the ferry—they was still slippin the last moorin rope over the last post when I stepped down onto the dock—and I went straight to the high school. I got the idear on my way up that I wasn't going to find her in the study-hall no matter what she and her home-room teacher said, that she'd be out behind the woodshop after all, with the rest of the thuds . . . all of em laughin and grab-assin around and maybe passin a bottle of cheap wine in a paper bag. If you ain't never been in a situation like that, you don't know what it's like and I can't describe it to you. All I can say is that I was findin out that there's no way you can prepare yourself for a broken heart. You just have to keep marchin forward and hope like hell it doesn't happen.

But when I opened the study-hall door and peeked in, she *was* there, sittin at a desk by the windows with her head bent over her algebra book. She didn't see me at first n I just stood there, lookin at her. She hadn't fallen in with bad comp'ny like I'd feared, but my heart broke a little just the same, Andy, because it looked like she'd fallen in with no comp'ny at all, and could be that's even worse. Maybe her home-room teacher didn't see anything wrong with a girl studyin all by herself after school in that great big room; maybe she even thought it was admirable. I didn't see nothing admirable about it, though, nor anything healthy, either. She didn't even have the detention kids to keep her comp'ny, because they keep the bad actors in the lib'ry at Jonesport-Beals High.

She should have been with her girlfriends, maybe listenin to records or moonin over some boy, and instead she was sittin there in a dusty ray of afternoon sun, sittin in the smell of chalk and floor-varnish and that nasty red sawdust they put down after all the kids have gone home, sittin with her head bent so close over her book that you'd've thought all the secrets of life n death was in there.

"Hello, Selena," I says. She cringed like a rabbit and knocked half her books off her desk turnin around to see who'd told her hello. Her eyes were so big they looked like they filled the whole top half of her face, and what I could see of her cheeks and forehead was as pale as buttermilk in a white cup. Except for the places where the new pimples were, that is. *They* stood out a bright red, like burn-marks.

Then she saw it was me. The terror went away, but

no smile come in its place. It was like a shutter dropped over her face . . . or like she was inside a castle and had just pulled up the drawbridge. Yes, like that. Do you see what I'm tryin to say?

"Mamma!" she says. "What are *you* doin here?"

I thought of sayin, "I've come to take you home on the ferry and get some answers out of you, my little sweetheart," but somethin told me it would have been wrong in that room—that empty room where I could smell the thing that was wrong with her just as clear as I could smell the chalk and the red sawdust. I could smell it, and I meant to find out what it was. From the look of her, I'd waited far too long already. I didn't think it was dope anymore, but whatever it was, it was hungry. It was eatin her alive.

I told her I'd decided to toss my afternoon's work out the door and come over and window-shop a little, but I couldn't find anything I liked. "So I thought maybe you and I could ride back on the ferry together," I said. "Do you mind, Selena?"

She finally smiled. I would have paid a thousand dollars for that smile, I can tell you . . . a smile that was just for me. "Oh no, Mommy," she said. "It would be nice, having company."

So we walked back down the hill to the ferry-landin together, and when I asked her about some of her classes, she told me more than she had in weeks. After that first look she gave me—like a cornered rabbit lookin at a tomcat—she seemed more like her old self than she had in months, and I began to hope.

Well, Nancy here may not know how empty that four-forty-five to Little Tall and the Outer Islands is,

but I guess you n Frank do, Andy. Most of the workin folk who live off the mainland go home on the five-thirty, and what comes on the four-forty-five is mostly parcel post, UPS, shop-goods, and groceries bound for the market. So even though it was a lovely autumn afternoon, nowhere near as cold and damp as I'd thought it was gonna be, we had the aft deck mostly to ourselves.

We stood there awhile, watchin the wake spread back toward the mainland. The sun was on the wester by then, beatin a track across the water, and the wake broke it up and made it look like pieces of gold. When I was a little girl, my Dad used to tell me it *was* gold, and that sometimes the mermaids came up and got it. He said they used those broken pieces of late-afternoon sunlight as shingles on their magic castles under the sea. When I saw that kind of broken golden track on the water, I always watched it for mermaids, and until I was almost Selena's age I never doubted there were such things, because my Dad had told me there were.

The water that day was the deep shade of blue you only seem to see on calm days in October, and the sound of the diesels was soothin. Selena untied the kerchief she was wearin over her head and raised her arms and laughed. "Isn't it beautiful, Mom?" she asked me.

"Yes," I said, "it is. And you used to be beautiful, too, Selena. Why ain't you anymore?"

She looked at me, and it was like she had two faces on. The top one was puzzled and still kinda laughin . . . but underneath there was a careful, distrustin sort of

look. What I saw in that underneath face was everythin Joe had told her that spring and summer, before she had begun to pull away from him, too. I don't have no friends, is what that underneath face said to me. Certainly not you, nor him, either. And the longer we looked at each other, the more that face came to the top.

She stopped laughin and turned away from me to look out over the water. That made me feel bad, Andy, but I couldn't let it stop me any more than I could let Vera get away with her bitchery later on, no matter how sad it all was at the bottom. The fact is, sometimes we *do* have to be cruel to be kind—like a doctor givin a shot to a child even though he knows the child will cry and not understand. I looked inside myself and saw I could be cruel like that if I had to. It scared me to know that then, and it still scares me a little. It's scary to know you can be as hard as you need to be, and never hesitate before or look back afterward and question what you did.

"I don't know what you mean, Mom," she says, but she was lookin at me with a careful eye.

"You've changed," I said. "Your looks, the way you dress, the way you act. All those things tell me you're in some kind of trouble."

"There's nothing wrong," she said, but all the time she was sayin it she was backin away from me. I grabbed her hands in mine before she could get too far away to reach.

"Yes there is," I said, "and neither of us is steppin off this ferry until you tell me what it is."

"*Nothin!*" she yelled. She tried to yank her hands

free but I wouldn't let loose. "Nothin's wrong, now let go! Let me *go!*"

"Not yet," I says. "Whatever trouble you're in won't change my love for you, Selena, but I can't begin helpin you out of it until you tell me what it *is.*"

She stopped strugglin then and only looked at me. And I seen a third face below the first two—a crafty, miserable face I didn't like much. Except for her complexion, Selena usually takes after my side of the family, but right then she looked like Joe.

"Tell me somethin first," she says.

"I will if I can," I says back.

"Why'd you hit him?" she asks. "Why'd you hit him that time?"

I opened my mouth to ask "*What* time?"—mostly to get a few seconds to think—but all at once I knew somethin, Andy. Don't ask me how—it might have been a hunch, or what they call woman's intuition, or maybe I actually reached out somehow and read my daughter's mind—but I did. I knew that if I hesitated, even for a second, I was gonna lose her. Maybe only for that day, but all too likely for good. It was a thing I just *knew,* and I didn't hesitate a beat.

"Because he hit me in the back with a piece of stovewood earlier that evenin," I said. "Just about crushed my kidneys. I guess I just decided I wasn't going to be done that way anymore. Not ever again."

She blinked the way you do when somebody makes a quick move toward your face with their hand, and her mouth dropped open in a big surprised *O.*

"That ain't what he told you it was about, was it?"

She shook her head.

"What'd *he* say? His drinkin?"

"That and his poker games," she said in a voice almost too low to hear. "He said you didn't want him or anybody else to have any fun. That was why you didn't want him to play poker, and why you wouldn't let me go to Tanya's sleep-over last year. He said you want everyone to work eight days a week like you do. And when he stood up to you, you conked him with the creamer and then said you'd cut off his head if he tried to do anything about it. That you'd do it while he was sleepin."

I woulda laughed, Andy, if it hadn't been so awful.

"Did you believe him?"

"I don't know," she said. "Thinking about that hatchet made me so scared I didn't know what to believe."

That went in my heart like a knife-blade, but I never showed it. "Selena," I says, "what he told you was a lie."

"*Just leave me alone!*" she said, pullin back from me. That cornered-rabbit look come on her face again, and I realized she wasn't just hidin somethin because she was ashamed or worried—she was scared to death. "*I'll fix it myself! I don't want your help, so just leave me alone!*"

"You *can't* fix it yourself, Selena," I says. I was usin the low, soothin tone you'd use on a hoss or lamb that's gotten caught in a barbwire fence. "If you could have, you already would have. Now listen to me—I'm sorry you had to see me with that hatchet in my hand; I'm sorry about *everythin* you saw n heard that night. If I'd

known it was going to make you so scared and unhappy, I wouldn't have took after him no matter how much he provoked me."

"Can't you just stop it?" she asks, and then she finally pulled her hands out of mine and put em over her ears. "I don't want to hear any more. I *won't* hear any more."

"I can't stop because that's over and done with, beyond reach," I says, "but this ain't. So let me help, dear heart. Please." I tried to put an arm around her and draw her to me.

"*Don't! Don't you hit me! Don't you even* touch *me, you bitch!*" she screams, and shoved herself backward. She stumbled against the rail, and I was sure she was gonna go flip-flop right over it and into the drink. My heart stopped, but thank God my hands never did. I reached out, caught her by the front of the coat, and drug her back toward me. I slipped in some wet and almost fell. I caught my balance, though, and when I looked up, she hauled off and slapped me across the side of the face.

I never minded, just grabbed hold of her again and hugged her against me. You quit at a time like that with a child Selena's age, I think a lot of what you had with that child is gonna be over for good. Besides, that slap didn't hurt a bit. I was just scared of losin her—and not just from my heart, neither. For that one second I was sure she was gonna go over the rail with her head down and her feet up. I was so sure I could see it. It's a wonder all my hair didn't go gray right then.

Then she was cryin and tellin me she was sorry, that she never meant to hit me, that she never *ever* meant to do that, and I told her I knew it. "Hush awhile," I says, and what she said back almost froze me solid. "You should have let me go over, Mommy," she said. "You should have let me go."

I held her out from me at arms' length—by then we was both cryin—and I says, "*Nothin* could make me do a thing like that, sweetheart."

She was shakin her head back and forth. "I can't stand it anymore, Mommy . . . I can't. I feel so dirty and confused, and I can't be happy no matter how hard I try."

"What is it?" I says, beginnin to be frightened all over again. "What is it, Selena?"

"If I tell you," she says, "you'll probably push me over the rail yourself."

"You know better," I says. "And I'll tell you another thing, dear heart—you ain't steppin foot back on dry land until you've come clean with me. If goin back n forth on this ferry for the rest of the year is what it takes, then that's what we'll do . . . although I think we'll both be frozen solid before the end of November, if we ain't died of ptomaine from what they serve in that shitty little snack-bar."

I thought that might make her laugh, but it didn't. Instead she bowed her head so she was lookin at the deck and said somethin, real low. With the sound of the wind and the engines, I couldn't quite hear what it was.

"What did you say, sweetheart?"

She said it again, and I heard it that second time, even though she didn't speak much louder. All at once I understood everythin, and Joe St. George's days were numbered from that moment on.

"I never wanted to do anything. He made me." That's what she said.

For a minute I could only stand there, and when I finally did reach for her, she flinched away. Her face was as white as a sheet. Then the ferry—the old *Island Princess*, that was—took a lurch. The world had already gone slippery on me, and I guess I would have gone on my skinny old ass if Selena hadn't grabbed me around the middle. The next second it was me holdin her again, and she cryin against my neck.

"Come on," I says. "Come on over here and sit down with me. We've had enough rammin from one side of this boat to the other to last us awhile, haven't we?"

We went over to the bench by the aft companionway with our arms around each other, shufflin like a pair of invalids. I don't know if Selena felt like an invalid or not, but I sure did. I was only leakin from the eyes a little, but Selena was cryin s'hard it sounded like she'd pull her guts loose from their moorins if she didn't quit pretty soon. I was glad to hear her cry that way, though. It wasn't until I heard her sobbin and seen the tears rollin down her cheeks that I realized how much of her *feelins* had gone away, too, like the light in her eyes and the shape inside her clothes. I would have liked hearin her laugh one frig of a lot better'n I liked hearin her cry, but I was willin to take what I could get.

We sat down on the bench and I let her cry awhile longer. When it finally started to ease off a little, I gave her the hanky from my purse. She didn't even use it at first. She just looked at me, her cheeks all wet and deep brown hollows under her eyes, and she says, "You don't hate me, Mommy? You really don't?"

"No," I says. "Not now, not never. I promise on my heart. But I want to get this straight. I want you to tell me the whole thing, all the way through. I see on your face that you don't think you can do that, but I know you can. And remember this—you'll never have to tell it again, not even to your own husband, if you don't want to. It will be like drawin a splinter. I promise *that* on my heart, too. Do you understand?"

"Yes, Mommy, but he said if I ever told . . . sometimes you get so mad, he said . . . like the night you hit him with the cream-pot . . . he said if I ever felt like telling I'd better remember the hatchet . . . and . . ."

"No, that's not the way," I says. "You need to start at the beginning and go right through her. But I want to be sure I got one thing straight from the word go. Your Dad's been at you, hasn't he?"

She just hung her head and didn't say nothing. It was all the answer *I* needed, but I think *she* needed to hear herself sayin it right out loud.

I put my finger under her chin and lifted her head until we were lookin each other right in the eye. "Hasn't he?"

"Yes," she said, and broke out sobbin again. This time it didn't last so long nor go so deep, though. I let her go on awhile just the same because it took me awhile to see how *I* should go on. I couldn't ask "What's he done to you?" because I thought the chances were pretty good she wouldn't know for sure. For a little while the only thing I could think of was "Has he fucked you?" but I thought she might not know for sure even if I put it just that way, that

crude. And the sound of it was so damned ugly in my head.

At last I said, "Has he had his penis into you, Selena? Has he had it in your pussy?"

She shook her head. "I haven't let him." She swallowed back a sob. "Not yet, anyway."

Well, we were both able to relax a little after that—with each other, anyway. What I felt inside was pure rage. It was like I had an eye inside, one I never knew about before that day, and all I could see with it was Joe's long, horsey face, with his lips always cracked and his dentures always kind of yellow and his cheeks always chapped and red high up on the cheekbones. I saw his face pretty near all the time after that, that eye wouldn't close even when my other two did and I was asleep, and I began to know it *wouldn't* close until he was dead. It was like bein in love, only inside out.

Meantime, Selena was tellin her story, from beginnin to end. I listened and didn't interrupt even once, and accourse it started with the night I hit Joe with the creamer and Selena come to the door in time to see him with his hand over his bleedin ear and me holdin the hatchet over him like I really did intend to cut his head off with it. All I wanted to do was make him *stop,* Andy, and I risked my life to do it, but she didn't see none of that. Everything she saw stacked up on *his* side of the ledger. The road to hell's paved with good intentions, they say, and I know it's true. I know it from bitter experience. What I don't know is *why*—why it is that tryin to do good so often leads to ill. That's for wider heads than mine, I guess.

I ain't gonna tell that whole story here, not out of

respect to Selena, but because it's too long and it hurts too much, even now. But I'll tell you the first thing she said. I'll never forget it, because I was struck again by what a difference there is between how things look and how they really are . . . between the outside and the inside.

"He looked so sad," she said. "There was blood running between his fingers and tears in his eyes and he just looked so *sad.* I hated you more for that look than for the blood and tears, Mommy, and I made up my mind to make it up to him. Before I went to bed, I got down on my knees and prayed. 'God,' I said, 'if you keep her from hurting him any more, I'll make it up to him. I swear I will. For Jesus' sake, amen.' "

You got any idear how I felt, hearin that from my daughter a year or more after I thought the door was shut on that business? Do you, Andy? Frank? What about you, Nancy Bannister from Kennebunk? No—I see you don't. I pray to God you never will.

She started bein nice to him—bringin him special treats when he was out in the back shed, workin on somebody's snowmobile or outboard motor, sittin beside him while we were watchin TV at night, sittin with him on the porch step while he whittled, listenin while he talked all his usual line of Joe St. George bullshit politics—how Kennedy was lettin the Jews n Catholics run everythin, how it was the Commies tryin to get the niggers into the schools n lunchrooms down south, and pretty soon the country would be ruined. She listened, she smiled at his jokes, she put Cornhuskers on his hands when they chapped, and he wasn't too deaf to hear opportunity knockin. He quit givin her the

lowdown on politics in favor of givin her the lowdown on me, how crazy I could be when I was riled, and everythin that was wrong with our marriage. Accordin to him it was mostly me.

It was in the late spring of 1962 that he started touchin her in a way that was a little more'n just fatherly. That was all it was at first, though—little strokes along the leg while they were sittin on the couch together and I was out of the room, little pats on the bottom when she brought him his beer out in the shed. That's where it started, and it went on from there. By the middle of July, poor Selena'd gotten as scared of him as she already was of me. By the time I finally took it into my head to go across to the mainland and get some answers out of her, he'd done just about everything a man can do to a woman short of fucking her . . . and frightened her into doing any number of things to him, as well.

I think he would have picked her cherry before Labor Day if it hadn't been for Joe Junior and Little Pete bein out of school and underfoot a lot of the time. Little Pete was just there and in the way, but I think Joe Junior had more'n half an idear of what was up, and set out to put himself in the way of it. God bless him if he did, is all I can say. I was certainly no help, workin twelve and sometimes fourteen hours a day like I was back then. And all the time I was gone, Joe was around her, touchin her, askin her for kisses, askin her to touch him in his "special places" (that's what he called em), and tellin her that he couldn't help it, he *had* to ask—she was nice to him, I wasn't, a man had certain needs, and that was all there was to it. But she

couldn't tell. If she did, he said, I might kill both of them. He kep remindin her about the creamer and the hatchet. He kep tellin her about what a cold, bad-tempered bitch I was and about how he couldn't help it because a man had certain needs. He drilled those things into her, Andy, until she was half-crazy with em. He—

What, Frank?

Yes, he worked, all right, but his kind of work didn't slow him down much when it came to chasin his daughter. A jack of all trades, I called him, and that's just what he was. He did chores for any number of the summer people and caretook two houses (I hope the people who hired him to do *that* kep a good inventory of their possessions); there were four or five different fishermen who'd call him to crew when they were busy—Joe could haul traps with the best of em, if he wa'ant too hung over—and accourse he had his small engines for a sideline. In other words, he worked the way a lot of island men work (although not as hard as most)—a drib here n a drab there. A man like that can pretty much set his own hours, and that summer and early fall, Joe set his so's to be around the house as much as he could when I was gone. To be around Selena.

Do you understand what I need you to understand, I wonder? Do you see that he was workin as hard to get into her *mind* as he was into her pants? I think it was seein me with that goddam hatchet in my hand that had the most power over her, so that was what he used the most. When he saw he couldn't use it anymore to gain her sympathy, he used it to scare her with. He

told her over n over again that I'd drive her out of the house if I ever found out what they was doin.

What *they* was doin! Gorry!

She said she didn't *want* to do it, and he said that was just too bad, but it was too late to stop. He told her she'd teased him until he was half-crazy, and said that kind of teasin's why most rapes happen, and good women (meanin bad-tempered, hatchet-wavin bitches like me, I guess) knew it. Joe kep tellin her he'd keep *his* end quiet as long as she kep *hers* quiet . . . "But," he told her, "you have to understand, baby, that if *some* comes out, *all* comes out."

She didn't know what he meant by *all,* and she didn't understand how bringin him a glass of iced tea in the afternoon and tellin him about Laurie Langill's new puppy had given him the idear that he could reach between her legs n squeeze her there whenever he wanted, but she was convinced she must have done *somethin* to make him act so bad, and it made her ashamed. That was the worst of it, I think—not the fear but the shame.

She said she set out one day to tell the whole story to Mrs. Sheets, the guidance counsellor. She even made an appointment, but she lost her nerve in the outside office when another girl's appointment ran a little overtime. That had been less than a month before, just after school let back in.

"I started to think how it would sound," she told me as we sat there on the bench by the aft companionway. We were halfway across the reach by then, and we could see the East Head, all lit up with the afternoon sun. Selena was finally done her cryin. She'd give out a big watery sniffle every now n then, and my hanky was wet clear through, but she mostly had herself under control, and I was damned proud of her. She never let go of my hand, though. She held it in a death-grip all the time we was talkin. I had bruises on it the next day. "I thought about how it'd be to sit down and say, 'Mrs. Sheets, my Dad is trying to do you-know-what to me.' And she's so dense—and so *old*—she'd probably say, 'No, I *don't* know-what, Selena. What are you talking about?' Only she'd say *TAWkeen about,* like she does when she gets up on her high horse. And then I'd have to tell her that my own father was trying to screw me, and she wouldn't believe me, because people don't do things like that where she comes from."

"I think it happens all over the world," I said. "Sad, but true. And I think a school guidance counsellor would know it, too, unless she's an out-and-out fool. Is Mrs. Sheets an out-and-out fool, Selena?"

"No," Selena says, "I don't think so, Mommy, but—"

"Sweetheart, *did* you think you were the first girl this ever happened to?" I asks, and she said something again I couldn't hear on account of she talked so low. I had to ask her to say it again.

"I didn't know if I was or not," she says, and hugs me. I hugged her back. "Anyway," she went on at last, "I found out sitting there that I couldn't say it. Maybe if I'd been able to march right in I could have gotten it out, but not once I had time to sit and turn it over in my mind, and to wonder if Daddy was right, and you'd think I was a bad girl—"

"I'd never think that," I says, and give her another hug.

She gave me a smile back that warmed my heart. "I know that now," she said, "but then I wasn't so sure. And while I was sitting there, watching through the glass while Mrs. Sheets finished up with the girl that was before me, I thought up a good reason not to go in."

"Oh?" I asked her. "What was that?"

"Well," she says, "it wasn't school business."

That struck me funny and I started to giggle. Pretty soon Selena was gigglin with me, and the giggles kep gettin louder until we was settin there on that bench, holdin hands and laughin like a couple of loons in matin season. We was so loud that the man who sells snacks n cigarettes down below poked his head up for a second or two to make sure we were all right.

There were two other things she said on the way back—one with her mouth and one with her eyes. The one she said out loud was that she'd been thinkin of packin her things and runnin away; that seemed at least like a way out. But runnin won't solve your problems if you've been hurt bad enough—wherever you run, you take your head n your heart with you, after all—and the thing I saw in her eyes was that the thought of suicide had done more'n just cross her mind.

I'd think of that—of seein the thought of suicide in my daughter's eyes—and then I'd see Joe's face even clearer with that eye inside me. I'd see how he must've looked, pesterin her and pesterin her, tryin to get a hand up under her skirt until she wore nothin but jeans in self-defense, not gettin what he wanted (or not *all* of what he wanted) because of simple luck, her good n his bad, and not for any lack of tryin. I thought about what might've happened if Joe Junior hadn't cut his playin with Willy Bramhall short a few times n come home early, or if I hadn't finally opened my eyes enough to get a really good look at her. Most of all I thought about how he'd driven her. He'd done it the way a bad-hearted man with a quirt or a greenwood stick might drive a horse, and never stop once, not for love and not for pity, until that animal lay dead at his feet . . . and him prob'ly standin above it with the stick in his hand, wonderin why in hell *that* happened. This was where wantin to touch his forehead, wantin to see if it felt as smooth as it looked, had gotten me; this was where it all come out. My eyes were all the way open, and I saw I was livin with a loveless, pitiless man who believed anything he could reach with his arm and grasp with his hand was his to take, even his own daughter.

I'd got just about that far in my thinkin when the thought of killin him crossed my mind for the first time. That wasn't when I made up my mind to do it —gorry, no—but I'd be a liar if I said the thought was only a daydream. It was a *lot* more than that.

Selena must've seen some of that in my eyes, because she laid her hand on my arm and says, "Is there going to be trouble, Mommy? Please say there isn't—he'll know I told, and he'll be mad!"

I wanted to soothe her heart by tellin her what she wanted to hear, but I couldn't. There *was* going to be trouble—just how much and how bad would probably be up to Joe. He'd backed down the night I hit him

with the creamer, but that didn't mean he would again.

"I don't know what's going to happen," I said, "but I'll tell you two things, Selena: none of this is your fault, and his days of pawin and pesterin you are over. Do you understand?"

Her eyes filled up with tears again, and one of em spilled over and rolled down her cheek. "I just don't want there to be trouble," she said. She stopped a minute, her mouth workin, and then she busts out: "Oh, I *hate* this! Why did you ever hit him? Why did he ever have to start up with me? Why couldn't things stay like they were?"

I took her hand. "Things never do, honey—sometimes they go wrong, and then they have to be fixed. You know that, don't you?"

She nodded her head. I saw pain in her face, but no doubt. "Yes," she said. "I guess I do."

We were comin into the dock then, and there was no more time for talk. I was just as glad; I didn't want her lookin at me with those tearful eyes of hers, wantin what I guess every kid wants, for everything to be made right but with no pain and nobody hurt. Wantin me to make promises I couldn't make, because they were promises I didn't know if I could keep. I wasn't sure that inside eye would *let* me keep em. We got off the ferry without another word passin between us, and that was just as fine as paint with me.

That evenin, after Joe got home from the Carstairs place where he was buildin a back porch, I sent all three kids down to the market. I saw Selena castin little glances back at me all the way down the drive, and her face was just as pale as a glass of milk. Every time she

turned her head, Andy, I saw that double-damned hatchet in her eyes. But I saw somethin else in them, too, and I believe that other thing was relief. At least things are gonna quit just goin around n around like they have been, she musta been thinkin; scared as she was, I think part of her *musta* been thinkin that.

Joe was sittin by the stove readin the *American*, like he done every night. I stood by the woodbox, lookin at him, and that eye inside seemed to open wider'n ever. Lookit him, I thought, sittin there like the Grand High Poobah of Upper Butt-Crack. Sittin there like he didn't have to put on his pants one leg at a time like the rest of us. Sittin there as if puttin his hands all over his only daughter was the most natural thing in all the world and any man could sleep easy after doin it. I tried to think of how we'd gotten from the Junior-Senior Prom at The Samoset Inn to where we were right now, him sittin by the stove and readin the paper in his old patched bluejeans and dirty thermal undershirt and me standin by the woodbox with murder in my heart, and I couldn't do it. It was like bein in a magic forest where you look back over your shoulder and see the path has disappeared behind you.

Meantime, that inside eye saw more n more. It saw the crisscross scars on his ear from when I hit him with the creamer; it saw the squiggly little veins in his nose; it saw the way his lower lip pooched out so he almost always looked like he was havin a fit of the sulks; it saw the dandruff in his eyebrows and the way he'd pull at the hairs growin out of his nose or give his pants a good tug at the crotch every now and then.

All the things that eye saw were bad, and it come to

me that marryin him had been a lot more than the biggest mistake of my life; it was the only mistake that really mattered, because it wasn't just me that would end up payin for it. It was Selena he was occupied with then, but there were two boys comin along right behind her, and if he wouldn't stop at tryin to rape their big sister, what might he do to them?

I turned my head and that eye inside saw the hatchet, layin on the shelf over the woodbox just the same as always. I reached out for it n closed my fingers around the handle, thinkin, I ain't just going to put it in your hand this time, Joe. Then I thought of Selena turnin back to look at me as the three of em walked down the driveway, and I decided that whatever happened, the goddam hatchet wasn't going to be any part of it. I bent down and took a chunk of rock maple out of the woodbox instead.

Hatchet or stovelength, it almost didn't matter—Joe's life come within a whisker of endin right then and there. The longer I looked at him sittin in his dirty shirt, tuggin at the hairs stickin outta his nose and readin the funnypages, the more I thought of what he'd been up to with Selena; the more I thought about that, the madder I got; the madder I got, the closer I came to just walkin over there and breakin his skull open with that stick of wood. I could even see the place I'd hit the first lick. His hair had started to get real thin, especially in back, and the light from the lamp beside his chair made a kind of gleam there. You could see the freckles on the skin between the few strands of hair that was left. Right there, I thought, that very place. The blood'll jump up n splatter all over the

lampshade, but I don't care; it's an ugly old thing, anyway. The more I thought about it, the more I *wanted* to see the blood flyin up onto the shade like I knew it would. And then I thought about how drops would fly onto the light-bulb, too, and make a little sizzlin sound. I thought about those things, and the more I thought, the more my fingers bore down on that chunk of stovewood, gettin their best grip. It was crazy, oh yes, but I couldn't seem to turn away from him, and I knew that inside eye would go on lookin at him even if I did.

I told myself to think of how Selena would feel if I did it—all her worst fears come true—but that didn't work, either. As much as I loved her and as much as I wanted her good regard, it didn't. That eye was too strong for love. Not even wonderin what would happen to the three of em if he was dead and I was in South Windham for killin him would make that inside eye close up. It stayed wide open, and it kep seein more and more ugly things in Joe's face. The way he scraped white flakes of skin up from his cheeks when he shaved. A blob of mustard from his dinner dryin on his chin. His big old horsey dentures, which he got from mail-order and didn't fit him right. And every time I saw somethin else with that eye, my grip on that stove-length would tighten down a little more.

At the last minute I thought of somethin else. If you do this right here and right now, you won't be doin it for Selena, I thought. You wouldn't be doin it for the boys, either. You'd be doin it because all that grabbin was goin on under your very nose for three months or more and you was too dumb to notice. If you're going

to kill him and go to prison and only see your kids on Sat'dy afternoons, you better understand why you're doin it: not because he was at Selena, but because he fooled you, and that's one way you're just like Vera—you hate bein fooled worse'n anything.

That finally put a damper on me. The inside eye didn't close, but it dimmed down and lost a little of its power. I tried to open my hand and let that chunk of rock maple fall, but I'd been squeezin it too tight and couldn't seem to let go. I had to reach over with my other hand and pry the first two fingers off before it dropped back into the woodbox, and the other three fingers stayed curled, like they were still holdin on. I had to flex my hand three or four times before it started to feel normal again.

After it did, I walked over to Joe and tapped him on the shoulder. "I want to talk to you," I says.

"So talk," he says from behind the paper. "I ain't stoppin you."

"I want you lookin at me when I do," I says. "Put that rag down."

He dropped the paper into his lap and looked at me. "Ain't you got the *busiest* mouth on you these days," he says.

"I'll take care of my mouth," I says, "you just want to take care of your hands. If you don't, they're gonna get you in more trouble than you could handle in a year of Sundays."

His brows went up and he asked me what that was supposed to mean.

"It means I want you to leave Selena alone," I says.

He looked like I'd hoicked my knee right up into

his family jewels. That was the best of a sorry business, Andy—the look on Joe's face when he found out he was found out. His skin went pale and his mouth dropped open and his whole body kinda jerked in that shitty old rocker of his, the way a person's body will jerk sometimes when they are just fallin off to sleep and have a bad thought on their way down.

He tried to pass it off by actin like he'd had a muscle-twinge in his back, but he didn't fool either one of us. He actually looked a little ashamed of himself, too, but that didn't win him any favor with me. Even a stupid hound-dog has sense enough to look ashamed if you catch it stealin eggs out of a henhouse.

"I don't know what you're talkin about," he says.

"Then how come you look like the devil just reached into your pants and squeezed your balls?" I asked him.

The thunder started to come onto his brow then. "If that damned Joe Junior's been tellin lies about me—" he begun.

"Joe Junior ain't been sayin yes, no, aye, nor maybe about you," I says, "and you can just drop the act, Joe. Selena told me. She told me everything—how she tried to be nice to you after the night I hit you with the cream-pitcher, how you repaid her, and what you said would happen if she ever told."

"She's a little liar!" he says, throwin his paper on the floor like that proved it. "A little liar and a goddam tease! I'm gonna get my belt, and when she shows her face again—if she ever *dares* to show it around here again—"

He started to get up. I took one hand and shoved him back down again. It's awful easy, shovin a person

who's tryin to get out of a rockin chair; it surprised me a little how easy it was. Accourse, I'd almost bashed his head in with a stovelength not three minutes before, and that mighta had somethin to do with it.

His eyes went down to narrow little slits and he said I'd better not fool with him. "You've done it before," he says, "but that don't mean you can bell the cat *every* time you want to."

I'd been thinkin that very thing myself, and not so long before, but that wasn't hardly the time to tell him so. "You can save your big talk for your friends," I says instead. "What you want to do right now isn't talk but listen . . . and hear what I say, because I mean every word. If you ever fool with Selena again, I'll see you in State Prison for molesting a child or statutory rape, whichever charge will keep you in cold storage the longest."

That flummoxed him. His mouth fell open again and he just sat there for a minute, starin up at me.

"You'd never," he begun, and then stopped. Because he seen that I *would.* So he went into a pet, with his lower lip poochin out farther than ever. "You take her part, don't you?" he says. "You never even ast for my side of it, Dolores."

"Do you *have* one?" I asked him back. "When a man just four years shy of forty asks his fourteen-year-old daughter to take off her underpants so he can see how much hair she has growin on her pussy, can you say that man *has* a side?"

"She'll be fifteen next month," he says, as if that somehow changed everything. He was a piece of work, all right.

"Do you hear yourself?" I asked him. "Do you hear what's runnin out of your own mouth?"

He stared at me a little longer, then bent over and picked his newspaper up off the floor. "Leave me alone, Dolores," he says in his best sulky poor-old-me voice. "I want to finish this article."

I felt like tearin the damned paper out of his hands and throwin it in his face, but there would have been a blood-flowin tussle for sure if I had, and I didn't want the kids—especially not Selena—comin in on somethin like that. So I just reached out and pulled down the top of it, gentle, with my thumb.

"First you're gonna promise me you'll leave Selena alone," I said, "so we can put this shit-miserable business behind us. You promise me you ain't gonna touch her that way ever again in your life."

"Dolores, you ain't—" he starts.

"Promise, Joe, or I'll make your life hell."

"You think that scares me?" he shouts. "You've made my life hell for the last fifteen years, you bitch—your ugly face can't hold a candle to your ugly disposition! If you don't like the way I am, blame yourself!"

"You don't know what hell is," I said, "but if you don't promise to leave her alone, I'll see you find out."

"All right!" he yells. "All right, I promise! There! Done! Are you satisfied?"

"Yes," I says, although I wasn't. He wasn't ever gonna be able to satisfy me again. It wouldn't have mattered if he'd worked the miracle of the loaves and fishes. I meant to get the kids out of that house or see him dead before the turn of the year. Which way it

went didn't make much difference to me, but I didn't want him to know somethin was comin his way until it was too late for him to do anythin about it.

"Good," he says. "Then we're all done and buttoned up, ain't we, Dolores?" But he was lookin at me with a funny little gleam in his eyes that I didn't much like. "You think you're pretty smart, don't you?"

"I dunno," I says. "I used to think I had a fair amount of intelligence, but look who I ended up keepin house with."

"Oh, come on," he says, still lookin at me in that funny half-wise way. "You think you're such hot shit you prob'ly look over your shoulder to make sure your ass ain't smokin before you wipe yourself. But you don't know everything."

"What do you mean by that?"

"*You* figure it out," he says, and shakes his paper out like some rich guy who wants to make sure the stock market didn't use him too bad that day. "It shouldn't be no trouble for a smartypants like you."

I didn't like it, but I let it go. Partly it was because I didn't want to spend any more time knockin a stick against a hornet's nest than I had to, but that wasn't all of it. I *did* think I was smart, smarter'n him, anyway, and that was the rest of it. I figured if he tried to get his own back on me, I'd see what he was up to about five minutes after he got started. It was pride, in other words, pride pure n simple, and the idea that he'd *already* got started never crossed my mind.

When the kids came back from the store, I sent the boys into the house and walked around to the back with Selena. There's a big tangle of blackberry bushes

there, mostly bare by that time of the year. A little breeze had come up, and it made them rattle. It was a lonesome sound. A little creepy, too. There's a big white stone stickin out of the ground there, and we sat down on it. A half-moon had risen over East Head, and when she took my hands, her fingers were just as cold as that half-moon looked.

"I don't dare go in, Mommy," she said, and her voice was tremblin. "I'll go to Tanya's, all right? Please say I can."

"You don't have to be afraid of a thing, sweetheart," I says. "It's all taken care of."

"I don't believe you," she whispered, although her face said she wanted to—her face said she wanted to believe it more than anythin.

"It's true," I said. "He's promised to leave you alone. He doesn't always keep his promises, but he'll keep this one, now that he knows I'm watchin and he can't count on you to keep quiet. Also, he's scared to death."

"Scared to dea—why?"

"Because I told him I'd see him in Shawshank if he got up to any more nasty business with you."

She gasped, and her hands bore down on mine again. "Mommy, you *didn't!*"

"Yes I did, and I meant it," I says. "Best for you to know that, Selena. But I wouldn't worry too much; Joe probably won't come within ten feet of you for the next four years . . . and by then you'll be in college. If there's one thing on this round world he respects, it's his own hide."

She let go of my hands, slow but sure. I saw the hope comin into her face, and somethin else, as well.

It was like her youth was comin back to her, and it wasn't until then, sittin in the moonlight by the blackberry patch with her, that I realized how old she'd come to look that fall.

"He won't strap me or anything?" she asked.

"No," I says. "It's done."

Then she believed it all and put her head down on my shoulder and started to cry. Those were tears of relief, pure and simple. That she should have to cry that way made me hate Joe even more.

I think that, for the next few nights, there was a girl in my house sleepin better'n she had for three months or more . . . but I laid awake. I'd listen to Joe snorin beside me, and look at him with that inside eye, and feel like turnin over and bitin his goddam throat out. But I wasn't crazy anymore, like I'd been when I almost poleaxed him with that stick of stovewood. Thinkin of the kids and what would happen to em if I was taken up for murder hadn't had any power over that inside eye then, but later on, after I'd told Selena she was safe and had a chance to cool off a little myself, it did. Still, I knew that what Selena most likely wanted—for things to go on like what her Dad had been up to had never happened—couldn't be. Even if he kep his promise and never touched her again, that couldn't be . . . and in spite of what I'd told Selena, I wasn't completely sure he'd keep his promise. Sooner or later, men like Joe usually persuade themselves that they can get away with it next time; that if they're only a little more careful, they can have whatever they like.

Lyin there in the dark and calm again at last, the answer seemed simple enough: I had to take the kids

and move to the mainland, and I had to do it soon. I was calm enough right then, but I knew I wasn't gonna stay that way; that inside eye wouldn't let me. The next time I got hot, it would see even better and Joe would look even uglier and there might not be any thought on earth that could keep me from doin it. It was a new way of bein mad, at least for me, and I was just wise enough to see the damage it could do, if I let it. I had to get us away from Little Tall before that madness could break all the way out. And when I made my first move in that direction, I found out what that funny half-wise look in his eyes meant. Did I ever!

I waited awhile for things to settle, then I took the eleven o'clock ferry across to the mainland one Friday mornin. The kids were in school and Joe was out on the boundin main with Mike Stargill and his brother Gordon, playin with the lobster-pots—he wouldn't be back til almost sundown.

I had the kids' savins account passbooks with me. We'd been puttin money away for their college ever since they were born . . . *I* had, anyway; Joe didn't give a squitter if they went to college or not. Whenever the subject came up—and it was always me who brought it up, accourse—he'd most likely be sittin there in his shitty rocker with his face hid behind the Ellsworth *American* and he'd poke it out just long enough to say, "Why in *Christ's* name are you so set on sendin those kids to college, Dolores? *I* never went, and I did all right."

Well, there's some things you just can't argue with, ain't there? If Joe thought that readin the paper, minin for boogers, and wipin em on the runners of his rockin

chair was doin all right, there wasn't no room at all for discussion; it was hopeless from the word go. That was all right, though. As long as I could keep makin him kick in his fair share if he happened to fall into somethin good, like when he got on the county road crew, I didn't give a shit if he thought every college in the country was run by the Commies. The winter he worked on the road crew on the mainland, I got him to put five hundred dollars in their bank accounts, and he whined like a pup. Said I was takin all his dividend. I knew better, though, Andy. If that sonofawhore didn't make two thousand, maybe twenty-five hundred, dollars that winter, I'll smile n kiss a pig.

"Why do you always want to nag me so, Dolores?" he'd ask.

"If you were man enough to do what's right for your kids in the first place, I wouldn't have to," I'd tell him, and around n around it'd go, blah-blah-blahdy-blah. I got pretty sick of it from time to time, Andy, but I almost always got out of him what I thought the kids had comin. I couldn't get too sick of it to do that, because they didn't have nobody else to make sure their future'd still be there for em when they got to it.

There wasn't a lot in those three accounts by today's standards—two thousand or so in Selena's, about eight hundred in Joe Junior's, four or five hundred in Little Pete's—but this is 1962 I'm talkin about, and in those days it was a fairish chunk of change. More'n enough to get away on, that was for sure. I figured to draw Little Pete's in cash and take cashier's checks for the other two. I'd decided to make a clean break and move us all the way down to Portland—find a place to live

and a decent job. We wasn't none of us used to city livin, but people can get used to damned near anything if they have to. Besides, Portland wasn't really much more than a big town back then—not like it is now.

Once I got settled, I could start puttin back the money I'd had to take, and I thought I could do it. Even if I couldn't, they was bright kids, and I knew there were such things as scholarships. If they missed out on those, I decided I wasn't too proud to fill out a few loan applications. The major thing was to get them *away*—right then doin that seemed a lot more important than college. First things first, as the bumper sticker on Joe's old Farmall tractor used to say.

I've run m'gums for pretty near three-quarters of an hour about Selena, but it wasn't only her who'd suffered from him. She got the worst of it, but there was plenty of black weather left over for Joe Junior. He was twelve in 1962, a prime age for a boy, but you wouldn't know it lookin at him. He hardly ever smiled or laughed, and it really wasn't any wonder. He'd no more'n come into the room and his Dad'd be on him like a weasel on a chicken, tellin him to tuck in his shirt, to comb his hair, to quit slouchin, to grow up, stop actin like a goddam sissy with his nose always stuck in a book, to be a man. When Joe Junior didn't make the Little League All-Star team the summer before I found out what was wrong with Selena, you would have thought, listenin to his father, that he'd been kicked off the Olympic track team for takin pep-pills. Add to that whatever he'd seen his father gettin up to with his big sister, and you got a real mess on your hands, Sunny Jim. I'd sometimes look at Joe Junior lookin at his

father and see real hate in that boy's face—hate, pure n simple. And durin the week or two before I went across to the mainland with those passbooks in my pocket, I realized that, when it came to his father, Joe Junior had his own inside eye.

Then there was Little Pete. By the time he was four, he'd go swaggerin around right behind Joe, with the waist of his pants pulled up like Joe wore his, and he'd pull at the end of his nose and his ears, just like Joe did. Little Pete didn't have any hairs there to pull, accourse, so he'd just pretend. On his first day at first grade, he come home snivellin, with dirt on the seat of his pants and a scratch on his cheek. I sat down beside him on the porch step, put my arm around his shoulders, and asked him what happened. He said that goddam little sheeny Dicky O'Hara pushed him down. I told him goddam was swearin and he shouldn't say it, then asked him if he knew what a sheeny was. I was pretty curious to hear what might pop out of his mouth, to tell you the truth.

"Sure I do," he says. "A sheeny's a stupid jerk like Dicky O'Hara." I told him no, he was wrong, and he asked me what it *did* mean, then. I told him to never mind, it wasn't a nice word and I didn't want him sayin it anymore. He just sat there glarin at me with his lip pooched out. He looked just like his old man. Selena was scared of her father, Joe Junior hated him, but in some ways it was Little Pete who scared me the most, because Little Pete wanted to grow up to be just like him.

So I got their passbooks from the bottom drawer of my little jewelry box (I kep em there because it was the only thing I had in those days with a lock on it; I wore the key around my neck on a chain) and walked into the Coastal Northern Bank in Jonesport at about half-past noon. When I got to the front of the line, I pushed the passbooks across to the teller, said I meant to close all three accounts out, and explained how I wanted the money.

"That'll be just a moment, Mrs. St. George," she says, and goes to the back of the tellers' area to pull the accounts. This was long before computers, accourse, and they had to do a lot more fiddlin and diddlin.

She got em—I saw her pull all three—and then she opened em up and looked at em. A little line showed up down the middle of her brow, and she said somethin to one of the other women. Then they both looked for awhile, with me standin out there on the other side of the counter, watchin em and tellin myself there wasn't a reason in the world to feel nervous and feelin pretty goddam nervous just the same.

Then, instead of comin back to me, the teller went into one of those jumped-up little cubbyholes they called offices. It had glass sides, and I could see her talkin to a little bald man in a gray suit and a black tie. When she came back to the counter, she didn't have the account files anymore. She'd left them on the bald fella's desk.

"I think you'd better discuss your children's savings accounts with Mr. Pease, Mrs. St. George," she says, and pushes the passbooks back to me. She did it with the side of her hand, like they were germy and she might get infected if she touched em too much or too long.

"Why?" I asked. "What's wrong with em?" By then I'd given up the notion that I didn't have anythin to feel nervous about. My heart was rappin away double-time in my chest and my mouth had gone all dry.

"Really, I couldn't say, but I'm sure that if there's a misunderstanding, Mr. Pease will straighten it right out," she says, but she wouldn't look me in the eye and I could tell she didn't think any such thing.

I walked to that office like I had a twenty-pound cake of cement on each foot. I already had a pretty good idear of what must have happened, but I didn't see how in the world it *could* have happened. Gorry, I had the passbooks, didn't I? Joe hadn't got em outta my jewelry box and then put em back, either, because the lock woulda been busted and it wasn't. Even if he'd picked it somehow (which is a laugh; that man couldn't get a forkful of lima beans from his plate to his mouth without droppin half of em in his lap), the passbooks would either show the withdrawals or be stamped ACCOUNT CLOSED in the red ink the bank uses . . . and they didn't show neither one.

Just the same, I knew that Mr. Pease was gonna tell me my husband had been up to fuckery, and once I got into his office, that was just what he *did* tell me. He said that Joe Junior's and Little Pete's accounts had been closed out two months ago and Selena's less'n two weeks ago. Joe'd done it when he did because he knew I never put money in their accounts after Labor Day until I thought I had enough squirreled away in the big soup-kettle on the top kitchen shelf to take care of the Christmas bills.

Pease showed me those green sheets of ruled paper accountants use, and I saw Joe had scooped out the last big chunk—five hundred dollars from Selena's account—the day after I told him I knew what he'd been up to with her and he sat there in his rocker and told me I didn't know everything. He sure was right about that.

I went over the figures half a dozen times, and when I looked up, Mr. Pease was sittin acrost from me, rubbin his hands together and lookin worried. I could see little drops of sweat on his bald head. He knew what'd happened as well as I did.

"As you can see, Mrs. St. George, those accounts have been closed out by your husband, and—"

"How can that be?" I asks him. I threw the three passbooks down on his desk. They made a whacking noise and he kinda blinked his eyes and jerked back. "How can that be, when I got the Christly savings account books right here?"

"Well," he says, lickin his lips and blinkin like a lizard sunnin itself on a hot rock, "you see, Mrs. St. George, those are—*were*—what we call 'custodial savings accounts.' That means the child in whose name the account is held can—could—draw from it with either you or your husband to countersign. It also means that either of you can, as parents, draw from any of these three accounts when and as you like. As you would have done today, if the money had still, ahem, been in the accounts."

"But these don't *show* any goddam withdrawals!" I says, and I must have been shoutin, because people in

the bank were lookin around at us. I could see em through the glass walls. Not that I cared. "How'd he get the money without the goddam *passbooks?*"

He was rubbin his hands together faster n faster. They made a sandpapery kind of sound, and if he'd had a dry stick between em, I b'lieve he coulda set fire to the gum-wrappers in his ashtray. "Mrs. St. George, if I could ask you to keep your voice down—"

"*I'll* worry about my voice," I says, louder'n ever. "*You* worry about the way this beshitted bank does business, chummy! The way it looks to me, you got a lot to worry *about.*"

He took a sheet of paper off his desk and looked at it. "According to this, your husband stated the pass-books were lost," he says finally. "He asked to be issued new ones. It's a common enough—"

"Common-be-damned!" I yelled. "You never called me! *No one* from the bank called me! Those accounts were held *between* the two of us—that's how it was explained to me when we opened Selena's and Joe Junior's back in '51, and it was still the same when we opened Peter's in '54. You want to tell me the rules have been changed since then?"

"Mrs. St. George—" he started, but he might as well have tried whistlin through a mouthful of crackers; I meant to have my say.

"He told you a fairy-story and you believed it—asked for new passbooks and you gave em to him. Gorry sakes! Who the hell do you think put that money in the bank to begin with? If you think it was Joe St. George, you're a lot dumber'n you look!"

By then everybody in the bank'd quit even *pretendin*

to be goin about their business. They just stood where they were, lookin at us. Most of em must have thought it was a pretty good show, too, judgin by the expressions on their faces, but I wonder if they would have been quite so entertained if it had been *their* kids' college money that'd just flown away like a bigass bird. Mr. Pease had gone as red as the side of old dad's barn. Even his sweaty old bald head had turned bright red.

"*Please*, Mrs. St. George," he says. By then he was lookin like he might break down n cry. "I assure you that what we did was not only perfectly legal, but standard bank practice."

I lowered my voice then. I could feel all the fight runnin outta me. Joe had fooled me, all right, fooled me good, and this time I didn't have to wait for it to happen twice to say shame on me.

"Maybe it's legal and maybe it ain't," I says. "I'd have to haul you into court to find out one way or the other, wouldn't I, and I ain't got either the time or the money to do it. Besides, it ain't the question what's legal or what ain't that's knocked me for a loop here . . . it's how you never once thought that someone else might be concerned about what happened to that money. Don't 'standard bank practice' ever allow you folks to make a single goddam phone call? I mean, the number's right there on all those forms, and it ain't changed."

"Mrs. St. George, I'm very sorry, but—"

"If it'd been the other way around," I says, "if *I'd* been the one with a story about how the passbooks was lost and ast for new ones, if *I'd* been the one who started drawin out what took eleven or twelve years to put in . . . wouldn't you have called *Joe*? If the

money'd still been here for me to withdraw *today,* like I came in meanin to do, wouldn't you have called him the minute I stepped out the door, to let him know—just as a courtesy, mind you!—what his wife'd been up to?"

Because I'd expected just that, Andy—that was why I'd picked a day when he was out with the Stargills. I'd expected to go back to the island, collect the kids, and be long gone before Joe come up the driveway with a six-pack in one hand and his dinnerpail in the other.

Pease looked at me n opened his mouth. Then he closed it again and didn't say nothing. He didn't have to. The answer was right there on his face. *Accourse* he—or someone else from the bank—would have called Joe, and kep on tryin until he finally got him. Why? Because Joe was the man of the house, that's why. And the reason nobody'd bothered to tell *me* was because I was just his wife. What the hell was *I* s'posed to know about money, except how to earn some down on my knees scrubbin floors n baseboards n toilet-bowls? If the man of the house decided to draw out all his kids' college money, he must have had a damned good reason, and even if he didn't, it didn't matter, because he was the man of the house, and in charge. His wife was just the little woman, and all *she* was in charge of was baseboards, toilet-bowls, and chicken dinners on Sunday afternoons.

"If there's a problem, Mrs. St. George," Pease was sayin, "I'm very sorry, but—"

"If you say you're sorry one more time, I'll kick your butt up so high you'll look like a hunchback," I says,

but there was no real danger of me doin anything to him. Right about then I didn't feel like I had enough strength to kick a beer-can across the road. "Just tell me one thing and I'll get out of your hair: is the money spent?"

"I would have no way of knowing!" he says in this prissy little shocked voice. You'da thought I'd told him I'd show him mine if he'd show me his.

"This is the bank Joe's done business with his whole life," I says. "He *could* have gone down the road to Machias or Columbia Falls and stuck it in one of those banks, but he didn't—he's too dumb and lazy and set in his ways. No, he's either stuck it in a couple of Mason jars and buried it somewhere or put it right back in here. *That's* what I want to know—if my husband's opened some kind of new account here in the last couple of months." Except it felt more like I *had* to know, Andy. Findin out how he'd fooled me made me feel sick to my stomach, and that was bad, but not knowin if he'd pissed it all away somehow . . . *that* was killin me.

"If he's . . . that's privileged information!" he says, and by then you'da thought I'd told him I'd *touch* his if he'd touch mine.

"Ayuh," I says. "Figured it was. I'm askin you to break a rule. I know just lookin at you that you're not a man who does that often; I can see it runs against your grain. But that was my kids' money, Mr. Pease, and he lied to get it. You know he did; the proof's right there on your desk blotter. It's a lie that wouldn't have worked if this bank—*your* bank—had had the common courtesy to make a telephone call."

He clears his throat and starts, "We are not required—"

"I know you ain't," I says. I wanted to grab him and shake him, but I saw it wouldn't do no good—not with a man like him. Besides, my mother always said you c'n catch more flies with honey than you ever can with vinegar, and I've found it to be true. "I know that, but think of the grief and heartache you'da saved me with that one call. And if you'd like to make up for some of it—I know you don't *have* to, but if you'd *like* to—please tell me if he's opened an account here or if I've got to start diggin holes around my house. Please—I'll never tell. I swear on the name of God I won't."

He sat there lookin at me, drummin his fingers on those green accountants' sheets. His nails were all clean and it looked like he'd had a professional manicure, although I guess that ain't too likely—it's Jonesport in 1962 we're talkin about, after all. I s'pose his wife did it. Those nice neat nails made little muffled thumps on the papers each time they came down, n I thought, He ain't gonna do nothin for me, not a man like him. What's he care about island folk and their problems? His ass is covered, n that's all he cares about.

So when he *did* speak up, I felt ashamed for what I'd been thinkin about men in general and him in particular.

"I can't check something like that with you sitting right here, Mrs. St. George," he says. "Why don't you go down to The Chatty Buoy and order yourself a cruller and a nice hot cup of coffee? You look like you could use something. I'll join you in fifteen minutes. No, better make it half an hour."

"Thank you," I said. "Thank you so very much."

He sighed and began shufflin the papers back together. "I must be losin my mind," he says, then laughed kinda nervous-like.

"No," I told him. "You're helpin a woman who don't have nowhere else to turn, that's all."

"Ladies in distress have always been a weakness of mine," he says. "Give me half an hour. Maybe even a little longer."

"But you'll come?"

"Yes," he said. "I will."

He did, too, but it was closer to forty-five minutes than half an hour, and by the time he finally got to the Buoy, I'd pretty well made up my mind he was gonna leave me in the lurch. Then, when he finally came in, I thought he had bad news. I thought I could read it in his face.

He stood in the doorway a few seconds, takin a good look around to make sure there was nobody in the restaurant who might make trouble for him if we was seen together after the row I made in the bank. Then he came over to the booth in the corner where I was sittin, slid in acrost from me, and says, "It's still in the bank. Most of it, anyway. Just under three thousand dollars."

"Thank God!" I said.

"Well," he says, "that's the good part. The bad part is that the new account is in his name only."

"Accourse it is," I said. "He sure didn't give me no new passbook account card to sign. That woulda tipped me off to his little game, wouldn't it?"

"Many women wouldn't know one way or the other,"

he says. He cleared his throat, gave a yank on his tie, then looked around quick to see who'd come in when the bell over the door jingled. "Many women sign anything their husbands put in front of them."

"Well, I ain't many women," I says.

"I've noticed," he says back, kinda dry. "Anyway, I've done what you asked, and now I really have to get back to the bank. I wish I had time to drink a coffee with you."

"You know," I says, "I kinda doubt that."

"Actually, so do I," he says back. But he gave me his hand to shake, just like I was another man, and I took that as a bit of a compliment. I sat where I was until he was gone, and when the girl came back n asked me if I wanted a fresh cup of coffee, I told her no thanks, I had the acid indigestion from the first one. I had it, all right, but it wasn't the coffee that give it to me.

A person can always find *somethin* to be grateful for, no matter how dark things get, and goin back on the ferry, I was grateful that at least I hadn't packed nothing; this way I didn't have all that work to undo again. I was glad I hadn't told Selena, either. I'd set out to, but in the end I was afraid the secret might be too much for her and she'd tell one of her friends and word might get back to Joe that way. It had even crossed my mind that she might get stubborn and say she didn't want to go. I didn't think that was likely, not the way she flinched back from Joe whenever he came close to her, but when it's a teenage girl you're dealin with, anythin's possible—anythin at all.

So I had a few blessings to count, but no idears. I

couldn't very well take the money outta the joint savings account me n Joe had; there was about forty-six dollars in it, and our checkin account was an even bigger laugh—if we weren't overdrawn, we were damned close. I wasn't gonna just grab the kids up and go off, though; no sir and no ma'am. If I did that, Joe'd spend the money just for spite. I knew that as well's I knew my own name. He'd already managed to get through three hundred dollars of it, accordin to Mr. Pease . . . and of the three thousand or so left, I'd put at least twenty-five hundred away myself—I earned it scrubbin floors and warshin windows and hangin out that damned bitch Vera Donovan's sheets—*six* pins, not just four—all summer long. It wasn't as bad then as it turned out to be in the wintertime, but it still wasn't no day in the park, not by a long shot.

Me n the kids were still gonna go, my mind was made up on that score, but I was damned if we was gonna go broke. I meant my children to have their money. Goin back to the island, standin on the foredeck of the *Princess* with a fresh open-water wind cuttin itself in two on my face and blowin my hair back from my temples, I *knew* I was going to get that money out of him again. The only thing I didn't know was *how*.

Life went on. If you only looked at the top of things, it didn't look like anything had changed. Things never *do* seem to change much on the island . . . if you only look at the top of things, that is. But there's lots more to a life than what a body can see on top, and for me, at least, the things underneath seemed completely different that fall. The way I *saw* things had changed, and I s'pose that was the biggest part of it. I'm not just

talkin about that third eye now; by the time Little Pete's paper witch had been taken down and his pitchers of turkeys and Pilgrims had gone up, I was seein all I needed to with my two good natural eyes.

The greedy, piggy way Joe'd watch Selena sometimes when she was in her robe, for instance, or how he'd look at her butt if she bent over to get a dishcloth out from under the sink. The way she'd swing wide of him when he was in his chair and she was crossin the livin room to get to her room; how she'd try to make sure her hand never touched his when she passed him a dish at the supper-table. It made my heart ache for shame and pity, but it also made me so mad that I went around most days feelin sick to my stomach. He was her *father*, for Christ's sake, his blood was runnin in her veins, she had his black Irish hair and double-jointed little fingers, but his eyes'd get all big and round if her bra-strap so much as fell down the side of her arm.

I seen the way Joe Junior also swung wide of him, and wouldn't answer what Joe asked him if he could get away without doin it, and answered in a mutter when he couldn't. I remember the day Joe Junior brought me his report on President Roosevelt when he got it back from the teacher. She'd marked it A-plus and wrote on the front that it was the only A-plus she'd given a history paper in twenty years of teachin, and she thought it might be good enough to get published in a newspaper. I asked Joe Junior if he'd like to try sendin it to the Ellsworth *American* or maybe the Bar Harbor *Times.* I said I'd be glad to pay for the postage. He just shook his head and laughed. It wasn't a laugh I liked much; it was hard n cynical, like his

father's. "And have *him* on my back for the next six months?" he asks. "No thanks. Haven't you ever heard Dad call him Franklin D. Sheenyvelt?"

I can see him now, Andy, only twelve but already purt-near six feet tall, standin on the back porch with his hands stuffed deep in his pockets, lookin down at me as I held his report with the A-plus on it. I remember the little tiny smile on the corners of his mouth. There was no good will in that smile, no good humor, no happiness. It was his father's smile, although I could never have told the boy that.

"Of all the Presidents, Dad hates Roosevelt the most," he told me. "That's why I picked him to do my report on. Now give it back, please. I'm going to burn it in the woodstove."

"No you ain't, Sunny Jim," I says, "and if you want to see what it feels like to be knocked over the porch rail and into the dooryard by your own Mom, you just try to get it away from me."

He shrugged. He done that like Joe, too, but his smile got wide, and it was sweeter than any his father ever wore in his life when it did that. "Okay," he said. "Just don't let him see it, okay?"

I said I wouldn't, and he run off to shoot baskets with his friend Randy Gigeure. I watched him go, holdin his report and thinkin about what had just passed between us. Mostly what I thought about was how he'd gotten his teacher's only A-plus in twenty years, and how he'd done it by pickin the President his father hated the most to make his report on.

Then there was Little Pete, always swaggerin around with his butt switchin and his lower lip pooched out, callin people sheenies and bein kept after school three afternoons outta every five for gettin in trouble. Once I had to go get him because he'd been fightin, and hit some other little boy on the side of the head so hard he made his ear bleed. What his father said about it that night was "I guess he'll know to get out of your way the next time he sees you comin, won't he, Petey?" I saw the way the boy's eyes lit up when Joe said that, and I saw how tenderly Joe carried him to bed an hour or so later. That fall it seemed like I could see everything but the one thing I wanted to see most . . . a way to get clear of him.

You know who finally gave me the answer? Vera. That's right—Vera Donovan herself. She was the only one who ever knew what I did, at least up until now. And she was the one who gave me the idear.

All through the fifties, the Donovans—well, Vera n the kids, anyway—were the summer people of all summer people—they showed up Memorial Day weekend, never left the island all summer long, and went back to Baltimore on Labor Day weekend. I don't know's you could set your watch by em, but I know damn well you could set your *calendar* by em. I'd take a cleanin crew in there the Wednesday after they left and swamp the place out from stem to stern, strippin beds, coverin furniture, pickin up the kids' toys, and stackin the jigsaw puzzles down in the basement. I believe that by 1960, when the mister died, there must have been over three hundred of those puzzles down there, stacked up between pieces of cardboard and growin mildew. I could do a complete cleanin like that because I knew that the chances were good no one would step foot into that house again until Memorial Day weekend next year.

There were a few exceptions, accourse; the year that Little Pete was born they come up n had their Thanksgiving on the island (the place was fully winterized, which we thought was funny, but accourse summer people mostly *are* funny), and a few years later they come up for Christmas. I remember the Donovan kids took Selena n Joe Junior sleddin with em Christmas afternoon, and how Selena come home from three hours on Sunrise Hill with her cheeks as red as apples and her eyes sparklin like diamonds. She couldn't have been no more'n eight or nine then, but I'm pretty sure she had a crush the size of a pickup truck on Donald Donovan, just the same.

So they took Thanksgiving on the island one year and Christmas on it another, but that was all. They were *summer* people . . . or at least Michael Donovan and the kids were. Vera was from away, but in the end she turned out to be as much an island woman as I am. Maybe more.

In 1961 things started out just as they had all those other years, even though her husband had died in that car-crash the year before—she n the kids showed up on Memorial Day and Vera went to work knittin n doin jigsaw puzzles, collectin shells, smokin cigarettes, and havin her special Vera Donovan brand of cocktail hour, which started at five and finished around nine-thirty. But it wasn't the same, even I could see that, n I was only the hired help. The kids were drawn-in and quiet, still mournin their Dad, I guess, and not long after the Fourth of July, the three of em had a real

wowser of an argument while they were eatin at The Harborside. I remember Jimmy DeWitt, who waited table there back then, sayin he thought it had somethin to do with the car.

Whatever it was, the kids left the next day. The hunky took em across to the mainland in the big motorboat they had, and I imagine some other hired hand grabbed onto em there. I ain't seen neither one of em since. Vera stayed. You could see she wasn't happy, but she stayed. That was a bad summer to be around her. She must have fired half a dozen temporary girls before Labor Day finally came, and when I seen the *Princess* leavin the dock with her on it, I thought, I bet we don't see her next summer, or not for as long. She'll mend her fences with her kids—she'll have to, they're all she's got now—and if they're sick of Little Tall, she'll bend to them and go somewheres else. After all, it's comin to be their time now, and she'll have to recognize that.

Which only shows you how little I knew Vera Donovan back then. As far as *that* kitty was concerned, she didn't have to recognize Jack Shit on a hill of beans if she didn't want to. She showed up on the ferry Memorial Day afternoon in 1962—by herself—and stayed right through until Labor Day. She came by herself, she hadn't a good word for me or anybody else, she was drinkin more'n ever and looked like death's Gramma most days, but she came n she stayed n she did her jigsaw puzzles n she went down—all by herself now—n collected her shells on the beach, just like she always had. Once she told me that she believed Donald and Helga would be spending August at Pinewood

(which was what they always called the house; you prob'ly know that, Andy, but I doubt if Nancy does), but they never showed up.

It was durin 1962 that she started comin up regular *after* Labor Day. She called in mid-October and asked me to open the house, which I did. She stayed three days—the hunky come with her, and stayed in the apartment over the garage—then left again. Before she did, she called me on the phone and told me to have Dougie Tappert check the furnace, and to leave the dust-sheets off the furniture. "You'll be seeing a lot more of me now that my husband's affairs are finally settled," she says. "P'raps more of me than you like, Dolores. And I hope you'll be seeing the children, too." But I heard somethin in her voice that makes me think she knew that part was wishful thinkin, even back then.

She come the next time near the end of November, about a week after Thanksgivin, and she called right away, wantin me to vacuum and make up the beds. The kids weren't with her, accourse—this was durin the school week—but she said they might decide at the last minute to spend the weekend with her instead of in the boardin schools where they were. She prob'ly knew better, but Vera was a Girl Scout at heart—believed in bein prepared, she did.

I was able to come right away, that bein a slack time on the island for folks in my line of work. I trudged up there in a cold rain with my head down and my mind fumin away like it always did in the days after I found out what had happened to the kids' money. My trip to the bank had been almost a whole month before, and it had been eatin away at me ever since, the way

bat'try acid will eat a hole in your clothes or your skin if you get some on you.

I couldn't eat a decent meal, couldn't sleep more'n three hours at a stretch before some nightmare woke me up, couldn't hardly remember to change m'own underwear. My mind was never far from what Joe'd been up to with Selena, and the money he'd snuck out of the bank, and how was I gonna get it back again. I understood I had to stop thinkin about those things awhile to find an answer—if I could, one might come on its own—but I couldn't seem to do it. Even when my mind *did* go somewheres else for a little bit, the least little thing would send it tumblin right back down that same old hole. I was stuck in one gear, it was drivin me crazy, and I s'pose that's the real reason I ended up speakin to Vera about what had happened.

I surely didn't *mean* to speak to her; she'd been as sore-natured as a lioness with a thorn in her paw ever since she showed her face the May after her husband died, and I didn't have no interest in spillin my guts to a woman who acted like the whole world had turned to shit on her. But when I come in that day, her mood had finally changed for the better.

She was in the kitchen, pinnin an article she'd cut out of the front page of the Boston *Globe* to the cork bulletin board hung on the wall by the pantry door. She says, "Look at this, Dolores—if we're lucky and the weather cooperates, we're going to see something pretty amazing next summer."

I still remember the headline of that article word for word after all these years, because when I read it, it felt like somethin turned over inside me. TOTAL

ECLIPSE TO DARKEN NORTHERN NEW ENGLAND SKIES NEXT SUMMER, it said. There was a little map that showed what part of Maine would be in the path of the eclipse, and Vera'd made a little red pen-mark on it where Little Tall was.

"There won't be another one until late in the next century," she says. "Our great-grandchildren might see it, Dolores, but we'll be long gone . . . so we better appreciate this one!"

"It'll prob'ly rain like a bugger that day," I says back, hardly even thinkin about it, and with the dark temper Vera'd been in almost all the time since her husband died, I thought she'd snap at me. Instead she just laughed and went upstairs, hummin. I remember thinkin that the weather in her head really *had* changed. Not only was she hummin, she didn't have even a trace of a hangover.

About two hours later I was up in her room, changin the bed where she'd spend so much time layin helpless in later years. She was sittin in her chair by the window, knittin an afghan square n still hummin. The furnace was on but the heat hadn't really took yet—those big houses take donkey's years to get warm, winterized or not—and she had her pink shawl thrown over her shoulders. The wind had come up strong from the west by then, and the rain hittin the window beside her sounded like handfuls of thrown sand. When I looked out that one, I could see the gleam of light comin from the garage that meant the hunky was up there in his little apartment, snug as a bug in a rug.

I was tuckin in the corners of the ground sheet (no fitted sheets for Vera Donovan, you c'n bet your bot-

tom dollar on that—fitted sheets woulda been too easy), not thinkin about Joe or the kids at all for a change, and my lower lip started to tremble. Quit that, I told myself. Quit it right now. But that lip wouldn't quit. Then the upper one started to shimmy, too. All at once my eyes filled up with tears n my legs went weak n I sat down on the bed n cried.

No. No.

If I'm gonna tell the truth, I might's well go whole hog. The fact is I didn't just *cry*; I put my apron up over my face and *wailed.* I was tired and confused and at the end of my thinkin. I hadn't had anything but scratch sleep in weeks and couldn't for the life of me see how I was going to go on. And the thought that kept comin into my head was Guess you were wrong, Dolores. Guess you were thinkin about Joe n the kids after all. And accourse I was. It had got so I wasn't able to think of nothin else, which was exactly why I was bawlin.

I dunno how long I cried like that, but I know when it finally stopped I had snot all over my face and my nose was plugged up n I was so out of breath I felt like I'd run a race. I was afraid to take my apron down, too, because I had an idear that when I did, Vera would say, "That was quite a performance, Dolores. You can pick up your final pay envelope on Friday. Kenopensky"—there, that was the hunky's name, Andy, I've finally thought of it—"will give it to you." That woulda been just like her. Except *anythin* was just like her. You couldn't predict Vera even back in those days, before her brains turned mostly to mush.

When I finally took the apron off my face, she was

sittin there by the window with her knittin in her lap, lookin at me like I was some new and int'restin kind of bug. I remember the crawly shadows the rain slidin down the windowpanes made on her cheeks and forehead.

"Dolores," she said, "please tell me you haven't been careless enough to allow that mean-spirited creature you live with to knock you up again."

For a second I didn't have the slightest idear what she was talkin about—when she said "knock you up," my mind flashed to the night Joe'd hit me with the stovelength and I hit him with the creamer. Then it clicked, and I started to giggle. In a few seconds I was laughin every bit as hard as I'd cried before, and not able to help that any more'n I'd been able to help the other. I knew it was mostly horror—the idear of bein pregnant again by Joe was about the worst thing I could think of, and the fact that we weren't doin the thing that makes babies anymore didn't change it—but knowin what was makin me laugh didn't do a thing about stoppin it.

Vera looked at me a second or two longer, then picked her knittin up out of her lap and went back to it, as calm as you please. She even started to hum again. It was like havin the housekeeper sittin on her unmade bed, bellerin like a calf in the moonlight, was the most natural thing in the world to her. If so, the Donovans must have had some peculiar house-help down there in Baltimore.

After awhile the laughin went back to cryin again, the way rain sometimes turns to snow for a little while durin winter squalls, if the wind shifts the right way.

Then it finally wound down to nothin and I just sat there on her bed, feelin tired n ashamed of myself . . . but cleaned out somehow, too.

"I'm sorry, Mrs. Donovan," I says. "I truly am."

"Vera," she says.

"I beg pardon?" I ast her.

"Vera," she repeated. "I insist that all women who have hysterics on my bed call me by my Christian name thenceforward."

"I don't know what came over me," I said.

"Oh," she says right back, "I imagine you do. Clean yourself up, Dolores—you look like you dunked your face in a bowl of pureed spinach. You can use my bathroom."

I went in to warsh my face, and I stayed in there a long time. The truth was, I was a little afraid to come out. I'd quit thinkin she was gonna fire me when she told me to call her Vera instead of Mrs. Donovan—that ain't the way you behave to someone you mean to let go in five minutes—but I didn't know what she *was* gonna do. She could be cruel; if you haven't gotten at least that much out of what I been tellin you, I been wastin my time. She could poke you pretty much when n where she liked, and when she did it, she usually did it hard.

"Did you drown in there, Dolores?" she calls, and I knew I couldn't delay any longer. I turned off the water, dried my face, and went back into her bedroom. I started to apologize again right away, but she waved that off. She was still lookin at me like I was a kind of bug she'd never seen before.

"You know, you startled the *shit* out of me, woman,"

she says. "All these years I wasn't sure you *could* cry —I thought maybe you were made of stone."

I muttered somethin about how I hadn't been gettin my rest lately.

"I can see you haven't," she says. "You've got a matching set of Louis Vuitton under your eyes, and your hands have picked up a piquant little quiver."

"I got *what* under my eyes?" I asked.

"Never mind," she says. "Tell me what's wrong. A bun in the oven was the only cause of such an unexpected outburst I could think of, and I must confess it's *still* the only thing I can think of. So enlighten me, Dolores."

"I can't," I says, and I'll be goddamned if I couldn't feel the whole thing gettin ready to kick back on me again, like the crank of my Dad's old Model-A Ford used to do when you didn't grab it right; if I didn't watch out, pretty soon I was gonna be settin there on her bed again with my apron over my face.

"You can and you will," Vera said. "You can't spend the day howling your head off. It'll give me a headache and I'll have to take an aspirin. I hate taking aspirin. It irritates the lining of the stomach."

I sat down on the edge of the bed n looked at her. I opened my mouth without the slightest idear of what was gonna come out. What did was this: "My husband is trying to screw his own daughter, and when I went to get their college money out of the bank so I could take her n the boys away, I found he'd scooped up the whole kit n caboodle. No, I ain't made out of stone. I ain't made out of stone at all."

I started to cry again, and I cried for quite awhile,

but not so hard as before and without feelin the need to hide my face behind my apron. When I was down to sniffles, she said to tell her the whole story, right from the beginnin and without leavin a single thing out.

And I did. I wouldn't have believed I could have told *anyone* that story, least of all Vera Donovan, with her money and her house in Baltimore and her pet hunky, who she didn't keep around just to Simonize her car, but I *did* tell her, and I could feel the weight on my heart gettin lighter with every word. I spilled all of it, just like she told me to do.

"So I'm stuck," I finished. "I can't figure out what to do about the son of a bitch. I s'pose I could catch on someplace if I just packed the kids up and took em to the mainland—I ain't never been afraid of hard work—but that ain't the point."

"What *is* the point, then?" she asked me. The afghan square she was workin on was almost done—her fingers were about the quickest I've ever seen.

"He's done everything but rape his own daughter," I says. "He's scared her so bad she may never get all the way over it, and he's paid himself a reward of purtnear three thousand dollars for his own bad behavior. I ain't gonna let him get away with it—*that's* the friggin point."

"*Is* it?" she says in that mild voice of hers, and her needles went click-click-click, and the rain went rollin down the windowpanes, and the shadows wiggled n squiggled on her cheek and forehead like black veins. Lookin at her that way made me think of a story my grandmother used to tell about the three sisters in the

stars who knit our lives . . . one to spin and one to hold and one to cut off each thread whenever the fancy takes her. I think that last one's name was Atropos. Even if it's not, that name has always given me the shivers.

"Yes," I says to her, "but I'll be goddamned if I see a way to do him the way he deserves to be done."

Click-click-click. There was a cup of tea beside her, and she paused long enough to have a sip. There'd come a time when she'd like as not try to drink her tea through her right ear n give herself a Tetley shampoo, but on that fall day in 1962 she was still as sharp as my father's cutthroat razor. When she looked at me, her eyes seemed to bore a hole right through to the other side.

"What's the worst of it, Dolores?" she says finally, puttin her cup down and pickin up her knittin again. "What would you say is the worst? Not for Selena or the boys, but for *you*?"

I didn't even have to stop n think about it. "That sonofawhore's *laughin* at me," I says. "That's the worst of it for me. I see it in his face sometimes. I never told him so, but he knows I checked at the bank, he knows damned well, and he knows what I found out."

"That could be just your imagination," she says.

"I don't give a frig if it is," I shot right back. "It's how I *feel*."

"Yes," she says, "it's how you feel that's important. I agree. Go on, Dolores."

What do you mean, go on? I was gonna say. That's all there is. But I guess it wasn't, because somethin else popped out, just like Jack out of his box. "He

wouldn't be laughin at me," I says, "if he knew how close I've come to stoppin his clock for good a couple of times."

She just sat there lookin at me, those dark thin shadows chasin each other down her face and gettin in her eyes so I couldn't read em, and I thought of the ladies who spin in the stars again. Especially the one who holds the shears.

"I'm scared," I says. "Not of him—of myself. If I don't get the kids away from him soon, somethin bad is gonna happen. I know it is. There's a thing inside me, and it's gettin worse."

"Is it an eye?" she ast calmly, and such a chill swept over me then! It was like she'd found a window in my skull and used it to peek right into my thoughts. "Something like an eye?"

"How'd you know that?" I whispered, and as I sat there my arms broke out in goosebumps n I started to shiver.

"I know," she says, and starts knittin a fresh row. "I know all about it, Dolores."

"Well . . . I'm gonna do him in if I don't watch out. That's what I'm afraid of. Then I can forget all about that money. I can forget all about *everythin.*"

"Nonsense," she says, and the needles went click-click-click in her lap. "Husbands die every day, Dolores. Why, one is probably dying right now, while we're sitting here talking. They die and leave their wives their money." She finished her row and looked up at me but I still couldn't see what was in her eyes because of the shadows the rain made. They went creepin and crawlin all acrost her face like snakes. "I

should know, shouldn't I?" she says. "After all, look what happened to mine."

I couldn't say nothing. My tongue was stuck to the roof of my mouth like an inchbug to flypaper.

"An accident," she says in a clear voice almost like a schoolteacher's, "is sometimes an unhappy woman's best friend."

"What do you mean?" I asked. It was only a whisper, but I was a little surprised to find I could even get that out.

"Why, whatever you think," she says. Then she grinned—not a smile but a grin. To tell you the truth, Andy, that grin chilled my blood. "You just want to remember that what's yours is his and what's his is yours. If he had an accident, for instance, the money he's holding in his bank accounts would become yours. It's the law in this great country of ours."

Her eyes fastened on mine, and for just a second there the shadows were gone and I could see clear into them. What I saw made me look away fast. On the outside, Vera was just as cool as a baby sittin on a block of ice, but inside the temperature looked to be quite a bit hotter; about as hot as it gets in the middle of a forest fire, I'd say at a guess. Too hot for the likes of me to look at for long, that's for sure.

"The law is a great thing, Dolores," she says. "And when a bad man has a bad accident, that can sometimes be a great thing, too."

"Are you sayin—" I begun. I was able to get a little above a whisper by then, but not much.

"I'm not saying *anything*," she says. Back in those days, when Vera decided she was done with a subject,

she slammed it closed like a book. She stuck her knittin back in her basket and got up. "I'll tell you this, though—that bed's never going to get made with you sitting on it. I'm going down and put on the tea-kettle. Maybe when you get done here, you'd like to come down and try a slice of the apple pie I brought over from the mainland. If you're lucky, I might even add a scoop of vanilla ice cream."

"All right," I says. My mind was in a whirl, and the only thing I was completely sure of was that a piece of pie from the Jonesport Bakery sounded like just the thing. I was really hungry for the first time in over four weeks—gettin the business off my chest done that much, anyway.

Vera got as far as the door and turned back to look at me. "I feel no pity for you, Dolores," she said. "You didn't tell me you were pregnant when you married him, and you didn't have to; even a mathematical dunderhead like me can add and subtract. What were you, three months gone?"

"Six weeks," I said. My voice had sunk back to a whisper. "Selena come a little early."

She nodded. "And what does a conventional little island girl do when she finds the loaf's been leavened? The obvious, of course . . . but those who marry in haste often repent at leisure, as you seem to have discovered. Too bad your sainted mother didn't teach you that one along with there's a heartbeat in every potato and use your head to save your feet. But I'll tell you one thing, Dolores: bawling your eyes out with your apron over your head won't save your daughter's maidenhead if

that smelly old goat really means to take it, or your children's money if he really means to spend it. But sometimes men, especially drinking men, *do* have accidents. They fall downstairs, they slip in bathtubs, and sometimes their brakes fail and they run their BMWs into oak trees when they are hurrying home from their mistresses' apartments in Arlington Heights."

She went out then, closin the door behind her. I made up the bed, and while I did it I thought about what she'd said . . . about how when a bad man has a bad accident, sometimes that can be a great thing, too. I began to see what had been right in front of me all along—what I would have seen sooner if my mind hadn't been flyin around in a blind panic, like a sparrow trapped in an attic room.

By the time we'd had our pie and I'd seen her upstairs for her afternoon nap, the could-do part of it was clear in my mind. I wanted to be shut of Joe, I wanted my kids' money back, and most of all, I wanted to make him pay for all he'd put us through . . . especially for all he'd put Selena through. If the son of a bitch had an accident—the right *kind* of accident—all those things'd happen. The money I couldn't get at while he was alive would come to me when he died. He might've snuck off to get the money in the first place, but he hadn't ever snuck off to make a will cuttin me out. It wasn't a question of brains—the way he got the money showed me he was quite a bit slyer'n I'd given him credit for—but just the way his mind worked. I'm pretty sure that down deep, Joe St. George didn't think he was *ever* gonna die.

And as his wife, everything would come right back to me.

By the time I left Pinewood that afternoon the rain had stopped, and I walked home real slow. I wasn't even halfway there before I'd started to think of the old well behind the woodshed.

I had the house to myself when I got back—the boys were off playin, and Selena had left a note sayin she'd gone over to Mrs. Devereaux's to help her do a laundry . . . she did all the sheets from The Harborside Hotel in those days, you know. I didn't have any idear where Joe was and didn't care. The important thing was that his truck was gone, and with the muffler hangin by a thread the way it was, I'd have plenty of warnin if he came back.

I stood there a minute, lookin at Selena's note. It's funny, the little things that finally push a person into makin up her mind—sendin her from could-do to might-do to will-do, so's to speak. Even now I'm not sure if I really meant to kill Joe when I came home from Vera Donovan's that day. I meant to check on the well, yes, but that could have been no more than a game, the way kids play Let's Pretend. If Selena hadn't left that note, I might never have done it . . . and no matter what else comes of this, Andy, Selena must never know that.

The note went somethin like this: "Mom—I have gone over to Mrs. Devereaux's with Cindy Babcock to help do the hotel wash—they had lots more people over the holiday weekend than they expected, and you know how bad Mrs. D.'s arthritis has gotten. The poor

dear sounded at her wit's end when she called. I will be back to help with supper. Love and kisses, Sel."

I knew Selena'd come back with no more'n five or seven dollars, but happy as a lark to have it. She'd be happy to go back if Mrs. Devereaux or Cindy called again, too, and if she got offered a job as a part-time chambermaid at the hotel next summer, she'd prob'ly try to talk me into lettin her take it. Because money is money, and on the island in those days, tradin back n forth was still the most common way of life and cash a hard commodity to come by. Mrs. Devereaux *would* call again, too, and be delighted to write a hotel reference for Selena if Selena ast her to, because Selena was a good little worker, not afraid to bend her back or get her hands dirty.

She was just like me when I was her age, in other words, n look how I turned out—just another cleanin-witch with a permanent stoop in her walk and a bottle of pain-pills in the medicine cabinet for my back. Selena didn't see nothing wrong with that, but she'd just turned fifteen, and at fifteen a girl don't know what the hell she's seein even when she's lookin spang at it. I read that note over n over and I thought, Frig it—she ain't gonna end up like me, old n damn near used up at thirty-five. She ain't gonna do that even if I have to die to keep her from it. But you know something, Andy? I didn't think things'd have to go that far. I thought maybe Joe was gonna do all the dyin that needed to be done around our place.

I put her note back on the table, did up the snaps on my slicker again, and pulled on my gumrubber

boots. Then I walked around back n stood by the big white stone where me'n Selena sat the night I told her she didn't have to be afraid of Joe anymore, that he'd promised to let her alone. The rain'd stopped, but I could still hear the water drippin deep in the blackberry tangle behind the house, and see drops of water hangin off the bare branches. They looked like Vera Donovan's diamond-drop earrings, only not so big.

That patch covered better'n half an acre, and by the time I'd pushed my way in, I was damned glad I had on my slicker and tall boots. The wet was the least of it; those thorns were murder. In the late forties, that patch had been flowers and field-grass, with the well-head sittin on the shed side of it, but about six years after me n Joe were married and moved onto the place—which his Uncle Freddy left him when he died—the well went dry. Joe got Peter Doyon to come over and dowse us a new one, on the west side of the house. We've never had a spot of water-trouble since.

Once we stopped usin the old well, the half-acre behind the shed grew up in those chest-high snarls of scrub blackberry, and the thorns tore and pulled at my slicker as I walked back n forth, lookin for the board cap on the old well. After my hands got cut in three or four places, I pulled the sleeves down over em.

In the end, I almost found the damned thing by fallin into it. I took a step onto somethin that was both loose and kinda spongy, there was a cracklin noise under my foot, and I drew back just before the board I'd stepped on gave way. If I'd been unlucky, I'd've fallen forward, and the whole cap would most likely have collapsed. Ding-dong-bell, pussy's in the well.

I got down on my knees, keepin one hand up in front of my face so the blackberry thorns wouldn't scratch my cheeks or maybe put out one of my eyes, and took a good close look.

The cap was about four feet wide n five feet long; the boards were all white n warped n rotted. I pushed on one of em with my hand, and it was like pushin down on a licorice stick. The board I'd put my foot on was all bowed down, and I could see fresh splinters stickin up from it. I woulda fallen in, all right, and in those days I went about one-twenty. Joe weighed at least fifty pounds more'n that.

I had a handkerchief in my pocket. I tied it around the top of a bush on the shed side of the cap so I could find it again in a hurry. Then I went back into the house. That night I slept like a lamb, and I had no bad dreams for the first time since I'd found out from Selena what her Prince Charmin of a Dad had been up to with her.

That was in late November, and I didn't intend to do anythin more for quite awhile. I doubt if I need to tell you why, but I will, anyway: if anythin happened to him too soon after our talk on the ferry, Selena's eyes might turn to me. I didn't want that to happen, because there was a part of her that still loved him and prob'ly always would, and because I was afraid of how she'd feel if she even *suspected* what happened. Of how she'd feel about *me,* accourse—I guess that goes without sayin—but I was even more afraid of how she might feel about herself. As to how that turned out . . . well, never mind now. I'll get there, I guess.

So I let time go by, although that's always been the

hardest thing for me to do once I've made up my mind about a thing. Still, the days piled up into weeks, like they always do. Every now n then I'd ask Selena about him. "Is your Dad bein good?" is what I asked, and we both understood what I was really askin. She always said yes, which was a relief, because if Joe started up again, I'd have to get rid of him right away, and damn the risks. Or the consequences.

I had other things to worry about as Christmas passed and 1963 got started. One was the money—every day I'd wake up thinkin that this might be the day he'd start spendin it. Why *wouldn't* I worry about that? He'd got through the first three hundred right smart, and I had no way of keepin him from pissin away the rest while I was waitin for time to take time, as they like to say in his A.A. meetins. I can't tell you how many times I hunted for the goddam savins passbook they had to have given him when he opened his own account with that dough, but I never found it. So all I could do was watch for him to come home with a new chain-saw or an expensive watch on his wrist, and hope he hadn't already lost some of it or even all of it in one of the high-stakes poker games he claimed went on every weekend in Ellsworth n Bangor. I never felt s'helpless in my whole life.

Then there was the questions of when and how I was gonna do it . . . if I ended up havin the nerve to do it at all, that was. The idear of usin the old well as a pit-trap was all right as far as it went; the trouble was, it didn't go anywheres near far enough. If he died neat n clean, like people do on TV, everythin would be fine. But even thirty years ago I'd seen enough of life to

know that things hardly ever go the way they do on TV.

Suppose he fell down in there and started screamin, for instance? The island wasn't built up then the way it is now, but we still had three neighbors along that stretch of East Lane—the Carons, the Langills, and the Jolanders. They might not hear screams comin from the blackberry patch behind our house, but then again they might . . . especially if the wind was high and blowin the right way. Nor was that all. Runnin between the village and the Head like it does, East Lane could be pretty busy. There was trucks n cars goin past our place all the time, not as many of them back then, either, but enough to worry a woman who was thinkin about what I was thinkin about.

I'd about decided I couldn't use the well to settle his hash after all, that it was just too risky, when the answer came. It was Vera who gave it to me that time, too, although I don't think she knew it.

She was fascinated by the eclipse, you see. She was on the island most of that season, and as winter started to wear thin, there'd be a new clippin about it pinned to the kitchen bulletin board every week. When spring began with the usual high winds n cold slops, she was here even more, and those clippins showed up just about every other day. There were pieces from the local papers, from away papers like the *Globe* and the New York *Times*, and from magazines like *Scientific American.*

She was excited because she was sure the eclipse would finally lure Donald n Helga back to Pinewood —she told me that again n again—but she was excited

on her own account, too. By the middle of May, when the weather finally started to warm up, she had pretty well settled in completely—she never even *talked* about Baltimore. That friggin eclipse was the only thing she talked about. She had four cameras—I ain't talkin about Brownie Starflashes, either—in the entry closet, three of em already mounted on tripods. She had eight or nine pairs of special sunglasses, specially made open boxes she called "eclipse-viewers," periscopes with special tinted mirrors inside em, and I dunno what else.

Then, near the end of May, I came in and saw the article pinned to the bulletin board was from our own little paper—*The Weekly Tide.* HARBORSIDE TO BE "ECLIPSE CENTRAL" FOR RESIDENTS, SUMMER VISITORS, the headline said. The picture showed Jimmy Gagnon and Harley Fox doin some sort of carpentry on the hotel roof, which was as flat n broad then as it is now. And do you know what? I felt somethin turn over in me again, just like I'd felt when I saw that first article about the eclipse pinned up in the very same place.

The story said that the owners of The Harborside were plannin to turn the roof into a kind of open-air observatory on the day of the eclipse . . . except it sounded like the same old business-as-usual with a brand-new label on it to me. They said the roof was bein "specially renovated" for the occasion (the idear of Jimmy Gagnon n Harley Fox renovatin anythin is pretty funny, when you stop to think of it), and they expected to sell three hundred n fifty special "eclipse tickets." Summer residents would get the first pick, then year-round residents. The price was actually

pretty reasonable—two bucks a throw—but accourse they were plannin on servin food n havin a bar, and those are the places where hotels have always clipped folks. Especially the bar.

I was still readin the article when Vera come in. I didn't hear her, and when she spoke I went just about two feet into the air.

"Well, Dolores," she says, "which'll it be? The roof of The Harborside or the *Island Princess?*"

"What about the *Island Princess?*" I asked her.

"I've chartered it for the afternoon of the eclipse," she says.

"You never!" I says, but I knew the second after it was out of my mouth that she had; Vera had no use for idle talk, nor idle boastin, neither. Still, the thought of her charterin a ferry as big as the *Princess* kinda took my breath away.

"I did," she said. "It's costing me an arm and a leg, Dolores, most of it for the replacement ferry that will run the *Princess*'s regular routes that day, but I certainly did do it. And if you come on *my* excursion, you'll ride free with all drinks on the house." Then, kinda peekin at me from underneath her eyelids, she says, "That last part should appeal to your husband, wouldn't you agree?"

"My God," I says, "why'd you charter the damned *ferry*, Vera?" Her first name still sounded strange to me every time it came out of my mouth, but by then she'd made it clear she hadn't been jokin—she didn't mean to let me go back to Mrs. Donovan even if I wanted to, which I sometimes did. "I mean, I know you're excited about the eclipse and all, but you coulda

got an excursion boat almost as big down to Vinalhaven, and prob'ly at half the expense."

She gave a little shrug and shook her long hair back at the same time—it was her Kiss-My-Back-Cheeks look if I ever seen it. "I chartered it because I love that tubby old whore," she says. "Little Tall Island is my favorite place in all the world, Dolores—do you know that?"

As a matter of fact I *did* know it, so I nodded my head.

"Of course you do. And it's the *Princess* which has almost always brought me here—the funny, fat, waddling old *Princess.* I'm told it will hold four hundred comfortably and safely, fifty more than the roof of the hotel, and I'm going to take anyone who wants to go with me and the kids." Then she grinned, and *that* grin was all right; it was the grin of a girl who's glad just to be alive. "And do you know something else, Dolores?" she asked me.

"Nope," I says. "I'm flummoxed."

"You won't need to bow and scrape to anyone if you—" Then she stopped, and give me the queerest look. "Dolores? Are you all right?"

But I couldn't say anything. The most awful, most wonderful pitcher had filled my mind. In it I seen the big flat roof of The Harborside Hotel filled with people standin around with their necks craned back, and I seen the *Princess* stopped dead in the middle of the reach between the mainland and the island, her decks also chockablock with people lookin up, and above it all hung a big black circle surrounded by fire in a sky filled with daytime stars. It was a spooky pitcher, enough to

raise the hackles on a dead man, but that wasn't what had gut-punched me. It was thinkin about *the rest of the island* that done that.

"Dolores?" she ast, and put a hand on my shoulder. "Do you have a cramp? Feel faint? Come over and sit down at the table, I'll get you a glass of water."

I didn't have a cramp, but all at once I *did* feel a little faint, so I went where she wanted and sat down . . . except my knees were so rubbery I almost fell into the chair. I watched her gettin me the water and thought about somethin she'd said the last November—that even a mathematical dunderhead like her could add n subtract. Well, even one like me could add three hundred and fifty on the hotel roof and four hundred more on the *Island Princess* and come out with seven hundred and fifty. That wasn't *everybody* that'd be on the island in the middle of July, but it was an almighty slug of em, by the Jesus. I had a good idear that the rest would either be out haulin their traps or watchin the eclipse from the shingle and the town docks.

Vera brought me the water and I drank it down all at once. She sat down across from me, lookin concerned. "Are you all right, Dolores?" she ast. "Do you need to lie down?"

"No," I says, "I just come over funny for a few seconds there."

I had, too. All at once knowin what day you plan to kill your husband on, I guess that'd be apt to bring anyone over funny.

Three hours or so later, with the warsh done and the marketin done and the groceries put away and the

carpets vacuumed and a tiny casserole put away in the refrigerator for her solitary supper (she mighta shared her bed with the hunky from time to time, but I never saw her share her dinner-table with him), I was gatherin up my things to leave. Vera was sittin at the kitchen table, doin the newspaper crossword puzzle.

"Think about coming with us on the boat July twentieth, Dolores," she says. "It will be ever so much more pleasant out on the reach than on that hot roof, believe me."

"Thank you, Vera," I says, "but if I've got that day off, I doubt I'll go either place—I'll probably just stay home."

"Would you be offended if I said that sounds very dull?" she ast, lookin up at me.

When did you ever worry about offendin me or anyone else, you snooty bitch? I thought, but accourse I didn't say it. And besides, she really did look concerned when she thought I might be gonna faint, although that coulda been because she was afraid I'd go down on my nose n bleed all over her kitchen floor, which I'd waxed just the day before.

"Nope," I says. "That's me, Vera—dull as dishwater."

She gave me a funny look then. "Are you?" she says back. "Sometimes I think so . . . and sometimes I wonder."

I said goodbye n went on home, turnin the idear I'd had over n over as I went, lookin for holes. I didn't find none—only maybes, and maybes are a part of life, ain't they? Bad luck can always happen, but if people worried about that too much, nothin would ever get

done. Besides, I thought, if things go wrong, I c'n always cry it off. I c'n do that almost right up to the very end.

May passed, Memorial Day came n went, and school vacation rolled around. I got all ready to hold Selena off if she came pesterin about workin at The Harborside, but before we even had our first argument about it, the most wonderful thing happened. Reverend Huff, who was the Methodist minister back then, came around to talk to me n Joe. He said that the Methodist Church Camp in Winthrop had openins for two girl counsellors who had advanced-swimmin qualifications. Well, both Selena and Tanya Caron could swim like fish, Huffy knew it, and to make a long story at least a little shorter, me n Melissa Caron saw our daughters off on the ferry the week after school let out, them wavin from the boat and us wavin from the dock and all four of us crying like fools. Selena was dressed in a pretty pink suit for the trip, and it was the first time I got a clear look at the woman she was gonna be. It almost broke my heart, and does still. Does one of you happen to have a tissue?

Thank you, Nancy. So much. Now where was I?

Oh yes.

Selena was taken care of; that left the boys. I got Joe to call his sister in New Gloucester and ask if she and her husband would mind havin em for the last three weeks or so of July and the first week of August, as we'd had their two little hellions for a month or so in the summer a couple of times when they were younger. I thought Joe might balk at sendin Little Pete away, but he didn't—I s'pose he thought of how quiet

the place'd be with all three gone and liked the idear.

Alicia Forbert—that was his sister's married name—said they'd be glad to have the boys. I got an idear Jack Forbert was prob'ly a little less glad than she was, but Alicia wagged the tail on *that* dog, so there wasn't no problem—at least not there.

The problem was that neither Joe Junior nor Little Pete much wanted to go. I didn't really blame em; the Forbert boys were both teenagers, and wouldn't have so much as the time of day for a couple of squirts like them. I wasn't about to let that stop me, though—I couldn't *let* it stop me. In the end I just put down my head n bulldozed em into it. Of the two, Joe Junior turned out to be the tougher nut. Finally I took him aside and said, "Just think of it as a vacation from your father." That convinced him where nothin else would, and that's a pretty sad thing when you think about it, wouldn't you say?

Once I had the boys' midsummer trip settled, there was nothin to do but wait for em to be gone, and I think that in the end they were glad enough to go. Joe'd been drinkin a lot ever since the Fourth of July, and I don't think even Little Pete found him very pleasant to be around.

His drinkin wasn't no surprise to me; I'd been helpin him do it. The first time he opened the cupboard under the sink and saw a brand-new fifth of whiskey sittin in there, it struck him as odd—I remember him askin me if I'd fallen on my head or somethin. After that, though, he didn't ask any questions. Why would he? From the Fourth til the day he died, Joe St. George was all in the bag some of the time and half in the bag most of

the time, and a man in that condition don't take long to start seein his good fortune as one of his Constitutional rights . . . especially a man like Joe.

That was fine as paint with me, but the time after the Fourth—the week before the boys left and the week or so after—wasn't exactly pleasant, just the same. I'd go off to Vera's at seven with him layin in bed beside me like a lump of sour cheese, snorin away with his hair all stickin up n wild. I'd come home at two or three and he'd be plunked down out on the porch (he'd dragged that nasty old rocker of his out there), with his *American* in one hand and his second or third drink of the day in the other. He never had any comp'ny to help him with his whiskey; my Joe didn't have what you'd call a sharin heart.

There was a story about the eclipse on the front page of the *American* just about every day that July, but I think that, for all his newspaper-readin, Joe had only the fuzziest idear anything out of the ordinary was gonna happen later in the month. He didn't care squat about such things, you see. What Joe cared about were the Commies and the freedom-riders (only he called em "the Greyhound niggers") and that goddam Catholic kike-lover in the White House. If he'd known what was gonna happen to Kennedy four months later, I think he almost coulda died happy, that's how nasty he was.

I'd sit beside him just the same, though, and listen to him rant about whatever he'd found in that day's paper to put his fur up. I wanted him to get used to me bein around him when I come home, but if I was to tell you the work was easy, I'd be a goddamned liar.

I wouldn't have minded his drinkin half as much, you know, if he'd had a more cheerful disposition when he did it. Some men do, I know, but Joe wasn't one of em. Drinkin brought out the woman in him, and for the woman in Joe, it was always about two days before one godawful gusher of a period.

As the big day drew closer, though, leavin Vera's started to be a relief even though it was only a drunk smelly husband I was goin home to. She'd spent all of June bustlin around, jabberin away about this n that, checkin and recheckin her eclipse-gear, and callin people on the phone—she must have called the comp'ny caterin her ferry expedition at least twice a day durin the last week of June, and they was just one stop on her daily list.

I had six girls workin under me in June and eight after the Fourth of July; it was the most help Vera ever had, either before or after her husband died. The house was scrubbed from top to bottom—scrubbed until it shone—and every bed was made up. Hell, we added temporary beds in the solarium and on the second-floor porch as well. She was expectin at least a dozen overnight guests on the weekend of the eclipse, and maybe as many as twenty. There wasn't enough hours in the day for her and she went racin around like Moses on a motorcycle, but she was happy.

Then, right around the time I packed the boys off to their Aunt Alicia and Uncle Jack's—around the tenth or eleventh of July, that would be, and still over a week before the eclipse—her good mood collapsed.

Collapsed? Frig, no. That ain't right. It *popped*, like a balloon that's been stuck with a pin. One day she was

zoomin like a jet plane; the next she was steppin on the corners of her mouth and her eyes had taken on the mean, haunted look I'd seen a lot since she started spendin so much time on the island alone. She fired two girls that day, one for standin on a hassock to warsh the windows in the parlor, and the other for laughin in the kitchen with one of the caterers. That second one was especially nasty, cause the girl started to cry. She told Vera she'd known the young man in high school n hadn't seen him since n wanted to catch up a little on old times. She said she was sorry and begged not to be let go—she said her mother would be madder than a wet hen if that happened.

It didn't cut no ice with Vera. "Look on the bright side, dear," she says in her bitchiest voice. "Your mother may be angry, but you'll have *so* much time to talk about all the fun you had at good old Jonesport High."

The girl—it was Sandra Mulcahey—went down the driveway with her head dropped, sobbin like her heart was gonna break. Vera stood in the hall, bent over a little so she could watch her out the window by the front door. My foot itched to kick her ass when I seen her standin that way . . . but I felt a little sad for her, too. It wasn't hard to figure out what had changed her mood, and before much longer I knew for sure. Her kids weren't comin to watch the eclipse with her after all, chartered ferry or no chartered ferry. Maybe it was just that they'd made other plans, as kids will do with never a thought for any feelins their parents might have, but my guess was that whatever had gone wrong between her and them was still wrong.

Vera's mood improved as the first of her other guests started to show up on the sixteenth n seventeenth, but I was still glad to get away each day, and on Thursday the eighteenth she fired another girl—Karen Jolander, that one was. Her big crime was droppin a plate that had been cracked to begin with. Karen wasn't cryin when she went down the driveway, but you could tell she was just holdin on until she was over the first hill to let loose.

Well, I went and did somethin stupid—but you have to remember I was pretty strung-up myself by then. I managed to wait until Karen was out of sight, at least, but then I went lookin for Vera. I found her in the back garden. She'd yanked her straw sunhat on so hard the brim touched her ears, and she was takin such snaps with those garden-shears of hers that you'd'a thought she was Madam Dufarge choppin off heads instead of Vera Donovan cuttin roses for the parlor n dinin room.

I walked right up to her and said, "That was a boogery thing you done, firin that girl like that."

She stood up and give me her haughtiest lady-of-the-manor look. "Do you think so? I'm so glad to have your opinion, Dolores. I crave it, you know; each night when I go to bed, I lie there in the dark, reviewing the day and asking the same question as each event passes before my eyes: 'What would Dolores St. George have done?' "

Well, that made me madder'n ever. "I'll tell you one thing Dolores Claiborne *don't* do," I says, "and that's take it out on someone else when she's pissed off and disappointed about somethin. I guess I ain't enough of a high-riding bitch to do that."

Her mouth dropped open like somebody'd pulled the bolts that held her jaw shut. I'm pretty sure that was the first time I really surprised her, and I marched away in a hurry, before she could see how scared I was. My legs were shakin so bad by the time I got into the kitchen that I had to sit down and I thought, You're crazy, Dolores, tweakin her tail like that. I stood up enough to peek out the window over the sink, but her back was to me and she was workin her shears again for all she was worth; roses were fallin into her basket like dead soldiers with bloody heads.

I was gettin ready to go home that afternoon when she come up behind me and told me to wait a minute, she wanted to talk to me. I felt my heart sink all the way into my shoes. I hadn't no doubt at all that my time'd come—she'd tell me my services wouldn't be required anymore, give me one last Kiss-My-Back-Cheeks stare, and then down the road I'd go, this time for good. You'd think it'd been a relief to get shut of her, and I s'pose in some ways it woulda been, but I felt a pain around my heart just the same. I was thirty-six, I'd been workin hard since I was sixteen, and hadn't never been fired from a job. Just the same, there's some kinds of buggery-bullshit a person has to stand up to, and I was tryin with all my might to get ready to do that when I turned around to look at her.

When I saw her face, though, I knew it wasn't firin she'd come to do. All the makeup she'd had on that mornin was scrubbed off, and the way her eyelids were swole up gave me the idear she'd either been takin a nap or cryin in her room. She had a brown paper gro-

cery sack in her arms, and she kinda shoved it at me. "Here," she says.

"What's this?" I ast her.

"Two eclipse-viewers and two reflector-boxes," she says. "I thought you and Joe might like them. I happened to have—" She stopped then, and coughed into her curled-up fist before lookin me square in the eye again. One thing I admired about her, Andy—no matter what she was sayin or how hard it was for her, she'd look at you when she said it. "I happened to have two extras of each," she said.

"Oh?" I says. "I'm sorry to hear that."

She waved it away like it was a fly, then ast me if I'd changed my mind about goin on the ferry with her n her comp'ny.

"No," I says, "I guess I'll put up m'dogs on my own porch rail n watch it with Joe from there. Or, if he's actin out the Tartar, I'll go down to East Head."

"Speaking of acting out the Tartar," she says, still lookin right at me, "I want to apologize for this morning . . . and ask if you'd call Mabel Jolander and tell her I've changed my mind."

It took a lot of guts for her to say that, Andy—you didn't know her the way I did, so I guess you'll just have to take my word for it, but it took an *awful* lot of guts. When it came to apologizin, Vera Donovan was pretty much of a teetotaler.

"Sure I will," I said, speakin kind of gentle. I almost reached out n touched her hand, but in the end I didn't. "Only it's Karen, not Mabel. Mabel worked here six or seven years ago. She's in New Hampshire these

days, her mother says—workin for the telephone comp'ny and doin real well."

"Karen, then," she says. "Ask her back. Just say I've changed my mind, Dolores, not one word more than that. Do you understand?"

"Yes," I says. "And thanks for the eclipse-things. They'll come in handy, I'm sure."

"You're very welcome," she says. I opened the door to go out and she says, "Dolores?"

I looked back over my shoulder, and she give me a funny little nod, as if she knew things she had no business knowin.

"Sometimes you have to be a high-riding bitch to survive," she says. "Sometimes being a bitch is all a woman has to hold onto." And then she closed the door in my face . . . but gentle. She didn't slam it.

All right; here comes the day of the eclipse, and if I'm going to tell you what happened—*everything* that happened—I ain't going to do it dry. I been talkin for damn near two hours straight by my watch, long enough to burn the oil offa anyone's bearins, and I'm still a long way from bein done. So I tell you what, Andy—either you part with an inch of the Jim Beam you got in your desk drawer, or we hang it up for tonight. What do you say?

There—thank you. Boy, don't that just hit the spot! No; put it away. One's enough to prime the pump; two might not do anythin but clog the pipes.

All right—here we go again.

On the night of the nineteenth I went to bed so worried I was almost sick to my stomach with it, be-

cause the radio said there was a good chance it was gonna rain. I'd been so goddam busy plannin what I was gonna do and workin my nerve up to do it that the thought of rain'd never even crossed my mind. I'm gonna toss n turn all night, I thought as I laid down, and then I thought, No you ain't, Dolores, and I'll tell you why—you can't do a damn thing about the weather, and it don't matter, anyway. You know you mean to do for him even if it rains like a bastard all day long. You've gone too far to back out now. And I *did* know that, so I closed my eyes n went out like a light.

Saturday—the twentieth of July, 1963—come up hot n muggy n cloudy. The radio said there most likely wouldn't be any rain after all, unless it was just a few thundershowers late in the evenin, but the clouds were gonna hang around most of the day, and chances of the coastal communities actually seein the eclipse were no better'n fifty-fifty.

It felt like a big weight had slipped off my shoulders just the same, and when I went off to Vera's to help serve the big brunch buffet she had planned, my mind was calm and my worries behind me. It didn't matter that it was cloudy, you see; it wouldn't even matter if it showered off n on. As long as it didn't pour, the hotel-people would be up on the roof and Vera's people would be out on the reach, all of em hopin there'd be just enough of a break in the cloud-cover to let em get a look at what wasn't gonna happen again in their lifetimes . . . not in Maine, anyhow. Hope's a powerful force in human nature, you know—no one knows that better'n me.

As I remember, Vera ended up havin eighteen houseguests that Friday night, but there were even more at the Saturday-mornin buffet—thirty or forty, I'd say. The rest of the people who'd be goin with her on the boat (and they were island folk for the most part, not from away) would start gatherin at the town dock around one o'clock, and the old *Princess* was due to set out around two. By the time the eclipse actually began—four-thirty or so—the first two or three kegs of beer'd probably be empty.

I expected to find Vera all nerved up and ready to fly out of her own skin, but I sometimes think she made a damn career outta surprisin me. She was wearin a billowy red-n-white thing that looked more like a cape than a dress—a caftan, I think they're called—and she'd pulled her hair back in a simple hosstail that was a long way from the fifty-buck hairdos she usually sported in those days.

She went around and around the long buffet table that was set up on the back lawn near the rose garden, visitin and laughin with all her friends—most of em from Baltimore, judgin by the look n sound—but she was different that day than she had been durin the week leadin up to the eclipse. Remember me tellin you how she went zoomin back n forth like a jet plane? On the day of the eclipse, she was more like a butterfly visitin among a lot of plants, and her laugh wasn't so shrill or loud.

She seen me bringin out a tray of scrambled eggs n hurried over to give me some instructions, but she didn't walk like she had been walkin the last few days—like she really wanted to be runnin—and the

smile stayed on her face. I thought, She's happy—that's all it is. She's accepted that her kids aren't comin and has decided she can be happy just the same. And that *was* all . . . unless you knew her, and knew how rare a thing it was for Vera Donovan to be happy. Tell you somethin, Andy—I knew her another thirty years, almost, but I don't think I ever saw her really happy again. Content, yes, and resigned, but happy? Radiant n happy, like a butterfly wanderin a field of flowers on a hot summer afternoon? I don't think so.

"Dolores!" she says. "Dolores Claiborne!" It never occurred to me until a lot later that she'd called me by my maiden name, even though Joe was still alive n well that morning, and she never had before. When it *did* occur to me I shivered all over, the way you're s'posed to do when a goose walks acrost the place where you'll be buried someday.

"Mornin, Vera," I said back. "I'm sorry the day's so gray."

She glanced up at the sky, which was hung with low, humid summer clouds, then smiled. "The sun will be out by three o'clock," she says.

"You make it sound like you put in a work-order for it," I says.

I was only teasin, accourse, but she gave me a serious little nod and said, "Yes—that's just what I did. Now run into the kitchen, Dolores, and see why that stupid caterer hasn't brought out a fresh pot of coffee yet."

I set out to do as she ast, but before I got more'n four steps toward the kitchen door, she called after me just like she'd done two days before, when she told me that sometimes a woman has to be a bitch to survive.

I turned around with the idear in my head that she was gonna tell me that same thing all over again. She didn't though. She was standin there in her pretty red-n-white tent-dress, with her hands on her hips n that hosstail lyin over one shoulder, lookin not a year over twenty-one in that white mornin light.

"Sunshine by three, Dolores!" she says. "See if I'm not right!"

The buffet was over by eleven, and me n the girls had the kitchen to ourselves by noon, the caterer and his people havin moved on down to the *Island Princess* to start gettin ready for Act Two. Vera herself left fairly late, around twelve-fifteen, drivin the last three or four of her comp'ny down to the dock herself in the old Ford Ranch Wagon she kep on the island. I stuck with the warshin-up until one o'clock or so, then told Gail Lavesque, who was more or less my second in command that day, that I felt a little headachey n sick to my stomach, and I was gonna go on home now that the worst of the mess was ridded up. On my way out, Karen Jolander gave me a hug and thanked me. She was cryin again, too. I swan to goodness, that girl never stopped leakin around the eyes all the years I knew her.

"I don't know who's been talkin to you, Karen," I said, "but you don't have nothing to thank me for—I didn't do a single solitary thing."

"No one's said a word to me," she says, "but I know it was you, Missus St. George. No one else'd dare speak up to the old dragon."

I gave her a kiss on the cheek n told her I thought she wouldn't have nothing to worry about as long as

she didn't drop any more plates. Then I set out for home.

I remember everythin that happened, Andy—*everythin*—but from the time I stepped off Vera's driveway and onto Center Drive, it's like rememberin things that've happened in the brightest, most real-seemin dream you've ever had in your life. I kep thinkin "I'm goin home to kill my husband, I'm goin home to kill my husband," like I could pound it into my head the way you'd pound a nail into some thick wood like teak or mahogany, if I only kept at it long enough. But lookin back on it, I guess it was in my *head* all the time. It was my *heart* that couldn't understand.

Although it was only one-fifteen or so when I got to the village and the start of the eclipse still over three hours away, the streets were so empty it was spooky. It made me think of that little town down in the southern part of the state where they say no one lives. Then I looked up at the roof of The Harborside, and that was spookier still. There must've been a hundred people or more up there already, strollin around n checkin the sky like farmers at plantin time. I looked downhill to the dock and seen the *Princess* there, her gangplank down and the auto deck full of people instead of cars. They was walkin around with drinks in their hands, havin themselves a big open-air cocktail-party. The dock itself was crammed with people, and there musta been five hundred small boats—more'n I'd ever seen out there at one time anyway—on the reach already, anchored and waitin. And it seemed like everyone you saw, whether they was on the hotel roof or the town dock or the *Princess*, was wearin dark glasses and holdin

either a smoked-glass eclipse-viewer or a reflector-box. There's never been a day like it on the island before or since, and even if I hadn't had in mind what I *did* have in mind, I think it woulda felt like a dream to me.

The greenfront was open, eclipse or no eclipse—I expect *that* booger'll be doin business as usual even on Apocalypse Morn. I stopped in, bought a bottle of Johnnie Walker Red, then walked on out East Lane to the house. I gave the bottle to Joe first thing—didn't make any bones about it, just plopped it into his lap. Then I walked into the house n got the bag Vera had given me, the one with the eclipse-viewers and reflector-boxes in it. When I came out on the back porch again, he was holdin that bottle of Scotch up so he could see the color.

"Are you gonna drink it or just admire it?" I ast him.

He give me a look, kinda suspicious, and says, "Just what the hell *is* this, Dolores?"

"It's a present to celebrate the eclipse," I said. "If you don't want it, I c'n always pour it down the sink."

I made as if to reach for it n he yanked it back real quick.

"You been givin me one helluva lot of presents just lately," he says. "We can't afford stuff like this, eclipse or no eclipse." That didn't stop him from gettin out his pocket-knife and slittin the seal, though; didn't even seem to slow him down.

"Well, to tell you the truth, it's not just the eclipse," I says. "I've just been feelin so good and so relieved that I wanted to share some of my happiness. And since I've noticed that most of what seems to make *you* happy comes out of a bottle . . ."

I watched him take the cap off n pour himself a knock. His hand was shakin a little bit, and I wasn't sorry to see it. The raggeder he was, the better my chances would be.

"What have *you* got to feel good about?" he asks. "Did somebody invent a pill to cure ugly?"

"That's a pretty mean thing to say to someone who just bought you a bottle of premium Scotch," I said. "Maybe I really *should* take it back." I reached for it again and he pulled it back again.

"Fat chance," he says.

"Then be nice," I told him. "What happened to all that gratitude you were s'posed to be learnin in your A.A.?"

He never minded that, just went on lookin at me like a store-clerk tryin to decide if someone'd passed him a phony ten. "What's got you feelin so goddam good?" he asks again. "It's the brats, isn't it? Havin em outta the house."

"Nope, I miss em already," I said, and it was the truth, too.

"Yeah, you would," he says, n drinks his drink. "So what is it?"

"I'll tell you later," I says, n starts gettin up.

He grabbed my arm and said, "Tell me now, Dolores. You know I don't like it when you're fresh."

I looked down at him and says, "You better take your hand off me, or that expensive bottle of hooch might end up gettin broke over your head. I don't want to fight with you, Joe, especially not today. I've got some nice salami, some Swiss cheese, and some water-biscuits."

"Water-biscuits!" he says. "Jesus wept, woman!"

"Never mind," I says. "I'm gonna make us a tray of *hors d'oeuvres* every bit as nice as the ones Vera's guests are gonna have out on the ferry."

"Fancy food like that gives me the shits," he says. "Never mind any hosses' ovaries; just make me a sandwich."

"All right," I agreed. "I will."

He was lookin toward the reach by then—probably me mentionin the ferry'd put him in mind of it—with his lower lip poochin out in that ugly way it had. There were more boats out there than ever, and it looked to me like the sky over em had lightened up a little bit. "Lookit em!" he says in that sneerin way of his—the one his youngest son was tryin so goddam hard to copy. "Ain't nothin gonna happen that's any more'n a thunderhead goin across the sun, and they're all just about shootin off in their pants. I hope it rains! I hope it comes down s'hard it drowns that snooty cunt you work for, and the rest of em, too!"

"That's my Joe," I says. "Always cheery, always charitable."

He looked around at me, still holdin that bottle of Scotch curled against his chest like a bear with a chunk of honeycomb. "What in the name of *Christ* are you runnin on about, woman?"

"Nothin," I says. "I'm going inside to fix the food—a sandwich for you and some *hors d'oeuvres* for me. Then we'll sit n have a couple of drinks n watch the eclipse—Vera sent down a viewer and a reflector-box thingamajig for each of us—and when it's over, I'll tell you what's got me feeling so happy. It's a surprise."

"I don't like fucking surprises," he says.

"I know you don't," I told him. "But you'll get a kick out of this one, Joe. You'd never guess it in a thousand years." Then I went into the kitchen so he could really get started on that bottle I'd bought him at the greenfront. I wanted him to enjoy it—I really did. After all, it was the last liquor he was ever gonna drink. He wouldn't need A.A. to keep him off the sauce, either. Not where he was goin.

That was the longest afternoon of my life, and the strangest, too. There he was, sittin on the porch in his rocker, holdin the paper in one hand and a drink in the other, bitchin in the open kitchen window at me about somethin the Democrats were tryin to do down in Augusta. He'd forgot all about tryin to find out what I was happy about, and all about the eclipse, as well. I was in the kitchen, makin him a sandwich, hummin a tune, and thinkin, "Make it good, Dolores—put on some of that red onion he likes and just enough mustard to make it tangy. Make it good, cause it's the last thing he's ever gonna eat."

From where I was standin, I could look out along the line of the woodshed and see the white rock and the edge of the blackberry tangle. The handkerchief I'd tied to the top of one of the bushes was still there; I could see that, too. It went noddin back n forth in the breeze. Every time it did, I thought of that spongy wellcap right under it.

I remember how the birds sang that afternoon, and how I could hear some of the people out on the reach yellin back and forth to each other, their voices all tiny and far—they sounded like voices on the radio. I can

even remember what I was hummin: "Amazin Grace, how sweet the sound." I went on hummin it while I made my crackers n cheese (I didn't want em any more'n a hen wants a flag, but I didn't want Joe wonderin why I wasn't eatin, either).

It must have been quarter past two or so when I went back out on the porch with the tray of food balanced on one hand like a waitress and the bag Vera'd give me in the other. The sky was still overcast, but you could see it really had gotten quite a bit lighter.

That was a good little feed, as things turned out. Joe wasn't much for compliments, but I could see from the way he put down his paper n looked at his sandwich while he was eatin that he liked it. I thought of somethin I'd read in some book or saw in some movie: "The condemned man ate a hearty meal." Once I'd got that in my head, I couldn't get rid of the damned thing.

It didn't stop me from diggin into my own kip, though; once I got started, I kept goin until every one of those cheese-n-cracker things were gone, and I drank a whole bottle of Pepsi as well. Once or twice I found myself wonderin if most executioners have good appetites on the days when they have to do their job. It's funny what a person's mind will get up to when that person's nervin herself up to do somethin, isn't it?

The sun broke through the clouds just as we were finishin up. I thought of what Vera'd told me that mornin, looked down at my watch, and smiled. It was three o'clock, right on the button. About that same time, Dave Pelletier—he delivered mail on the island back in those days—drove back toward town, hell bent for election and pullin a long rooster-tail of dust behind

him. I didn't see another car on East Lane until long after dark.

I put the plates and my empty soda bottle on the tray, scoochin down to do it, n before I could stand up, Joe done somethin he hadn't done in years: put one of his hands on the back of my neck n give me a kiss. I've had better; his breath was all booze n onion n salami and he hadn't shaved, but it was a kiss just the same, and nothing mean or half-assed or peckish about it. It was just a nice kiss, n I couldn't remember the last time he'd give me one. I closed my eyes n let him do it. I remember that—closin my eyes and feelin his lips on mine and the sun on my forehead. One was as warm n nice as the other.

"That wa'ant half-bad, Dolores," he said—high praise, comin from him.

I had a second there when I kinda wavered—I ain't gonna sit here and say different. It was a second when it wasn't Joe puttin his hands all over Selena that I saw, but the way his forehead looked in study-hall back in 1945—how I saw that and wanted him to kiss me just the way he was kissin me now; how I thought, "If he kissed me I'd reach up and touch the skin there on his brow while he did it . . . see if it's as smooth as it looks."

I reached out my hand n touched it then, just like I'd dreamed of doin all those years before, when I'd been nothin but a green girl, and the minute I did, that inside eye opened wider'n ever. What it saw was how he'd go on if I let him go on—not just gettin what he wanted from Selena, or spendin the money he'd robbed out of his kids' bank accounts, but *workin* on em; belittlin Joe Junior for his good grades n his love of his-

tory; clappin Little Pete on the back whenever Pete called somebody a sheeny or said one of his classmates was lazy as a nigger; workin on em; always workin on em. He'd go on until they were broke or spoiled, if I let him, and in the end he'd die n leave us with nothin but bills and a hole to bury him in.

Well, *I* had a hole for him, one thirty feet deep instead of just six, and lined with chunks of fieldstone instead of dirt. You bet I had a hole for him, and one kiss after three years or maybe even five wasn't gonna change it. Neither was touchin his forehead, which had been a lot more the cause of all my trouble than his pulin little dingus ever was . . . but I touched it again, just the same; traced one finger over it and thought about how he kissed me on the patio of The Samoset Inn while the band inside played "Moonlight Cocktail," and how I'd been able to smell his father's cologne on his cheeks when he did.

Then I hardened my heart.

"I'm glad," I said, n picked up the tray again. "Why don't you see what you can make of those viewers and the reflector-boxes while I do up these few dishes?"

"I don't give a fuck about anything that rich cunt gave you," he says, "and I don't give a fuck about the goddam eclipse, either. I've seen dark before. It happens every goddam night."

"All right," I says. "Suit yourself."

I got as far's the door and he says, "Maybe you n me can get up to dickens later on. What would you think about that, Dee?"

"Maybe," I says, all the time thinkin there was gonna be plenty of dickens, all right. Before it got dark for

the second time that day, Joe St. George was gonna get more dickens than he'd ever dreamed of.

I kept my good weather eye on him while I was standin at the sink and doin up our few dishes. He hadn't done anything in bed but sleep, snore, n fart for years, and I think he knew as well's I did that the booze had as much to do with that as my ugly face . . . prob'ly more. I was scared that maybe the idear of gettin his ashes hauled later on would cause him to put the cap back on that bottle of Johnnie Walker, but no such bad luck. For Joe, fuckin (pardon my language, Nancy) was just a fancy, like kissin me had been. The bottle was a lot realer to him. The bottle was right there where he could touch it. He'd gotten one of the eclipse-viewers out of the bag and was holdin it up by the handle, turnin it this way n that, squintin at the sun through it. He reminded me of a thing I saw on TV once—a chimpanzee tryin to tune a radio. Then he put it down and poured himself another drink.

When I came back out on the porch with my sewin basket, I saw he was already gettin that owly, red-around-the-eyes look he had when he was on his way from moderately tickled to thoroughly tanked. He looked at me pretty sharp just the same, no doubt wonderin if I was gonna bitch at him.

"Don't mind me," I says, sweet as sugar-pie, "I'm just gonna sit here and do a little mendin and wait for the eclipse to start. It's nice that the sun came out, isn't it?"

"Christ, Dolores, you must think this is my birthday," he says. His voice had started to get thick and furry.

"Well—somethin like it, maybe," I says, and began sewin up a rip in a pair of Little Pete's jeans.

The next hour and a half passed slower'n any time had since I was a little girl, and my Aunt Cloris promised to come n take me to my first movie down in Ellsworth. I finished Little Pete's jeans, sewed patches on two pairs of Joe Junior's chinos (even back then that boy would absolutely not wear jeans—I think part of him'd already decided he was gonna be a politician when he grew up), and hemmed two of Selena's skirts. The last thing I did was sew a new fly in one of Joe's two or three pairs of good slacks. They were old but not entirely worn out. I remember thinkin they would do to bury him in.

Then, just when I thought it was never gonna happen, I noticed the light on my hands seemed a little dimmer.

"Dolores?" Joe says. "I think this is what you n all the rest of the fools've been waitin for."

"Ayuh," I says. "I guess." The light in the dooryard had gone from that strong afternoon yellow it has in July to a kind of faded rose, and the shadow of the house layin across the driveway had taken on a funny *thin* kind of look I'd never seen before and never have since.

I took one of the reflector-boxes from the bag, held it out the way Vera'd showed me about a hundred times in the last week or so, and when I did I had the funniest thought: That little girl is doin this, too, I thought. The one who's sittin on her father's lap. She's doin this very same thing.

I didn't know what that thought meant then, Andy,

and I don't really know now, but I'm tellin you anyway—because I made up my mind I'd tell you everythin, and because I thought of her again later. Except in the next second or two I wasn't just *thinkin* of her; I was *seein* her, the way you see people in dreams, or the way I guess the Old Testament prophets must have seen things in their visions: a little girl maybe ten years old, with her own reflector-box in her hands. She was wearin a short dress with red n yellow stripes—a kind of sundress with straps instead of sleeves, you know—and lipstick the color of peppermint candy. Her hair was blonde, and put up in the back, like she wanted to look older'n she really was. I saw somethin else, as well, somethin that made me think of Joe: her Daddy's hand was on her leg, way up high. Higher'n it ought to've been, maybe. Then it was gone.

"Dolores?" Joe ast me. "You all right?"

"What do you mean?" I asks back. "Course I am."

"You looked funny there for a minute."

"It's just the eclipse," I says, and I really think that's what it was, Andy, but I also think that little girl I saw then n again later was a *real* little girl, and that she was sittin with her father somewhere else along the path of the eclipse at the same time I was sittin on the back porch with Joe.

I looked down in the box and seen a little tiny white sun, so bright it was like lookin at a fifty-cent piece on fire, with a dark curve bit into one side of it. I looked at it for a little while, then at Joe. He was holdin up one of the viewers, peerin into it.

"Goddam," he says. "She's disappearin, all right."

The crickets started to sing in the grass right about

then; I guess they'd decided sundown was comin early that day, and it was time for em to crank up. I looked out on the reach at all the boats, and saw the water they were floatin on looked a darker blue now—there was somethin about them that was creepy n wonderful at the same time. My brain kept tryin to believe that all those boats sittin there under that funny dark summer sky were just a hallucination.

I glanced at my watch and saw it was goin on ten til five. That meant for the next hour or so everyone on the island would be thinkin about nothin else and watchin nothin else. East Lane was dead empty, our neighbors were either on the *Island Princess* or the hotel roof, and if I really meant to do him, the time'd come. My guts felt like they were all wound into one big spring and I couldn't quite get that thing I'd seen—the little girl sittin on her Daddy's lap—out of my mind, but I couldn't let either of those things stop me or even distract me, not for a single minute. I knew if I didn't do it right then, I wouldn't never.

I put the reflector-box down beside my sewin and said, "Joe."

"What?" he ast me. He'd pooh-poohed the eclipse before, but now that it'd actually started, it seemed like he couldn't take his eyes off it. His head was tipped back and the eclipse-viewer he was lookin through cast one of those funny, faded shadows on his face.

"It's time for the surprise," I said.

"What surprise?" he ast, and when he lowered the eclipse-viewer, which was just this double layer of special polarized glass in a frame, to look at me, I saw it wasn't fascination with the eclipse after all, or not com-

pletely. He was halfway to bein shitfaced, and so groggy I got a little scared. If he didn't understand what I was sayin, my plan was buggered before it even got started. And what was I gonna do then? I didn't know. The only thing I *did* know scared the hell outta me: I wasn't gonna turn back. No matter how wrong things went or what happened later, I wasn't gonna turn back.

Then he reached out a hand, grabbed me by the shoulder, and shook me. "What in God's name're you talkin about, woman?" he says.

"You know the money in the kids' bank accounts?" I asks him.

His eyes narrowed a little, and I saw he wasn't anywhere near as drunk as I'd first thought. I understood something else, too—that one kiss didn't change a thing. Anyone can give a kiss, after all; a kiss was how Judas Iscariot showed the Romans which one was Jesus.

"What about it?" he says.

"You took it."

"Like hell!"

"Oh yes," I says. "After I found out you'd been foolin with Selena, I went to the bank. I meant to withdraw the money, then take the kids and get them away from you."

His mouth dropped open and for a few seconds he just gaped at me. Then he started to laugh—just leaned back in his rocker and let fly while the day went on gettin darker all around him. "Well, you got fooled, didn't you?" he says. Then he helped himself to a little more Scotch and looked up at the sky through the eclipse-viewer again. This time I couldn't hardly see

the shadow on his face. "Half gone, Dolores!" he says. "Half gone now, maybe a little more!"

I looked down into my reflector-box and seen he was right; only half of that fifty-cent piece was left, and more was goin all the time. "Ayuh," I says. "Half gone, so it is. As to the money, Joe—"

"You just forget that," he told me. "Don't trouble your pointy little head about it. That money's just about fine."

"Oh, I'm not worried about it," I says. "Not a bit. The way you fooled me, though—that weighs on my mind."

He nodded, kinda solemn n thoughtful, as if to show me he understood n even sympathized, but he couldn't hold onto the expression. Pretty soon he busted out laughin again, like a little kid who's gettin scolded by a teacher he ain't in the least afraid of. He laughed so hard he sprayed a little silver cloud of spit into the air in front of his mouth.

"I'm sorry, Dolores," he says when he was able to talk again, "I don't mean to laugh, but I *did* steal a march on you, didn't I?"

"Oh, ayuh," I agreed. It wasn't nothing but the truth, after all.

"Fooled you right and proper," he says, laughin and shakin his head the way you do when someone tells a real knee-slapper.

"Ayuh," I agreed along with him, "but you know what they say."

"Nope," he says. He dropped the eclipse-viewer into his lap n turned to look at me. He'd laughed s'hard

there were tears standin in his piggy little bloodshot eyes. "You're the one with a sayin for every occasion, Dolores. What *do* they say about husbands who finally put one over on their meddling busybody wives?"

" 'Fool me once, shame on you, fool me twice, shame on me,' " I says. "You fooled me about Selena, and then you fooled me about the money, but I guess I finally caught up to you."

"Well maybe you did and maybe you didn't," he says, "but if you're worried about it bein spent, you can just stop, because—"

I broke in there. "I *ain't* worried," I says. "I told you that already. I ain't a *bit* worried."

He give me a hard look then, Andy, his smile dryin up little by little. "You got that smart look on your face again," he says, "the one I don't much care for."

"Tough titty," I says.

He looked at me for a long time, tryin to figure out what was goin on inside my head, but I guess it was as much a mystery to him then as ever. He pooched his lip out again n sighed so hard he blew back the lock of hair that'd fallen on his forehead.

"Most women don't understand the first thing about money, Dolores," he says, "n you're no exception to the rule. I put it all together in one account, that's all . . . so it'd draw more interest. I didn't tell you because I didn't want to listen to a lot of your ignorant bullshit. Well, I've had to listen to some anyway, like I just about always do, but enough's enough." Then he raised up the eclipse-viewer again to show me the subject was closed.

"One account in your own name," I says.

"So what?" he ast. By then it was like we was sittin in a deep twilight, and the trees had begun fadin against the horizon. I could hear a whippoorwill singin from behind the house, and a nightjar from somewhere else. It felt like the temperature had begun to drop, too. It all gave me the strangest feelin . . . like livin in a dream that's somehow turned real. "Why *shouldn't* it be in my name? I'm their father, ain't I?"

"Well, your blood is in em. If that makes you a father, I guess you are one."

I could see him tryin to figure out if that one was worth pickin up and yankin on awhile, and decidin it wa'ant. "You don't want to talk about this anymore, Dolores," he says. "I'm warnin you."

"Well, maybe just a *little* more," I says back, smiling. "You forgot all about the surprise, you see."

He looked at me, suspicious again. "What the fuck're you babblin on about, Dolores?"

"Well, I went to see the man in charge of the savins department at Coastal Northern in Jonesport," I says. "A nice man named Mr. Pease. I explained what happened, and he was awful upset. Especially when I showed him the original savins books weren't missin, like you told him they were."

That was when Joe lost what little int'rest in the eclipse he'd had. He just sat there in that shitty old rocker of his, starin at me with his eyes wide open. There was thunder on his brow n his lips were pressed down into a thin white line like a scar. He'd dropped the eclipse-viewer back into his lap and his hands were openin and closin, real slow.

"It turned out you weren't supposed to do that," I

told him. "Mr. Pease checked to see if the money was still in the bank. When he found out it was, we both heaved a big sigh of relief. He ast me if I wanted him to call the cops n tell em what happened. I could see from his face he was hopin like hell I'd say no. I ast if he could issue that money over to me. He looked it up in a book n said he could. So I said, 'That's what we'll do, then.' And he did it. So that's why I ain't worried about the kids' money anymore, Joe—*I've* got it now instead of you. Ain't that a corker of a surprise?"

"You lie!" Joe shouted at me, n stood up so fast his rocker almost fell over. The eclipse-viewer fell out of his lap n broke to pieces when it hit the porch floor. I wish I had a pitcher of the way he looked just then; I'd stuck it to him, all right—and it went in all the way to the hilt. The expression on the dirty sonofawhore's face was purt-near worth everythin I'd been through since that day on the ferry with Selena. "They can't do that!" he yells. "You can't touch a cent of that dough, can't even look at the fuckin passbook—"

"Oh no?" I says. "Then how come I know you already spent three hundred of it? I'm thankful it wasn't more, but it still makes me mad as hell every time I think of it. You're nothing but a thief, Joe St. George—one so low he'd even steal from his own children!"

His face was as white as a corpse's in the gloom. Only his eyes was alive, and they were burnin with hate. His hands was held out in front of him, openin and closin. I glanced down for just a second and saw the sun—less'n half by then, just a fat crescent—reflected over n over in the shattered pieces of smoked

glass layin around his feet. Then I looked back at him again. It wouldn't do to take my eyes off him for long, not with the mood he was in.

"What did you spend that three hundred on, Joe? Whores? Poker? Some of both? I know it wa'ant another junker, because there ain't any new ones out back."

He didn't say nothin, just stood there with his hands openin and closin, and behind him I could see the first lightnin bugs stitchin their lights across the dooryard. The boats out on the reach were just ghosts by then, and I thought of Vera. I figured if she wasn't in seventh heaven already, she was prob'ly in the vestibule. Not that I had any business thinkin about Vera; it was Joe I had to keep my mind on. I wanted to get him movin, and I judged one more good push'd do it.

"I guess I don't care what you spent it on, anyway," I says. "I got the rest, and that's good enough for me. You can just go fuck yourself . . . if you can get your old limp noodle to stand up, that is."

He stumbled across the porch, crunchin the pieces of the eclipse-viewer under his shoes, and grabbed me by the arms. I could have gotten away from him, but I didn't want to. Not just then.

"You want to watch your fresh mouth," he whispered, blowin Scotch fumes down into my face. "If you don't, I'm apt to."

"Mr. Pease wanted me to put the money back in the bank, but I wouldn't—I figured if you were able to get it out of the kids' accounts, you might find a way to get it out of mine, too. Then he wanted to give me a check, but I was afraid that if you found out what I

was up to before I *wanted* you to find out, you might stop payment on it. So I told Mr. Pease to give it to me in cash. He didn't like it, but in the end he did it, and now I have it, every cent, and I've put it in a place where it's safe."

He grabbed me by the throat then. I was pretty sure he would, and I was scared, but I wanted it, too—it'd make him believe the last thing I had to say that much more when I finally said it. But even that wa'ant the most important thing. Havin him grab me by the throat like that made it seem more like self-defense, somehow—*that* was the most important thing. And it *was* self-defense, no matter what the law might say about it; I know, because I was there and the law wasn't. In the end I was defendin myself, and I was defendin my children.

He cut off my wind and throttled me back n forth, yellin. I don't remember all of it; I think he must have knocked my head against one of the porch posts once or twice. I was a goddam bitch, he said, he'd kill me if I didn't give that money back, that money was his—foolishness like that. I began to be afraid he really *would* kill me before I could tell him what he wanted to hear. The dooryard had gotten a lot darker, and it seemed *full* of those little stitchin lights, as if the hundred or two hundred fireflies I'd seen before had been joined by ten thousand or so more. And his voice sounded so far away that I thought it had all gone wrong, somehow—that I'd fallen down the well instead of him.

Finally he let me go. I tried to stay on my feet but my legs wouldn't hold me. I tried to fall back into the chair I'd been sittin in, but he'd yanked me too far

away from it and my ass just clipped the edge of the seat on my way down. I landed on the porch floor next to the litter of broken glass that was all that was left of his eclipse-viewer. There was one big piece left, with a crescent of sun shinin in it like a jewel. I started to reach for it, then didn't. I wasn't going to cut him, even if he gave me the chance. I *couldn't* cut him. A cut like that—a glass-cut—might not look right later. So you see how I was thinkin . . . not much doubt anyplace along the line about whether or not it was first-degree, is there, Andy? Instead of the glass, I grabbed hold of my reflector-box, which was made of some heavy wood. I could say I was thinkin it would do to bash him with if it came to that, but it wouldn't be true. Right then I really wasn't thinkin much at all.

I was coughin, though—coughin so damned hard it seemed a wonder to me that I wasn't sprayin blood as well as spit. My throat felt like it was on fire.

He pulled me back onto my feet so hard one of my slip straps broke, then caught the nape of my neck in the crook of his arm and yanked me toward him until we was close enough to kiss—not that he was in a kissin mood anymore.

"I told you what'd happen if you didn't leave off bein so fresh with me," he says. His eyes were all wet n funny, like he'd been cryin, but what scared me about em was the way they seemed to be lookin right through me, as if I wasn't really there for him anymore. "I told you a million times. Do you believe me now, Dolores?"

"Yes," I said. He'd hurt my throat s'bad I sounded like I was talkin through a throatful of mud. "Yes, I do."

"Say it again!" he says. He still had my neck caught in the crook of his elbow and now he squeezed so hard it pinched one of the nerves in there. I screamed. I couldn't help it; it hurt dreadful. That made him grin. "Say it like you mean it!" he told me.

"I *do!*" I screamed. "I *do* mean it!" I'd planned on actin frightened, but Joe saved me the trouble; I didn't have to do no actin that day, after all.

"Good," he says, "I'm glad to hear it. Now tell me where the money is, and every red cent better be there."

"It's out back of the woodshed," I says. I didn't sound like I was talkin through a mouthful of mud anymore; by then I sounded like Groucho Marx on *You Bet Your Life.* Which sort of fit the situation, if you see what I mean. Then I told him I put the money in a jar and hid the jar in the blackberry bushes.

"Just like a woman!" he sneers, and then give me a shove toward the porch steps. "Well, come on. Let's go get it."

I walked down the porch steps and along the side of the house with Joe right behind me. By then it was almost as dark as it gets at night, and when we reached the shed, I saw somethin so strange it made me forget everythin else for a few seconds. I stopped n pointed up into the sky over the blackberry tangle. "Look, Joe!" I says. "Stars!"

And there were—I could see the Big Dipper as clear as I ever saw it on a winter's night. It gave me goose-bumps all over my body, but it wasn't nothing to Joe. He gave me a shove so hard I almost fell over. "Stars?"

he says. "You'll see *plenty* of em if you don't quit stallin, woman—I guarantee you that."

I started walkin again. Our shadows had completely disappeared, and the big white rock where me n Selena had sat that evenin the year before stood out almost as bright as a spotlight, like I've noticed it does when there's a full moon. The light wasn't like moonlight, Andy—I can't describe *what* it was like, how gloomy n weird it was—but it'll have to do. I know that the distances between things had gotten hard to judge, like they do in moonlight, and that you couldn't pick out any single blackberry bush anymore—they were all just one big smear with those fireflies dancing back n forth in front of em.

Vera'd told me time n time again that it was dangerous to look straight at the eclipse; she said it could burn your retinas or even blind you. Still, I couldn't no more resist turnin my head n takin one quick glance up over my shoulder than Lot's wife could resist takin one last glance back at the city of Sodom. What I saw has stayed in my memory ever since. Weeks, sometimes whole months go by without me thinkin about Joe, but hardly a day goes by when I don't think of what I saw that afternoon when I looked up over my shoulder and into the sky. Lot's wife was turned into a pillar of salt because she couldn't keep her eyes front n her mind on her business, and I've sometimes thought it's a wonder I didn't have to pay the same price.

The eclipse wasn't total yet, but it was close. The sky itself was a deep royal purple, and what I saw hangin in it above the reach looked like a big black pupil with a gauzy veil of fire spread out most of the way around it. On one side there was a thin crescent of sun still left, like beads of molten gold in a blast furnace. I had no business lookin at such a sight and I knew it, but once I had, it seemed like I couldn't look away. It was like . . . well, you might laugh, but I'm gonna say it anyway. It was like that inside eye had gotten free of me somehow, that it had floated up into the sky and was lookin down to see how I was gonna make out. But it was so much bigger than I'd ever imagined! So much *blacker!*

I probably woulda looked at it until I went stone blind, except Joe gave me another shove and bashed me into the shed wall. That kinda woke me up n I started walkin again. There was a great big blue spot, the kind you see after someone takes a flash pitcher, hangin in front of me, and I thought, "If you burned your retinas and have to look at that for the rest of your life, it'll serve you right, Dolores—it wouldn't be no more than the mark Cain had to bear."

We walked past the white rock, Joe right behind me n holdin onto the neck of my dress. I could feel my slip slidin down on one side, where the strap had broken. What with the dark and that big blue spot hangin in the middle of things, everythin looked off-kilter and out of place. The end of the shed wa'ant nothing but a dark shape, like someone'd taken a pair of shears and cut a roof-shaped hole in the sky.

He pushed me toward the edge of the blackberry patch, and when the first thorn prinked my calf, I remembered that this time I'd forgot to put on my jeans. It made me wonder what else I might have forgot, but accourse it was too late to change anything then; I could see that little scrap of cloth flutterin in the last of the light, and had just time to remember how the wellcap lay beneath it. Then I tore out of his fist and pelted into the brambles, hellbent for election.

"*No you don't, you bitch!*" he bawls at me, n I could hear the bushes breakin as he trampled in after me. I felt his hand grab for the neck of my dress again and almost catch. I jerked loose and kep on goin. It was hard to run because my slip was fallin down and kep hookin on the brambles. In the end they unravelled a great long strip of it, and took plenty of meat off my legs, as well. I was bloody from knees to ankles, but I never noticed until I got back into the house, n that was a long time after.

"*Come back here!*" he bellowed, n this time I felt his hand on my arm. I yanked it free n so he grabbed at my slip, which was floatin out behind me like a bridal train by then. If it'd held, he mighta reeled me in like a big fish, but it was old n tired from bein warshed two or three hundred times. I felt the strip he'd got hold of tear away n heard him curse, kinda high n outta breath. I could hear the sound of the brambles breakin n snappin n whippin in the air, but couldn't see hardly anything; once we was in the blackberry tangle, it was darker'n a woodchuck's asshole, and in the end that hankie I tied up wasn't any help. I saw the edge of the wellcap instead—no more'n a glimmer of white in the darkness just ahead of me—and I jumped with all my

might. I just cleared it, and because I was facin away from him, I didn't actually see him step onto it. There was a big *crrr-aack!* sound, and then he hollered—

No, that ain't right.

He didn't *holler,* n I guess you know it as well's I do. He screamed like a rabbit with its foot caught in a slipwire. I turned around and seen a big hole in the middle of the cap. Joe's head was stickin out of it, and he was holdin onto one of those smashed boards with all his might. His hands were bleedin, and there was a little thread of blood runnin down his chin from the corner of his mouth. His eyes were the size of doorknobs.

"Oh Christ, Dolores," he says. "It's the old well. Help me out, quick, before I fall all the way in."

I just stood there, and after a few seconds his eyes changed. I seen the understandin of what it had all been about come into em. I was never so scared as I was then, standin there on the far side of the wellcap n starin at him with that black sun hangin in the sky to the west of us. I had forgot my jeans, and he hadn't fallen right in like he was s'posed to. To me it seemed like everything had started goin wrong.

"Oh," he said. "Oh, you bitch." Then he started to claw n wriggle his way up.

I told myself I had to run, but my legs wouldn't move. Where was there to run to, anyway, if he got out? One thing I found out on the day of the eclipse: if you live on an island and you try to kill someone, you better do a good job. If you don't, there's nowhere to run n nowhere to hide.

I could hear his fingernails scratchin up splinters in

that old board as he worked at pullin himself out, hand over hand. That sound is like what I saw when I looked up at the eclipse—somethin that's always been a lot closer to me than I ever wanted it to be. Sometimes I even hear it in my dreams, only in the dreams he gets out n comes after me again, and that ain't what really happened. What happened was the board he was clawin his way along all of a sudden snapped under his weight and he dropped. It happened so fast it was almost like he'd never been there in the first place; all at once there was nothin there but a saggy gray square of wood with a ragged black hole in the middle of it and fireflies zippin back n forth over it.

He screamed again goin down. It echoed off the sides of the well. That was somethin else I hadn't figured on—him screamin when he fell. Then there was a thud and he stopped. Just flat stopped. The way a lamp stops shinin if someone yanks the plug outta the wall.

I knelt on the ground n hugged my arms acrost my middle n waited to see if there was gonna be any more. Some time went by, I don't know how much or how long, but the last of the light went out of the day. The total eclipse had come and it was dark as night. There still wasn't any sound comin from the well, but there was a little breeze comin from it toward me, and I realized I could *smell* it—you know that smell you sometimes get in water that comes from shallow wells? It's a coppery smell, dank n not very nice. I could smell that, and it made me shiver.

I saw my slip was hangin down almost to the top of my left shoe. It was all torn n full of rips. I reached under the neck of my dress on the right side n popped that strap, too. Then I pulled the slip down n off. I was bundlin it into a ball beside me n tryin to see the best way to get around the wellcap when all at once I thought of that little girl again, the one I told you about before, and all at once I saw her just as clear as day. *She* was down on her knees, too, lookin under her bed, and I thought, "She's so unhappy, and she smells that same smell. The one that's like pennies and oysters. Only it didn't come from the well; it has something to do with her father."

And then, all at once, it was like she looked around at me, Andy . . . I think she *saw* me. And when she did, I understood why she was so unhappy: her father'd been at her somehow, and she was tryin to cover it up. On top of that, she'd all at once realized someone was lookin at her, that a woman God knows how many miles away but still in the path of the eclipse—a woman who'd just killed her husband—was lookin at her.

She spoke to me, although I didn't hear her voice with my ears; it came from deep in the middle of my head. "Who *are* you?" she ast.

I don't know if I would have answered her or not, but before I even had a chance to, a long, waverin scream came out of the well: *"Duh-lorrrrr-issss . . ."*

It felt like my blood froze solid inside me, and I *know* my heart stopped for a second, because when it started again, it had to catch up with three or four beats all crammed together. I'd picked the slip up, but my fingers relaxed when I heard that scream and it fell out of my hand n caught on one of those blackberry bushes.

"It's just your imagination workin overtime, Dolores," I told myself. "That little girl lookin under the

bed for her clothes and Joe screamin like that . . . you imagined em both. One was a hallucination that somehow come of catchin a whiff of stale air from the well, and the other was no more'n your own guilty conscience. Joe's layin at the bottom of that well with his head bashed in. He's dead, and he ain't gonna bother either you or the kids ever again."

I didn't believe it at first, but more time went by and there was no more sound, except for an owl callin somewhere off in a field. I remember thinkin it sounded like he was askin how come his shift was gettin started so early today. A little breeze ran through the blackberry bushes, makin em rattle. I looked up at the stars shinin in the daytime sky, then down at the wellcap again. It almost seemed to float in the dark, and the hole in the middle he'd fallen through looked like an eye to me. July 20th, 1963, was my day for seein eyes everywhere.

Then his voice come driftin outta the well again. "*Help me Duh-lorrrrr-isss . . .*"

I groaned n put my hands over my face. It wa'ant any good tryin to tell myself *that* was just my imagination or my guilty conscience or anythin else except what it was: Joe. To me he sounded like he was cryin.

"*Help meeeee pleeease . . . PLEEEEEEEASE . . .*" he moaned.

I stumbled my way around the wellcap and went runnin back along the path we'd beat in the brambles. I wasn't in a panic, not quite, and I'll tell you how I know that: I stopped long enough to pick up the reflector-box I'd had in my hand when we started out toward the blackberry-patch. I couldn't remember

droppin it as I ran, but when I saw it hangin off one of those branches, I grabbed it. Prob'ly a damned good thing, too, considerin how things went with that damned Dr. McAuliffe . . . but that's still a turn or two away from where I am now. I *did* stop to pick it up, that's the point, and to me that says I was still in possession of my wits. I could feel the panic trying to reach underneath em, though, the way a cat'll try to get its paw under the lid of a box, if it's hungry and it can smell food inside.

I thought about Selena, and that helped keep the panic away. I could imagine her standin on the beach of Lake Winthrop along with Tanya and forty or fifty little campers, each camper with his or her own reflector-box that they'd made in the Handicrafts Cabin, and the girls showin em exactly how to see the eclipse in em. It wasn't as clear as the vision I'd had out by the well, the one of the little girl lookin under the bed for her shorts n shirt, but it was clear enough for me to hear Selena talkin to the little ones in that slow, kind voice of hers, soothin the ones who were afraid. I thought about that, and about how I had to be here for her and her brothers when they got back . . . only if I gave in to the panic, I probably wouldn't be. I'd gone too far and done too much, and there wasn't nobody left I could count on except myself.

I went into the shed and found Joe's big six-cell flashlight on his worktable. I turned it on, but nothin happened; he'd let the batt'ries go flat, which was just like him. I keep the bottom drawer of his table stocked with fresh ones, though, because we lose the power so often in the winter. I got half a dozen and tried to fill the flashlight up again. My hands were tremblin so bad the first time that I dropped D-cells all over the floor and had to scramble for em. The second time I got em in, but I musta put one or two in bass-ackwards in my hurry, because the light wouldn't come on. I thought about just leavin it; the sun'd be comin out again pretty soon, after all. Except it'd be dark at the bottom of the well even after it *did* come out, and besides, there was a voice in the very back of my mind tellin me to keep on fiddlin and diddlin just as long's I wanted—that maybe if I took long enough, I'd find he'd finally given up the ghost when I did get back out there.

At last I got the flash to work. It made a fine bright light, and at least I was able to find my way back to the wellcap without scratchin my legs any worse'n they already were. I don't have the slightest idear how much time'd gone by, but it was still gloomy and there was still stars showin in the sky, so I guess it wasn't yet six and the sun still mostly covered.

I knew he wasn't dead before I was halfway back—I could hear him groanin and callin my name, beggin me to help him get out. I don't know if the Jolanders or the Langills or the Carons would've heard him if they'd been home or not. I decided it was best not to wonder; I had plenty of problems without takin *that* on. I had to figure out what to do with him, that was the biggest thing, but I couldn't seem to get far. Every time I tried to think of an answer, this voice inside started howlin at me. "It ain't fair," that voice yelled, "this wa'ant in the deal, he's supposed to be *dead,* goddammit, *dead!*"

"*Helllp, Duh-lorrrr-isss!*" his voice come driftin up. It had a flat, echoey sound, as if he was yellin inside a cave. I turned on the light n tried to look down, but I couldn't. The hole in the wellcap was too far out in the middle, and all the flashlight showed me was the top of the shaft—big granite rocks with moss growin all over em. The moss looked black and poisonous in the flashlight beam.

Joe seen the light. "Dolores?" he calls up. "For God's sake, help me! I'm all broken!"

Now *he* was the one who sounded like he was talkin through a throatful of mud. I wouldn't answer him. I felt like if I had to talk to him, I'd go crazy for sure. Instead, I put the flashlight aside, reached out as far as I could, and managed to get hold of one of the boards he'd broken through. I pulled on it and it snapped off as easy as a rotted tooth.

"Dolores!" he yelled when he heard that. "Oh God! Oh God be thanked!"

I didn't answer, just broke off another board, and another, and another. By then I could see that the day had started to brighten again, and birds were singin the way they do in the summer when the sun comes up. Yet the sky was still a lot darker'n it had any business bein at that hour. The stars had gone in again, but the flicker-flies were still circlin around. Meantime, I went on breakin off boards, workin my way toward the side of the well I was kneelin on.

"Dolores!" his voice come driftin up. "You can have the money! All of it! And I'll never touch Selena again, I swear before God Almighty and all the angels I won't! Please, honey, just help me get outta this hole!"

I got up the last board—I had to yank it outta the blackberry creepers to get it loose—and tossed it behind me. Then I shone the light down into the well.

The first thing the beam struck was his upturned face, n I screamed. It was a little white circle with two big black holes in it. For a second or two I thought he'd pushed stones into his eyes for some reason. Then he blinked and it was just his eyes, after all, starin up at me. I thought of what they must have been seein—nothin but the dark shape of a woman's head behind a bright circle of light.

He was on his knees, and there was blood all over his chin and neck and the front of his shirt. When he opened his mouth n screamed my name, more blood came pourin out. He'd broke most of his ribs when he fell, and they musta been stickin into his lungs on both sides like porcupine quills.

I didn't know what to do. I kinda crouched there, feelin the heat come back into the day, on my neck n arms n legs I could feel it, and shinin the light down on him. Then he raised his arms n kinda waved em, like he was drowndin, and I couldn't stand it. I snapped off the light and drew back. I sat there on the edge of the well, all huddled up in a little ball, holdin my bloody knees and shiverin.

"*Please!*" he called up; "*Please!*" n "*Pleeease*" n finally "*Pleeeeeeeeeeze, Duh-lorrr-issss!*"

Oh, it was awful, more awful than anyone could imagine, and it went on like that for a long time. It went on until I thought it would drive me mad. The eclipse ended and the birds stopped singin their good-mornin songs and the flicker-flies stopped circlin (or maybe it was just that I couldn't see em anymore) and out on the reach I could hear boats tootin at each other like they do sometimes, shave n a haircut, two-bits, mostly, and still he wouldn't quit. Sometimes he'd beg and call me honeybunch; he'd tell me all the things he was gonna do if I let him outta there, how he was gonna change, how he was gonna build us a new house and buy me the Buick he thought I'd always wanted. Then he'd curse me and tell me he was gonna tie me to the wall n stick a hot poker up my snatch n watch me wiggle on it before he finally killed me.

Once he ast if I'd throw down that bottle of Scotch. Can you believe that? He wanted his goddam bottle, and he cursed me and called me a dirty old used-up cunt when he seen I wasn't gonna give it to him.

At last it began to get dark again—*really* dark—so it must have been at least eight-thirty, maybe even nine o'clock. I'd started listenin for cars along East Lane again, but so far there was nothin. That was good, but I knew I couldn't expect my luck to hold forever.

I snapped my head up off my chest some time later and realized I'd dozed off. It couldn't have been for long because there was still a little afterglow in the sky, but the fireflies were back, doin business as usual, and the owl had started its hootin again. It sounded a little more comfortable about it the second time around.

I shifted my spot a little and had to grit my teeth at the pins n needles that started pokin as soon's I moved; I'd been kneelin so long I was asleep from the knees down. I couldn't hear nothing from the well, though, and I started to hope that he was finally dead—that he'd slipped away while I'd been dozin. Then I heard

little shufflin noises, and groans, and the sound of him cryin. That was the worst, hearin him cry because movin around gave him so much pain.

I braced m'self on my left hand and shone the light down into the well again. It was hard as hell to make myself do that, especially now that it was almost completely dark. He'd managed to get to his feet somehow, and I could see the flashlight beam reflectin back at me from three or four wet spots around the workboots he was wearin. It made me think of the way I'd seen the eclipse in those busted pieces of tinted glass after he got tired of chokin me and I fell on the porch.

Lookin down there, I finally understood what'd happened—how he'd managed to fall thirty or thirty-five feet and only get bunged up bad instead of bein killed outright. The well wasn't completely dry anymore, you see. It hadn't filled up again—if it'd done that I guess he woulda drowned like a rat in a rain-barrel—but the bottom was all wet n swampy. It had cushioned his fall a little, n it prob'ly didn't hurt that he was drunk, either.

He stood with his head down, swayin from side to side with his hands pressed against the rock walls so he wouldn't fall over again. Then he looked up and saw me and grinned. That grin struck a chill all the way through me, Andy, because it was the grin of a dead man—a dead man with blood all over his face n shirt, a dead man with what looked like stones pushed into his eyes.

Then he started to climb the wall.

I was lookin right at it n still I couldn't believe it. He jammed his fingers in between two of the big rocks

stickin out of the side and yanked himself up until he could get one of his feet wedged in between two more. He rested there a minute, and then I seen one of his hands go gropin up n over his head again. It looked like a fat white bug. He found another rock to hold onto, set his grip, and brought his other hand up to join it. Then he pulled himself up again. When he stopped to rest the next time, he turned his bloody face up into the beam of my light, and I saw little bits of moss from the rock he was holdin onto crumble down onto his cheeks n shoulders.

He was still grinnin.

Can I have another drink, Andy? No, not the Beam—no more of that tonight. Just water'll do me fine from here on out.

Thanks. Thanks very much.

Anyway, he was feelin around for his next hold when his feet slipped n he fell. There was a muddy squelchin sound when he landed on his ass. He screamed n grabbed at his chest like they do on TV when they're supposed to be havin heart-attacks, and then his head fell forward on his chest.

I couldn't stand any more. I stumbled my way outta the blackberry creepers n ran back to the house. I went into the bathroom n puked my guts. Then I went into the bedroom n laid down. I was shakin all over, and I kep thinkin, What if he *still* ain't dead? What if he stays alive all night, what if he stays alive for *days*, drinkin the seep comin out from between the rocks or up through the mud? What if he keeps screamin for help until one of the Carons or Langills or Jolanders hears him and calls Garrett Thibodeau? Or what if someone

comes to the house tomorrow—one of his drinkin buddies, or someone wantin him to crew on their boat or fix an engine—and hears screams comin outta the blackberry patch? What then, Dolores?

There was another voice that answered all those questions. I suppose it belonged to the inside eye, but to me it sounded a lot more like Vera Donovan than it did Dolores Claiborne; it sounded bright n dry n kiss-my-back-cheeks-if-you-don't-like-it. "Of course he's dead," that voice said, "and even if he isn't, he soon will be. He'll die of shock and exposure and punctured lungs. There are probably people who wouldn't believe a man could die of exposure on a July night, but they'd be people who've never spent a few hours thirty feet under the ground, sitting right on top of the dank island bedrock. I know none of that is pleasant to think of, Dolores, but at least it means you can quit your worrying. Sleep for awhile, and when you go back out there, you'll see."

I didn't know if that voice was makin sense or not, but it *seemed* to be makin sense, and I did try to go to sleep. I couldn't, though. Each time I'd drift a little, I'd think I could hear Joe stumblin his way up the side of the shed toward the back door, and every time the house creaked, I jumped.

At last I couldn't stand it anymore. I took off my dress, put on a pair of jeans n a sweater (lockin the barn door after the hoss has been stolen, I guess you'd say), and grabbed the flashlight off the bathroom floor from beside the commode, where I'd dropped it when I knelt down to vomit. Then I went back out.

It was darker'n ever. I don't know if there was any

kind of moon that night, but it wouldn't've mattered even if there was, because the clouds had rolled back in again. The closer I got to the blackberry tangle behind the shed, the heavier my feet got. By the time I could see the wellcap again in the flashlight beam, it seemed like I couldn't hardly lift em at all.

I did, though—I made myself walk right up to it. I stood there listenin for almost five minutes and there wasn't a sound but the crickets and the wind rattlin through the blackberry bushes and an owl hooty-hooin someplace . . . prob'ly the exact same one I'd heard before. Oh, and far off to the east I could hear the waves strikin the headland, only that's a sound you get so used to on the island you don't hardly hear it at all. I stood there with Joe's flashlight in my hand, the beam aimed at the hole in the wellcap, feelin greasy, sticky sweat creepin down all over my body, stingin in the cuts n digs the blackberry thorns had made, and I told myself to kneel down and look in the well. After all, wa'ant that what I'd come out there to do?

It was, but once I was actually out there, I couldn't do it. All I could do was tremble n make a high moanin sound in my throat. My heart wasn't really beatin, either, but only flutterin in my chest like a humminbird's wings.

And then a white hand all streaked with dirt n blood n moss snaked right outta that well n grabbed my ankle.

I dropped the flashlight. It fell in the bushes right at the edge of the well, which was lucky for me; if it'd fallen *into* the well, I'd've been in deep shit indeed. But I wasn't thinkin about the flashlight or my good luck, because the shit I was in right then was plenty

deep enough, and the only thing I was thinkin about was the hand on my ankle, the hand that was draggin me toward the hole. That, and a line from the Bible. It clanged in my head like a big iron bell: *I have digged a pit for mine enemies, and am fallen into it myself.*

I screamed n tried to pull away, but Joe had me so tight it felt like his hand'd been dipped in cement. My eyes had adjusted to the dark enough so I could see him even with the flashlight beam shinin off in the wrong direction. He'd almost managed to climb outta the well, after all. God knows how many times he musta fallen back, but in the end he got almost to the top. I think he prob'ly would've made it all the way out if I hadn't come back when I did.

His head was no more'n two feet below what was left of the board cap. He was still grinnin. His lower plate was stuck out of his mouth a little—I can still see that as clear as I see you sittin acrost from me right now, Andy—and it looked like a hoss's teeth when it grins at you. Some of em looked black with the blood that was on em.

"*Duh-lorrrr-isss,*" he panted, and kep pullin me. I screamed n fell down on my backside n went slidin toward that damned hole in the ground. I could hear the blackberry thorns tickin n snickin as my jeans went slidin past em and over em. "*Duh-lorrr-issss you biiiitch,*" he says, but by then it was more like he was singin to me. I remember thinkin, "Pretty soon he'll start in on 'Moonlight Cocktail.' "

I grabbed at the bushes n got my hands full of stickers n fresh blood. I kicked at his head with the foot he didn't have ahold of, but it was just a little too low to

hit; I parted his hair with the heel of my sneaker a couple of times, but that was just about all.

"*Come on Duh-lorrrr-issss*," he said, like he wanted to take me out for an ice cream soda or maybe dancin to the country n western over at Fudgy's.

My ass fetched up against one of the boards still left on the side of the well, and I knew if I didn't do somethin right away, we was gonna go tumblin down together, and there we'd stay, prob'ly wrapped in each other's arms. And when we was found, there'd be people—ninnies like Yvette Anderson, for the most part—who'd say it just went to show how much we loved each other.

That did it. I found a little extra strength and give one last tug backwards. He almost held on, but then his hand slipped off. My sneaker musta hit him in the face. He screamed, his hand beat at the end of my foot a couple of times, and then it was gone for good. I waited to hear him go tumblin to the bottom, but he didn't. The son of a bitch *never* gave up; if he'd lived the same way he died, I don't know that we'd ever've had any problems, him n me.

I got up on my knees n saw him go swayin backwards over the hole . . . but somehow he held on. He looked up at me, shook a bloody clump of hair outta his eyes, and grinned. Then his hand come up outta the well again n grabbed onto the ground.

"*Dul-OOH-russ*," he kinda groaned. "*Dul-OOOH-russ, Dul-OOOH-russ, Dul-OOOOOHHH-russs!*" And then he started to climb out.

"Brain him, you ninny," Vera Donovan said then. Not in my head, like the voice of the little girl I seen

earlier. Do you understand what I'm sayin? I heard that voice just like you three are hearin me now, and if Nancy Bannister's tape-recorder had been out there, you could've played that voice back over n over n over again. I know that as well's I know my own name.

Anyway, I grabbed one of the stones set into the ground at the edge of the well. He kinda clutched at my wrist, but I pulled the stone free before he could set his grip. It was a big stone, all crusted with dry moss. I raised it over my head. He looked up at it. His head was outta the hole by then, and it looked like his eyes was standin out on stalks. I brought the rock down on him with all my strength. I heard that lower plate of his bust. It sounded like when you drop a china plate on a brick hearth. And then he was gone, tumblin back down the well, and the rock went with him.

I fainted then. I don't *remember* faintin, just layin back and lookin up at the sky. There was nothin to see because of the clouds, so I closed my eyes . . . only when I opened em, the sky was full of stars again. It took me a little while to realize what'd happened, that I'd fainted and the clouds had blown away while I was passed out.

The flashlight was still layin in the brambles beside the well, and the beam was still nice n bright. I picked it up and shone it down into the well. Joe was layin at the bottom, his head cocked over on one shoulder, his hands in his lap, and his legs splayed out. The rock I'd brained him with was layin between em.

I held the light on him for five minutes, waitin to see if he'd move, but he never. Then I got up n made my way back to the house. I had to stop twice when

the world went foggy on me, but I finally made it. I walked into the bedroom, takin off my clothes as I went n leavin em just wherever they fell. I got into the shower n only stood there under spray as hot as I could take it for the next ten minutes or so, not soapin myself, not warshin my hair, not doin nothin but standin with my face up so the water'd hit all over it. I think I mighta fallen asleep right there in the shower, except the water started to cool off. I warshed my hair quick, before it could go all the way to stone cold, and got out. My arms n legs were all scratched up and my throat still hurt like hell, but I didn't think I was gonna die from none of that. It never occurred to me what somebody might make of all those scratches, not to mention the bruises on my throat, after Joe was found down the well. Not then, at least.

I pulled my nightgown on n fell on the bed n went fast asleep with the light on. I woke up screamin less'n an hour later with Joe's hand on my ankle. I had a moment of relief when I realized it was only a dream, but then I thought, "What if he's climbin the side of the well again?" I knew he wasn't—I'd finished him for good when I hit him with that rock and he fell down the second time—but part of me was sure he *was,* and that he'd be out in another minute or so. Once he was, he'd come for me.

I tried to lie there n wait it out, but I couldn't—that pitcher of him climbin up the side of the well just kept gettin clearer n clearer, and my heart was beatin so hard it felt like it might explode. Finally I put on my sneakers, grabbed the flashlight again, and went runnin out there in my nightgown. I *crawled* to the edge of

the well that time; I couldn't make myself walk, not for nothing. I was too afraid of his white hand snakin up outta the dark n grabbin onto me.

At last I shone the light down. He was layin there just the same as he had been, with his hands in his lap n his head cocked to one side. The rock was still layin in the same place, between his spread legs. I looked for a long time, and when I went back to the house that time, I'd begun to know he was really dead.

I crawled into bed, turned off the lamp, and pretty soon I corked off to sleep. The last thing I remember thinkin was "I'll be all right now," but I wasn't. I woke up a couple of hours later, sure I could hear someone in the kitchen. Sure I could hear *Joe* in the kitchen. I tried to jump outta bed and my feet tangled in the blankets and I fell on the floor. I got up n started feelin around for the switch on the lamp, sure I'd feel his hands slide around my throat before I could find it.

That didn't happen, accourse. I turned on the light n went through the whole house. It was empty. Then I put on my sneakers n grabbed the flashlight n ran back out to the well.

Joe was still layin on the bottom with his hands in his lap n his head on his shoulder. I had to look at him a long time, though, before I could convince myself it was layin on the *same* shoulder. And once I thought I saw his foot move, although that was most likely just a shadow movin. There were lots of those, because the hand holdin the flashlight wasn't none too steady, let me tell you.

As I crouched there with my hair tied back and prob'ly lookin like the lady on the White Rock labels, the funniest urge come over me—I felt like just lettin myself lean forward on my knees until I tumbled into the well. They'd find me with him—not the ideal way to finish up, s'far's I was concerned—but at least I wouldn't be found with his arms wrapped around me . . . n I wouldn't have to keep wakin up with the idear he was in the room with me, or feelin I had to run back out with the light to check n make sure he was still dead.

Then Vera's voice spoke up again, only this time it *was* in my head. I know that, just like I know that it spoke right into my ear the first time. "The only place you're going to tumble into is your own bed," that voice told me. "Get some sleep, and when you wake up, the eclipse really will be over. You'll be surprised how much better things will look with the sun out."

That sounded like good advice, and I set out to follow it. I locked both doors to the outside, though, and before I actually got into bed, I did somethin I ain't never done before or since: propped a chair underneath the doorknob. I'm ashamed to admit that—my cheeks feel all hot, so I guess I'm blushin—but it musta helped, because I was asleep the second my head hit the pillow. When I opened my eyes the next time, full daylight was streamin in through the window. Vera had told me to take the day off—she said Gail Lavesque and a few of the other girls could oversee puttin the house to rights after the big party she'd been plannin for the night of the twentieth—and I was some glad.

I got up n took another shower n then got dressed. It took me half an hour to do all those things because

I was so lamed up. It was my back, mostly; it's been my weak point ever since the night Joe hit me in the kidneys with that stovelength, and I'm pretty sure I strained it again first pullin that rock I clouted him with free of the earth, then h'istin it up over my head the way I did. Whatever it was, I can tell you it hurt a bitch.

Once I finally had my clothes on, I sat down at the kitchen table in the bright sunshine and drank a cup of black coffee n thought of the things I ought to do. There wasn't many, even though nothing had gone just the way I'd meant for it to go, but they'd have to be done right; if I forgot somethin or overlooked somethin, I'd go to prison. Joe St. George wa'ant much loved on Little Tall, and there weren't many who'd've blamed me for what I did, but they don't pin a medal on you n give you a parade for killin a man, no matter if he was a worthless piece of shit.

I poured myself a fresh slug of mud and went out on the back porch to drink it . . . and to cast my eye around. Both reflector-boxes and one of the viewers were back in the grocery sack Vera'd given me. The pieces of the other viewer were layin right where they'd been since Joe jumped up sudden and it slid out of his lap n broke on the porch boards. I thought for quite awhile about those pieces of glass. Finally I went inside, got the broom n the dustpan, and swep em up. I decided that, bein the way I am and so many folks on the island *knowin* the way I am, it'd be more suspicious if I left em layin.

I'd started off with the idear of sayin I'd never seen Joe at all that afternoon. I thought I'd tell folks he'd been gone when I got home from Vera's, without

s'much as a note left behind to say where he'd taken his country butt off to, and that I'd poured that bottle of expensive Scotch whiskey out on the ground because I was mad at him. If they did tests that showed he was drunk when he fell into the well, it wouldn't bother me none; Joe could have gotten booze lots of places, includin under our own kitchen sink.

One look into the mirror convinced me that wouldn't do—if Joe hadn't been home to put those bruises on my neck, then they'd want to know who *had* put em there, and what was I gonna say? Santy Claus did it? Luckily, I'd left myself an out—I'd told Vera that if Joe started actin out the Tartar, prob'ly I'd leave him to stew in his own sauce n watch the eclipse from East Head. I hadn't had any plan in mind when I said those words, but I blessed em now.

East Head itself wouldn't do—there'd been people there, and they'd know I hadn't been with em—but Russian Meadow's on the way to East Head, it's got a good western view, and there hadn't been nobody at all there. I'd seen that for myself from my seat on the porch, and again while I was warshin up our dishes. The only real question—

What, Frank?

No, I wa'ant worried a bit about his truck bein at the house. He had a string of three or four DWIs right close together back in '59, you see, and finally lost his driver's licence for a month. Edgar Sherrick, who was our constable back then, came around n told him that he could drink until the cows came home, if that was what he wanted, but the next time he got caught drinkin and drivin, Edgar'd hoe him into district court n try to get his driver's licence lifted for a year. Edgar n his wife lost a little girl to a drunk driver back in 1948 or '49, and although he was an easygoin man about other things, he was death on drunks behind the wheel. Joe knew it, and he quit drivin if he'd had more'n two drinks right after him n Edgar had their little chat on our porch. No, when I came back from Russian Meadow and found Joe gone, I thought one of his friends must've come by n taken him someplace to celebrate Eclipse Day—that was the story I meant to tell.

What I started to say was the only real question I had was what to do about the whiskey bottle. People knew I'd been buyin him his drink just lately, but that was all right; I knew they thought I'd been doin it so he'd lay off hittin me. But where would that bottle have ended up if the story I was makin up had been a true story? It might not matter, but then again it might. When you've done a murder, you never know what may come back to haunt you later on. It's the best reason I know not to do it. I put myself in Joe's place—it wa'ant as hard to do as you might think—and knew right off that Joe wouldn't have gone nowhere with no one if there'd been so much as a sip of whiskey left in that bottle. It had to go down the well with him, and that's where it *did* go . . . all but the cap, that was. That I dropped into the swill on top of the little pile of broken tinted glass.

I walked out to the well with the last of the Scotch swishin in the bottle, thinkin, "He put the old booze to him and that was all right, that was no more'n what I expected, but then he kinda mistook my neck for a

pump-handle, and that *wa'ant* all right, so I took my reflector-box and went up to Russian Meadow by m'self, cursin the impulse that made me stop n buy him that bottle of Johnnie Walker in the first place. When I got back, he was gone. I didn't know where or who with, n I didn't care. I just cleared up his mess and hoped he'd be in a better frame of mind when he got back." I thought that sounded meek enough, and that it'd pass muster.

I guess what I mostly disliked about that goddam bottle was gettin rid of it meant goin back out there and lookin at Joe again. Still, my likes n dislikes didn't make a whole lot of difference by then.

I was worried about the state the blackberry bushes might be in, but they wasn't trampled down as bad as I'd been afraid they might be, and some were springin back already. I figured they'd look pretty much like always by the time I reported Joe missin.

I'd hoped the well wouldn't look quite so scary in broad daylight, but it did. The hole in the middle of the cap looked even creepier. It didn't look s'much like an eye with some of the boards pulled back, but not even that helped. Instead of an eye, it looked like an empty socket where somethin had finally rotted so bad it'd fallen completely out. And I could smell that dank, coppery smell. It made me think of the girl I'd glimpsed in my mind, and I wondered how *she* was doin on the mornin after.

I wanted to turn around n go back to the house, but I marched right up to the well instead, without so much as a single dragged foot. I wanted to get the next part behind me as soon as I could . . . n not look back.

What I had to do from then on out, Andy, was to think about my kids and keep faced front no matter what.

I scooched down n looked in. Joe was still layin there with his hands in his lap and his head cocked over on one shoulder. There was bugs runnin around on his face, and it was seein those that made me know once n for good that he really was dead. I held the bottle out with a hanky wrapped around the neck—it wa'ant a question of fingerprints, I just didn't want to touch it—and dropped it. It landed in the mud beside him but didn't break. The bugs scattered, though; they ran down his neck and into the collar of his shirt. I never forgot that.

I was gettin up to leave—the sight of those bugs divin for cover had left me feelin pukey again—when my eye fixed on the jumble of boards I'd pulled up so I could get a look at him that first time. It wasn't no good leavin em there; they'd raise all sorts of questions if I did.

I thought about em for a little while, and then, when I realized the mornin was slippin away on me and somebody might drop by anytime to talk about either the eclipse or Vera's big doins, I said to hell with it n threw em down the well. Then I went back to the house. *Worked* my way back to the house, I should say, because there were pieces of my dress n slip hangin from a good many thorns, and I picked off as many as I could. Later on that day I went back and picked off the three or four I missed the first time. There were little bits of fluff from Joe's flannel shirt, too, but I left those. "Let Garrett Thibodeau make anything of em he can," I thought. "Let *anyone* make anything of em they can.

It's gonna look like he got drunk n fell down the well no matter what, and with the reputation Joe's got around here, whatever they decide on'll most likely go in my favor."

Those little pieces of cloth didn't go in the swill with the broken glass and the Johnnie Walker cap, though; those I threw in the ocean later on that day. I was across the dooryard and gettin ready to climb the porch steps when a thought hit me. Joe had grabbed onto the piece of my slip that'd been trailin out behind me—suppose he *still* had a piece of it? Suppose it was clutched in one of the hands that was layin curled up in his lap at the bottom of the well?

That stopped me cold . . . and cold's just what I mean. I stood there in the dooryard under that hot July sun, my back all prickles and feelin zero at the bone, as some poime I read in high school said. Then Vera spoke up inside my mind again. "Since you can't do anything about it, Dolores," she says, "I'd advise you to let it go." It seemed like pretty good advice, so I went on up the steps and back inside.

I spent most of the mornin walkin around the house n out on the porch, lookin for . . . well, I dunno. I dunno what I was lookin for, exactly. Maybe I was expectin that inside eye to happen on somethin else that needed to be done or taken care of, the way it had happened on that little pile of boards. If so, I didn't see anything.

Around eleven o'clock I took the next step, which was callin Gail Lavesque up at Pinewood. I ast her what she thought of the eclipse n all, then ast how things was goin over at Her Nibs'.

"Well," she says, "I can't complain since I haven't seen nobody but that older fella with the bald head and the toothbrush mustache—do you know the one I mean?"

I said I did.

"He come downstairs about nine-thirty, went out back in the garden, walkin slow and kinda holdin his head, but at least *up*, which is more than you c'n say for the rest of em. When Karen Jolander asked him if he'd like a glass of fresh-squeezed orange-juice, he ran over to the edge of the porch n puked in the petunias. You shoulda heard him, Dolores—*Bleeeeee-ahhh!*"

I laughed until I almost cried, and no laughter ever felt better to me.

"They must have had quite a party when they got back from the ferry," Gail says. "If I had a nickel for every cigarette butt I've dumped this mornin—just a *nickel*, mindja—I could buy a brand-new Chevrolet. But I'll have the place spick n spiffy by the time Missus Donovan drags her hangover down the front stairs, you can count on that."

"I know you will," I says, "and if you need any help, you know who to call, don't you?"

Gail give a laugh at that. "Never mind," she says. "You worked your fingers to the bone over the last week—and Missus Donovan knows it as well as I do. She don't want to see you before tomorrow mornin, and neither do I."

"All right," I says, and then I took a little pause. She'd be expectin me to say goodbye, and when I said somethin else instead, she'd pay particular mind to

it . . . which was what I wanted. "You haven't seen Joe over there, have you?" I ast her.

"Joe?" she says. "*Your* Joe?"

"Ayuh."

"No—I've never seen him up here. Why do you ask?"

"He didn't come home last night."

"Oh, Dolores!" she says, soundin horrified n int'rested at the same time. "Drinkin?"

"Coss," I says. "Not that I'm really worried—this ain't the first time he's stayed out all night howlin at the moon. He'll turn up; bad pennies always do."

Then I hung up, feelin I'd done a pretty fair job plantin the first seed.

I made myself a toasted cheese sandwich for lunch, then couldn't eat it. The smell of the cheese n fried bread made my stomach feel all hot n sweaty. I took two asp'rins instead n laid down. I didn't think I'd fall asleep, but I did. When I woke up it was almost four o'clock n time to plant a few more seeds. I called Joe's friends—those few that had phones, that is—and asked each one if they'd seen him. He hadn't come home last night, I said, he *still* wa'ant home, and I was startin to get worried. They all told me no, accourse, and every one of em wanted to hear all the gory details, but the only one I said anything to was Tommy Anderson—prob'ly because I knew Joe'd bragged to Tommy before about how he kep his woman in line, and poor simple Tommy'd swallowed it. Even there I was careful not to overdo it; I just said me n Joe'd had an argument and Joe'd most likely gone off mad. I made a few more calls that evenin, includin a few to people I'd already

called, and was happy to find that stories were already startin to spread.

I didn't sleep very well that night; I had terrible dreams. One was about Joe. He was standin at the bottom of the well, lookin up at me with his white face and those dark circles above his nose that made him look like he'd pushed lumps of coal into his eyes. He said he was lonely, and kep beggin me to jump down into the well with him n keep him company.

The other one was worse, because it was about Selena. She was about four years old, n wearin the pink dress her Gramma Trisha bought her just before she died. Selena come up to me in the dooryard, I saw she had my sewin scissors in her hand. I put out my hand for em, but she just shook her head. "It's my fault and I'm the one who has to pay," she said. Then she raised the scissors to her face and cut off her own nose with em—snip. It fell into the dirt between her little black patent-leather shoes n I woke up screamin. It was only four o'clock, but I was all done sleepin that night, and not too stupid to know it.

At seven I called Vera's again. This time Kenopensky answered. I told him I knew Vera was expectin me that mornin, but I couldn't come in, at least not til I found out where my husband was. I said he'd gone missin two nights, and one night out drunk had always been his limit before.

Near the end of our talk, Vera herself picked up on the extension and ast me what was goin on. "I seem to've misplaced my husband," I said.

She didn't say nothing for a few seconds, and I would've given a pie to know what she was thinkin of.

Then she spoke up n said that if she'd been in my place, misplacin Joe St. George wouldn't have bothered her at all.

"Well," I says, "we've got three kids, and I've kind of got used to him. I'll be in later on, if he turns up."

"That's fine," she says, and then, "Are you still there, Ted?"

"Yes, Vera," says he.

"Well, go do something manly," she says. "Pound something in or push something over. I don't care which."

"Yes, Vera," he repeats, and there was a little click on the line as he hung up.

Vera was quiet for a couple more seconds just the same. Then she says, "Maybe he's had an accident, Dolores."

"Yes," I says, "it wouldn't surprise me none. He's been drinkin heavy the last few weeks, and when I tried to talk to him about the kids' money on the day of the eclipse, he damned near choked the life outta me."

"Oh—really?" she says. Another couple of seconds went by, and then she said, "Good luck, Dolores."

"Thanks," I says. "I may need it."

"If there's anything I can do, let me know."

"That's very kind," I told her.

"Not at all," she says back. "I'd simply hate to lose you. It's hard to find help these days who don't sweep the dirt under the carpets."

Not to mention help that c'n remember to put the welcome mats back down pointin in the right direction,

I thought but didn't say. I only thanked her n hung up. I gave it another half hour, then I rang Garrett Thibodeau. Wasn't nothin so fancy n modern as a police chief on Little Tall in those days; Garrett was the town constable. He took over the job when Edgar Sherrick had his stroke back in 1960.

I told him Joe hadn't been home the last two nights, and I was gettin worried. Garrett sounded pretty muzzy—I don't think he'd been up long enough to have gotten outside his first cup of coffee yet—but he said he'd contact the State Police on the mainland n check with a few people on the island. I knew they'd be all the same people I'd already called—twice, in some cases—but I didn't say so. Garrett finished by sayin he was sure I'd see Joe by lunchtime. That's right, you old fart, I thought, hangin up, and pigs'll whistle. I guess that man *did* have brains enough to sing "Yankee Doodle" while he took a shit, but I doubt if he coulda remembered all the words.

It was a whole damned week before they found him, and I was half outta my mind before they did. Selena came back on Wednesday. I called her late Tuesday afternoon to say her father had gone missin and it was startin to look serious. I asked her if she wanted to come home n she said she did. Melissa Caron—Tanya's mother, you know—went n fetched her. I left the boys right where they were—just dealin with Selena was enough for a start. She caught me out in my little vegetable garden on Thursday, still two days before they finally found Joe, and she says, "Mamma, tell me somethin."

"All right, dear," I says. I think I sounded calm enough, but I had a pretty good idear of what was comin—oh yes indeed.

"Did you do anything to him?" she asks.

All of a sudden my dream came back to me—Selena at four in her pretty pink dress, raisin up my sewin scissors and cuttin off her own nose. And I thought—prayed—"God, please help me lie to my daughter. Please, God. I'll never ask You for nothing again if You'll just help me lie to my daughter so she'll believe me n never doubt."

"No," I says. I was wearin my gardenin gloves, but I took em off so I could put my bare hands on her shoulders. I looked her dead in the eye. "No, Selena," I told her. "He was drunk n ugly n he choked me hard enough to leave these bruises on my neck, but I didn't do nothing to him. All I did was leave, n I did that because I was scairt to stay. You can understand that, can't you? Understand and not blame me? You know what it's like, to be scairt of him. Don't you?"

She nodded, but her eyes never left mine. They were a darker blue than I've ever seen em—the color of the ocean just ahead of a squall-line. In my mind's eye I saw the blades of the scissors flashin, and her little button of a nose fallin plop into the dust. And I'll tell you what I think—I think God granted half my prayer that day. It's how He usually answers em, I've noticed. No lie I told about Joe later was any better'n the one I told Selena that hot July afternoon amongst the beans n cukes . . . but did she believe me? Believe me n never doubt? As much as I'd like to think the answer

to that is yes, I can't. It was doubt that made her eyes so dark, then n ever after.

"The worst I'm guilty of," I says, "is buyin him a bottle of booze—of tryin to bribe him to be nice—when I shoulda known better."

She looked at me a minute longer, then bent down n took hold of the bag of cucumbers I'd picked. "All right," she said. "I'll take these in the house for you."

And that was all. We never spoke of it again, not before they found him n not after. She must have heard plenty of talk about me, both on the island and at school, but we never spoke of it again. That was when the coldness started to come in, though, that afternoon in the garden. And when the first crack in the wall families put between themselves n the rest of the world showed up between us. Since then it's only gotten wider n wider. She calls and writes me just as regular as clockwork, she's good about that, but we're apart just the same. We're estranged. What I did was mostly done for Selena, not for the boys or because of the money her Dad tried to steal. It was mostly for Selena that I led him on to his death, and all it cost me to protect her from him was the deepest part of her love for me. I once heard my own Dad say God pitched a bitch on the day He made the world, and over the years I've come to understand what he meant. And do you know the worst of it? Sometimes it's funny. Sometimes it's so funny you can't help from laughin even while it's all fallin apart around you.

Meantime, Garrett Thibodeau and his barber-shop cronies kep busy not findin Joe. It'd gotten to the point where I thought I'd just have to stumble on him myself, as little as I liked the idear. If it hadn't been for the dough, I'd've been happy to leave him down there until the Last Trump blew. But the money was over there in Jonesport, sittin in a bank account with his name on it, and I didn't fancy waitin seven years to have him declared legally dead so I could get it back. Selena was gonna be startin college in just a little over two years, and she'd want some of that money to get herself goin.

The idear that Joe mighta taken his bottle into the woods behind the house n either stepped in a trap or taken a fall walkin home tipsy in the dark finally started to go the rounds. Garrett claimed it was *his* idear, but that's awful hard for me to believe, havin gone to school with him like I did. No matter. He put a sign-up sheet on the door of the town hall Thursday afternoon, and on Sat'dy mornin—a week after the eclipse, this was—he fielded a search-party of forty or fifty men.

They formed up a line by the East Head end of Highgate Woods and worked their way toward the house, first through the woods n then across Russian Meadow. I seen em crossin the meadow in a long line around one o'clock, laughin and jokin, but the jokin stopped and the cursin begun when they crossed over onto our property n got into the blackberry tangle.

I stood in the entry door, watchin em come with my heart beatin way up in my throat. I remember thinkin that at least Selena wa'ant home—she'd gone over to see Laurie Langill—and that was a blessin. Then I started thinkin that all those brambles would cause em to just say frig it n break off the search before they got anywhere near the old well. But they kept on comin.

All at once I heard Sonny Benoit scream: "Hey, Garrett! Over here! *Git over here!*" and I knew that, for better or worse, Joe had been found.

There was an autopsy, accourse. They did it the very day they found him, and I guess it might have still been goin on when Jack n Alicia Forbert brought the boys back around dusk. Pete was cryin, but he looked all confused—I don't think he really understood what'd happened to his Dad. Joe Junior did, though, and when he drew me aside, I thought he was gonna ask me the same question Selena had ast, n I steeled myself to tell the same lie. But he ast me somethin entirely different.

"Ma," he says, "if I was glad he was dead, would God send me to hell?"

"Joey, a person can't much help his feelins, and I think God knows that," I said.

Then he started to cry, and he said somethin that broke my heart. "I *tried* to love him" is what he told me. "I *always* tried, but he wouldn't let me."

I swep him into my arms n hugged him as hard as I could. I think that was about as close as I come to cryin in the whole business . . . but accourse you have to remember that I hadn't been sleepin too well n still hadn't the slightest idear of how things was going to play out.

There was to be an inquest on Tuesday, and Lucien Mercier, who ran the only mortuary on Little Tall back then, told me I'd finally be allowed to bury Joe in The Oaks on Wednesday. But on Monday, the day before the inquest, Garrett called me on the telephone n ast if I could come down to his office for a few minutes. It was the call I'd been expectin and dreadin, but there

wasn't nothing to do but go, so I ast Selena if she'd give the boys their lunch, and off I went. Garrett wasn't alone. Dr. John McAuliffe was with him. I'd more or less expected that, too, but my heart still sank a little in my breast.

McAuliffe was the county medical examiner back then. He died three years later when a snowplow hit his little Volkswagen Beetle. It was Henry Briarton took over the job when McAuliffe died. If Briarton had been the county man in '63, I'd've felt a good deal easier in my mind about our little talk that day. Briarton's smarter than poor old Garrett Thibodeau was, but only by a little. John McAuliffe, though . . . he had a mind like the lamp that shines outta Battiscan Light.

He was a genuine bottled-in-bond Scotsman who turned up in these parts right after World War II ended, hoot-mon burr n all. I guess he musta been an American citizen, since he was both doctorin and holdin a county position, but he sure didn't sound much like folks from around here. Not that it mattered to me; I knew I'd have to face him down, no matter if he was an American or a Scotsman or a heathen Chinee.

He had snowy white hair even though he couldn't have been more'n forty-five, and blue eyes so bright n sharp they looked like drillbits. When he looked at you, you felt like he was starin right into your head and puttin the thoughts he saw there into alphabetical order. As soon as I seen him sittin beside Garrett's desk n heard the door to the rest of the Town Office Building click closed behind me, I knew that what happened the next day over on the mainland didn't matter a tinker's damn. The real inquest was gonna

happen right there in that tiny town constable's office, with a Weber Oil calendar hangin on one wall and a pitcher of Garrett's mother hangin on another.

"I'm sorry to bother you in your time of grief, Dolores," Garrett said. He was rubbin his hands together, kinda nervous, and he reminded me of Mr. Pease over at the bank. Garrett musta had a few more calluses on his hands, though, because the sound they made goin back n forth was like fine sandpaper rubbin along a dry board. "But Dr. McAuliffe here has a few questions he'd like to ask you."

I seen by the puzzled way Garrett looked at the doc that he didn't know what those questions might be, though, and that scared me even more. I didn't like the idear of that canny Scotsman thinkin matters were serious enough for him to keep his own counsels n not give poor old Garrett Thibodeau any chance at all to frig up the works.

"Ma deepest sympathies, Mrs. St. George," McAuliffe says in that thick Scots accent of his. He was a little man, but compact n well put together for all that. He had a neat little mustache, as white's the hair on his head, he was wearin a three-piece wool suit, n he didn't look no more like home folks than he sounded like em. Those blue eyes went drillin away at my forehead, and I seen he didn't have a bit of sympathy for me, no matter what he was sayin. Prob'ly not for nobody else, either . . . includin himself. "I'm verra, verra sorry for your grief and misfortune."

Sure, and if I believe that, you'll tell me one more, I thought. The last time you was really sorry, doc, was the last time you needed to use the pay toilet and the

string on your pet dime broke. But I made up my mind right then that I wasn't goin to show him how scared I was. Maybe he had me n maybe he didn't. You've got to remember that, for all I knew, he was gonna tell me that when they laid Joe on the table there in the basement of County Hospital n opened his hands, a little piece of white nylon fell outta one; a scrid of a lady's slip. That could be, all right, but I still wasn't gonna give him the satisfaction of squirmin under his eyes. And he was *used* to havin people squirm when he looked at em; he'd come to take it as his due, and he liked it.

"Thank you very much," I said.

"Will ye sit doon, madam?" he asks, like it was his office instead of poor old confused Garrett's.

I sat down and he ast me if I'd kindly give him permission to smoke. I told him the lamp was lit as far's as I was concerned. He chuckled like I'd made a funny . . . but his *eyes* didn't chuckle. He took a big old black pipe out of his coat pocket, a briar, and stoked it up. His eyes never left me while he was doin it, either. Even after he had it clamped between his teeth and the smoke was risin outta the bowl, he never took his eyes off me. They gave me the willies, peerin at me through the smoke like they did, and made me think of Battiscan Light again—they say that one shines out almost two mile even on a night when the fog's thick enough to carve with your hands.

I started to squirm under that look of his in spite of all my good intentions, and then I thought of Vera Donovan sayin "Nonsense—husbands die every day,

Dolores." It occurred to me that McAuliffe could stare at Vera until his eyes fell out n never get her to so much as cross her legs the other way. Thinkin of that eased me a little, and I grew quiet again; just folded my hands on top of my handbag n waited him out.

At last, when he seen I wasn't just gonna fall outta my chair onto the floor n confess to murderin my husband—through a rain of tears is how he would've liked it, I imagine—he took the pipe out of his mouth n said, "You told the constable 'twas your husband who put those bruises on your neck, Mrs. St. George."

"Ayuh," I says.

"That you and he had sat down on the porch to watch the eclipse, and there commenced an argument."

"Ayuh."

"And what, may I ask, was the argument about?"

"Money on top," I says, "booze underneath."

"But you yourself bought him the liquor he got drunk on that day, Mrs. St. George! Isna that right?"

"Ayuh," I says. I could feel myself wantin to say somethin more, to explain myself, but I didn't, even though I could. That's what McAuliffe wanted, you see—for me to go on rushin ahead. To explain myself right into a jail-cell someplace.

At last he give up waitin. He twiddled his fingers like he was annoyed, then fixed those lighthouse eyes of his on me again. "After the choking incident, you left your husband; you went up to Russian Meadow, on the way to East Head, to watch the eclipse by yourself."

"Ayuh."

He leaned forward all of a sudden, his little hands on his little knees, and says, "Mrs. St. George, do you know what direction the wind was from that day?"

It was like the day in November of '62, when I almost found the old well by fallin into it—I seemed to hear the same crackin noise, and I thought, "You be careful, Dolores Claiborne; you be oh so careful. There's wells everywhere today, and this man knows where every goddam one of em is."

"No," I says, "I don't. And when I don't know where the wind's quarterin from, that usually means the day's calm."

"Actually wasn't much more than a breeze—" Garrett started to say, but McAuliffe raised his hand n cut him off like a knife-blade.

"It was out of the west," he said. "A west wind, a west *breeze*, if you so prefer, seven to nine miles an hour, with gusts up to fifteen. It seems strange to me, Mrs. St. George, that that wind didna bring your husband's cries to you as you stood in Russian Meadow, not half a mile away."

I didn't say anything for at least three seconds. I'd made up my mind that I'd count to three inside my head before I answered *any* of his questions. Doin that might keep me from movin too quick and payin for it by fallin into one of the pits he'd dug for me. But McAuliffe musta thought he had me confused from the word go, because he leaned forward in his chair, and I'll declare and vow that for one or two seconds there, his eyes went from blue-hot to white-hot.

"It don't surprise me," I says. "For one thing, seven miles an hour ain't much more'n a puff of air on a

muggy day. For another, there were about a thousand boats out on the reach, all tootin to each other. And how do you know he called out at all? *You* sure as hell didn't hear him."

He sat back, lookin a little disappointed. "It's a reasonable deduction to make," he says. "We know the fall itself didna kill him, and the forensic evidence strongly suggests that he had at least one extended period of consciousness. Mrs. St. George, if *you* fell into a disused well and found yourself with a broken shin, a broken ankle, four broken ribs, and a sprained wrist, wouldn't *you* call for aid and succor?"

I gave it three seconds with a my-pretty-pony between each one, n then said, "It wasn't *me* who fell down the well, Dr. McAuliffe. It was Joe, and he'd been drinkin."

"Yes," Dr. McAuliffe comes back. "You bought him a bottle of Scotch whiskey, even though everyone I've spoken to says you hated it when he drank, even though he became unpleasant and argumentative when he drank; you bought him a bottle of Scotch, and he had not just been drinking, he was drunk. He was *verra* drunk. His mouth was also filled wi' bluid, and his shirt was matted wi' bluid all the way down to his belt-buckle. When you combine the fact o' this bluid wi' a knowledge of the broken ribs and the concomitant lung injuries he had sustained, do ye know what that suggests?"

One, my-pretty-pony . . . two, my-pretty-pony . . . three, my-pretty-pony. "Nope," I says.

"Several of the fractured ribs had punctured his lungs. Such injuries always result in bleeding, but rarely

bleeding this extensive. Bleeding of this sort was probably caused, I deduce, by the deceased crying repeatedly for riscue." That was how he said it, Andy—riscue.

It wasn't a question, but I counted three all the same before sayin, "You think he was down there callin for help. That's what it all comes to, ain't it?"

"No, madam," he says. "I do na just *think* so; I have a moral *sairtainty.*"

This time I didn't take no wait. "Dr. McAuliffe," I says, "do you think I pushed my husband down into that well?"

That shook him up a little. Those lighthouse eyes of his not only blinked, for a few seconds there they dulled right over. He fiddled n diddled with his pipe some more, then stuck it back in his mouth n drew on it, all the time tryin to decide how he should handle *that.*

Before he could, Garrett spoke up. His face had gone as red as a radish. "Dolores," he says, "I'm sure no one thinks . . . that is to say, that no one has even *considered* the idea that—"

"Aye," McAuliffe breaks in. I'd put his train of thought off on a sidin for a few seconds, but I saw he'd got it back onto the main line without no real trouble. "*I've* considered it. Ye'll understand, Mrs. St. George, that part of my job—"

"Oh, never mind no more Mrs. St. George," I says. "If you're gonna accuse me of first pushin my husband down the well n then standin over him while he screamed for help, you go right on ahead n call me Dolores."

I wasn't exactly *tryin* to plink him that time, Andy,

but I'll be damned if I didn't do it, anyway—second time in as many minutes. I doubt if he'd been used that hard since medical school.

"Nobody is *accusing* you of anything, Mrs. St. George," he says all stiff-like, and what I seen in his eyes was "Not yet, anyway."

"Well, that's good," I says. "Because the idear of me pushin Joe down the well is just silly, you know. He outweighed me by at least fifty pounds—prob'ly a fair-ish bit more. He larded up considerable the last few years. Also, he wa'ant afraid to use his fists if somebody crossed him or got in his way. I'm tellin you that as his wife of sixteen years, and you'll find plenty of people who'll tell you the same thing."

Accourse Joe hadn't hit me in a long while, but I'd never tried to correct the general impression on the island that he made a pretty steady business of it, and right then, with McAuliffe's blue eyes tryin to bore in through my forehead, I was damned glad of it.

"Nobody is saying you pushed him into the well," the Scotsman said. He was backin up fast now. I could see by his face that he knew he was, but didn't have no idear how it had happened. His face said that *I* was the one who was supposed to be backin up. "But he must have been crying out, you know. He must have done it for some time—hours, perhaps—and quite loudly, too."

One, my-pretty-pony . . . two, my-pretty-pony . . . three. "Maybe I'm gettin you now," I says. "Maybe you think he fell into the well by accident, and I heard him yellin n just turned a deaf ear. Is that what you been gettin at?"

I seen by his face that that was *exactly* what he'd been gettin at. I also seen he was mad things weren't goin the way he'd expected em to go, the way they'd always gone before when he had these little interviews. A tiny ball of bright red color had showed up in each of his cheeks. I was glad to see em, because I wanted him mad. A man like McAuliffe is easier to handle when he's mad, because men like him are used to keepin their composure while other people lose theirs.

"Mrs. St. George, it will be verra difficult to accomplish anything of value here if you keep responding to my questions with questions of your own."

"Why, you didn't *ask* a question, Dr. McAuliffe," I says, poppin my eyes wide n innocent. "You told me Joe must have been yellin—'cryin out' was what you actually said—so *I* just ast if—"

"All right, all right," he says, and put his pipe down in Garrett's brass ashtray hard enough to make it clang. Now his eyes were blazin, and he'd grown a red stripe acrost his forehead to go along with the balls of color in his cheeks. "*Did* you hear him calling for help, Mrs. St. George?"

One, my-pretty-pony . . . two, my-pretty-pony . . .

"John, I hardly think there's any call to *badger* the woman," Garrett broke in, soundin more uncomfortable than ever, and damn if it didn't break that little bandbox Scotsman's concentration *again.* I almost laughed right out loud. It woulda been bad for me if I had, I don't doubt it, but it was a near thing, all the same.

McAuliffe whipped around and says to Garrett, "You agreed to let me handle this."

Poor old Garrett jerked back in his chair s'fast he almost tipped it over, and I'm sure he gave himself a whiplash. "Okay, okay, no need to get hot under the collar," he mumbles.

McAuliffe turned back to me, ready to repeat the question, but I didn't bother lettin him. By then I'd had time to count to ten, pretty near.

"No," I says. "I didn't hear nothing but people out on the reach, tootin their boat-horns and yellin their fool heads off once they could see the eclipse had started to happen."

He waited for me to say some more—his old trick of bein quiet and lettin people rush ahead into the puckerbrush—and the silence spun out between us. I just kep my hands folded on top of my handbag and let her spin. He looked at me and I looked back at him.

"You're gonna talk to me, woman," his eyes said. "You're going to tell me everything I want to hear . . . twice, if that's the way I want it."

And my own eyes were sayin back, "No I ain't, chummy. You can sit there drillin on me with those diamond-bit baby-blues of yours until hell's a skatin rink and you won't get another word outta me unless you open your mouth n ask for it."

We went on that way for damned near a full minute, duellin with our eyes, y'might say, and toward the end of it I could feel myself weakenin, wantin to say somethin to him, even if it was only "Didn't your Ma ever teach you it ain't polite to stare?" Then Garrett spoke up—or rather his stomach did. It let out a long *goiiiinnnnggg* sound.

McAuliffe looked at him, disgusted as hell, and Garrett got out his pocket-knife and started to clean under his fingernails. McAuliffe pulled a notebook from the inside pocket of his wool coat (*wool!* in *July!*), looked at somethin in it, then put it back.

"He tried to climb out," he says at last, as casual as a man might say "I've got a lunch appointment."

It felt like somebody'd jabbed a meatfork into my lower back, where Joe hit me with the stovelength that time, but I tried not to show it. "Oh, ayuh?" I says.

"Yes," McAuliffe says. "The shaft of the well is lined with large stones (only he said "stanes," Andy, like they do), and we found bluidy handprints on several of them. It appears that he gained his feet, then slowly began to make his way up, hand over hand. It must have been a Herculean effort, made despite a pain more excruciating than I can imagine."

"I'm sorry to hear he suffered," I said. My voice was as calm as ever—at least I think it was—but I could feel the sweat startin to break in my armpits, and I remember bein scairt it'd spring out on my brow or in the little hollows of my temples where he could see it. "Poor old Joe."

"Yes indaid," McAuliffe says, his lighthouse eyes borin n flashin away. "Poor . . . auld . . . Joe. I think he might have actually gotten out on his own. He probably would have died soon after even if he had, but yes; I think he might have gotten out. Something prevented him from doing so, however."

"What was it?" I ast.

"He suffered a fractured skull," McAuliffe said. His

eyes were as bright as ever, but his voice'd become as soft as a purrin cat. "We found a large rock between his legs. It was covered wi' your husband's bluid, Mrs. St. George. And in that bluid we found a small number of porcelain fragments. Do you know what I deduce from them?"

One . . . two . . . three.

"Sounds like that rock must have busted his false teeth as well's his head," I says. "Too bad—Joe was partial to em, and I don't know how Lucien Mercier's gonna make him look just right for the viewin without em."

McAuliffe's lips drew back when I said that n I got a good look at *his* teeth. No dentures there. I s'pose he meant it to look like a smile, but it didn't. Not a bit.

"Yes," he says, showin me both rows of his neat little teeth all the way to the gumline. "Yes, that's my conclusion, as well—those porcelain shards are from his lower plate. Now, Mrs. St. George—do you have any idea of how that rock might have come to strike your husband just as he was on the verge of escaping the well?"

One . . . two . . . three.

"Nope," I says. "Do you?"

"Yes," he says. "I rather suspect someone pulled it out of the earth and smashed it cruelly and wi' malice aforethought into his upturned, pleading face."

Wasn't nobody said anything after that. I *wanted* to, God knows; I wanted to jump in as quick as ever I could n say, "It wasn't me. Maybe somebody did it,

but it wasn't me." I couldn't, though, because I was back in the blackberry tangles and this time there was friggin wells everyplace.

Instead of talkin I just sat there lookin at him, but I could feel the sweat tryin to break out on me again and I could feel my clasped hands wantin to lock down on each other. The fingernails'd turn white if they did that . . . and he'd notice. McAuliffe was a man *built* to notice such things; it'd be another chink to shine his version of the Battiscan Light into. I tried to think of Vera, and how she woulda looked at him—as if he was only a little dab of dogshit on one of her shoes—but with his eyes borin into me like they was just then, it didn't seem to do any good. Before, it'd been like she was almost there in the room with me, but it wasn't like that anymore. Now there was no one there but me n that neat little Scots doctor, who probably fancied himself just like the amateur detectives in the magazine stories (and whose testimony had already sent over a dozen people up n down the coast to jail, I found out later), and I could feel myself gettin closer n closer to openin my mouth n blurtin somethin out. And the hell of it was, Andy, I didn't have the slightest idear what it'd be when it finally came. I could hear the clock on Garrett's desk tickin—it had a big hollow sound.

And I *was* gonna say somethin when the one person I'd forgot—Garrett Thibodeau—spoke up instead. He spoke in a worried, fast voice, and I realized *he* couldn't stand no more of that silence, either—he musta thought it was gonna go on until somebody had to scream just to relieve the tension.

"Now John," he says, "I thought we agreed that, if Joe pulled on that stone just right, it could have come out on its own and—"

"*Mon, will ye not shut op!*" McAuliffe yelled at him in a high, frustrated sort of voice, and I relaxed. It was all over. I knew it, and I believe that little Scotsman knew it, too. It was like the two us had been in a black room together, and him ticklin my face with what might have been a razor-blade . . . n then clumsy old Constable Thibodeau stubbed his toe, fell against the window, and the shade went up with a bang n a rattle, lettin in the daylight, and I seen it was only a feather he'd been touchin me with, after all.

Garrett muttered somethin about how there was no call for McAuliffe to talk to him that way, but the doc didn't pay him no mind. He turned back to me and said "Well, Mrs. St. George?" in a hard way, like he had me in a corner, but by then we both knew better. All he could do was hope I'd make a mistake . . . but I had three kids to think about, and havin kids makes you careful.

"I've told you what I know," I says. "He got drunk while we were waitin for the eclipse. I made him a sandwich, thinkin it might sober him up a little, but it didn't. He got yellin, then he choked me n batted me around a little, so I went up to Russian Meadow. When I come back, he was gone. I thought he'd gone off with one of his friends, but he was down the well all the time. I s'pose he was tryin to take a short-cut out to the road. He might even have been lookin for me, wantin to apologize. That's somethin I won't never

know . . . n maybe it's just as well." I give him a good hard look. "You might try a little of that medicine yourself, Dr. McAuliffe."

"Never mind yer advice, madam," McAuliffe says, and those spots of color in his cheeks was burnin higher n hotter'n ever. "Are ye glad he's dead? Tell me that!"

"What in holy tarnal hell has that got to do with what happened to him?" I ast. "Jesus Christ, what's *wrong* with you?"

He didn't answer—just picked up his pipe in a hand that was shakin the tiniest little bit and went to work lightin it again. He never ast another question; the last question that was ast of me that day was ast by Garrett Thibodeau. McAuliffe didn't ask it because it didn't matter, at least not to him. It meant somethin to Garrett, though, and it meant even more to me, because nothing was going to end when I walked out of the Town Office Building that day; in some ways, me walkin out was gonna be just the beginning. That last question and the way I answered it mattered plenty, because it's usually the things that wouldn't mean squat in a courtroom that get whispered about the most over back fences while women hang out their warsh or out on the lobster-boats while men are sittin with their backs against the pilothouse n eatin their lunches. Those things may not send you to prison, but they can hang you in the eyes of the town.

"Why in God's name did you buy him a bottle of liquor in the first place?" Garrett kinda bleated. "What got into you, Dolores?"

"I thought he'd leave me alone if he had somethin

to drink," I said. "I thought we could sit together in peace n watch the eclipse n he'd leave me alone."

I didn't cry, not really, but I felt one tear go rollin down my cheek. I sometimes think that's the reason I was able to go on livin on Little Tall for the next thirty years—that one single tear. If not for that, they mighta driven me out with their whisperin and carpin and pointin at me from behind their hands—ayuh, in the end they mighta. I'm tough, but I don't know if anyone's tough enough to stand up to thirty years of gossip n little anonymous notes sayin things like "You got away with murder." I did get a few of those—and I got a pretty good idear of who sent em, too, although that ain't neither here nor there at this late date—but they stopped by the time school let back in that fall. And so I guess you could say that I owe all the rest of my life, includin this part here, to that single tear . . . and to Garrett puttin the word out that in the end I hadn't been too stony-hearted to cry for Joe. There wasn't nothing calculated about it, either, and don't you go thinkin there was. I was thinkin about how sorry I was that Joe'd suffered the way the little bandbox Scotsman said he had. In spite of everything he'd done and how I'd come to hate him since I'd first found out what he was tryin to do to Selena, I'd never intended for him to suffer. I thought the fall'd kill him, Andy—I swear on the name of God I thought the fall'd kill him outright.

Poor old Garrett Thibodeau went as red's a stop-sign. He fumbled a wad of Kleenex out of the box of em on his desk and kinda groped it out at me without

lookin—I imagine he thought that first tear meant I was gonna go a gusher—and apologized for puttin me through "such a stressful interrogation." I bet those were just about the biggest words he knew.

McAuliffe gave out a *humph!* sound at that, said somethin about how he'd be at the inquest to hear my statement taken, and then he left—stalked out, actually, n slammed the door behind him hard enough to rattle the glass. Garrett gave him time to clear out n then walked me to the door, holdin my arm but still not lookin at me (it was actually sorta comical) and mutterin all the time. I ain't sure what he was mutterin *about*, but I s'pose that, whatever it was, it was really Garrett's way of sayin he was sorry. That man had a tender heart and couldn't stand to see someone unhappy, I'll say that for him . . . and I'll say somethin else for Little Tall: where else could a man like that not only be constable for almost twenty years but get a dinner in his honor complete with a standin ovation at the end of it when he finally retired? I'll tell you what I think—a place where a tender-hearted man can succeed as an officer of the law ain't such a bad place to spend your life. Not at all. Even so, I was never gladder to hear a door close behind me than I was when Garrett's clicked shut that day.

So that was the bugger, and the inquest the next day wasn't nothing compared to it. McAuliffe ast me many of the same questions, and they were hard questions, but they didn't have no power over me anymore, and we both knew it. My one tear was all very well, but McAuliffe's questions—plus the fact that everyone could see he was pissed like a bear at me—went a long

way toward startin the talk which has run on the island ever since. Oh well; there would have been some talk no matter what, ain't that right?

The verdict was death by misadventure. McAuliffe didn't like it, and at the end he read his findins in a dead-level voice, without ever lookin up once, but what he said was official enough: Joe fell down the well while drunk, had prob'ly called for help for quite awhile without gettin an answer, then tried to climb out on his own hook. He got most of the way to the top, then put his weight on the wrong stone. It pulled free, bashed him in the head hard enough to fracture his skull (not to mention his dentures), and knocked him back down to the bottom again, where he died.

Maybe the biggest thing—and I never realized this until later—was they couldn't find no motive to hang on me. Of course, the people in town (and Dr. McAuliffe too, I have no doubt) thought that if I *had* done it, I did it to get shut of him beatin me, but all by itself that didn't carry enough weight. Only Selena and Mr. Pease knew how much motive I'd really had, and no one, not even smart old Dr. McAuliffe, thought of questionin Mr. Pease. He didn't come forward on his own hook, either. If he had've, our little talk in The Chatty Buoy would've come out, and he'd most likely have been in trouble with the bank. I'd talked him into breakin the rules, after all.

As for Selena . . . well, I think Selena tried me in her own court. Every now n then I'd see her eyes on me, dark n squally, and in my mind I'd hear her askin, "Did you do anything to him? Did you, Mamma? Is it my fault? Am I the one who has to pay?"

I think she *did* pay—that's the worst part. The little island girl who was never out of the state of Maine until she went to Boston for a swim-meet when she was eighteen has become a smart, successful career-woman in New York City—there was an article about her in the New York *Times* two years ago, did you know that? She writes for all those magazines and still finds time to write me once a week . . . but they feel like duty-letters, just like the phone-calls twice a month feel like duty-calls. I think the calls n the chatty little notes are the way she pays her heart to be quiet about how she don't ever come back here, about how she's cut her ties with me. Yes, I think she paid, all right; I think the one who was the most blameless of all paid the most, and that she's payin still.

She's forty-four years old, she's never married, she's too thin (I can see that in the pitchers she sometimes sends), and I think she drinks—I've heard it in her voice more'n once when she calls. I got an idear that might be one of the reasons she don't come home anymore; she doesn't want me to see her drinkin like her father drank. Or maybe because she's afraid of what she might say if she had one too many while I was right handy. What she might ask.

But never mind; it's all water over the dam now. I got away with it, that's the important thing. If there'd been insurance, or if Pease hadn't kep his mouth shut, I'm not sure I woulda. Of the two, a fat insurance policy prob'ly woulda been worse. The last thing in God's round world I needed was some smart insurance investigator hookin up with that smart little Scots doctor who was already mad as hell at the idear of bein beaten

by an ignorant island woman. Nope, if there'd been two of em, I think they might've got me.

So what happened? Why, what I imagine *always* happens in cases like that, when a murder's been done and not found out. Life went on, that's all. Nobody popped up with last-minute information, like in a movie, I didn't try to kill nobody else, n God didn't strike me dead with a lightnin-bolt. Maybe He felt hittin me with lightnin over the likes of Joe St. George woulda been a waste of electricity.

Life just went on. I went back to Pinewood n to Vera. Selena took up her old friendships when she went back to school that fall, and sometimes I heard her laughin on the phone. When the news finally sunk in, Little Pete took it hard . . . and so did Joe Junior. Joey took it harder'n I expected, actually. He lost some weight n had some nightmares, but by the next summer he seemed mostly all right again. The only thing that really changed durin the rest of 1963 was that I had Seth Reed come over n put a cement cap on the old well.

Six months after he died, Joe's estate was settled in County Probate. I wa'ant even there. A week or so later I got a paper tellin me that everythin was mine —I could sell it or swap it or drop it in the deep blue sea. When I'd finished goin through what he'd left, I thought the last of those choices looked like the best one. One kinda surprisin thing I discovered, though: if your husband dies sudden, it can come in handy if all his friends were idiots, like Joe's were. I sold the old shortwave radio he'd been tinkerin on for ten years to Norris Pinette for twenty-five dollars, and the three junk trucks settin in the back yard to Tommy Anderson. That fool was more'n glad to have em, and I used the money to buy a '59 Chevy that had wheezy valves but ran good otherwise. I also had Joe's savins passbook made over to me, and re-opened the kids' college accounts.

Oh, and one other thing—in January of 1964, I started goin by my maiden name again. I didn't make no particular fanfare about it, but I was damned if I was gonna drag St. George around behind me the rest of my life, like a can tied to a dog's tail. I guess you could say I cut the string holdin the can . . . but I didn't get rid of *him* as easy as I got rid of his name, I can tell you that.

Not that I expected to; I'm sixty-five, and I've known for at least fifty of those years that most of what bein human's about is makin choices and payin the bills when they come due. Some of the choices are pretty goddam nasty, but that don't give a person leave to just walk away from em—especially not if that person's got others dependin on her to do for em what they can't do for themselves. In a case like that, you just have to make the best choice you can n then pay the price. For me, the price was a lot of nights when I woke up in a cold sweat from bad dreams n even more when I never got to sleep at all; that and the sound the rock made when it hit him in the face, bustin his skull and his dentures—that sound like a china plate on a brick hearth. I've heard it for thirty years. Sometimes it's what wakes me up, and sometimes it's what keeps me outta sleep and sometimes it surprises me in broad daylight. I might be sweepin the porch at home or

polishin the silver at Vera's or sittin down to my lunch with the TV turned to the Oprah show and all at once I'll hear it. That sound. Or the thud when he hit bottom. Or his voice, comin up outta the well: "*Duh-lorrrr-issss . . .*"

I don't s'pose those sounds I sometimes hear are so different from whatever it was that Vera really saw when she screamed about the wires in the corners or the dust bunnies under the bed. There were times, especially after she really began to fail, when I'd crawl in bed with her n hold her n think of the sound the rock made, n then close my eyes n see a china plate strikin a brick hearth and shatterin all to bits. When I saw that I'd hug her like she was my sister, or like she was myself. We'd lie in that bed, each with her own fright, and finally we'd drowse off together—her with me to keep the dust bunnies away, and me with her to keep away the sound of the china plate—and sometimes before I went to sleep I'd think, "This is how. This is how you pay off bein a bitch. And it ain't no use sayin if you hadn't been a bitch you wouldn't've had to pay, because sometimes the world *makes* you be a bitch. When it's all doom n dark outside and only you inside to first make a light n then tend it, you *have* to be a bitch. But oh, the price. The terrible price."

Andy, do you s'pose I could have one more tiny little nip from that bottle of yours? I'll never tell a soul.

Thank you. And thank *you*, Nancy Bannister, for puttin up with such a long-winded old broad as me. How your fingers holdin out?

Are they? Good. Don't lose your courage now; I've gone at it widdershins, I know, but I guess I've finally

gotten around to the part you really want to hear about, just the same. That's good, because it's late and I'm tired. I've been workin my whole life, but I can't remember ever bein as tired as I am right now.

I was out hangin laundry yest'y mornin—it seems like six years ago, but it was only yest'y—and Vera was havin one of her bright days. That's why it was all so unexpected, and partly why I got so flustered. When she had her bright days she sometimes got bitchy, but that was the first n last time she got *crazy.*

So I was down below in the side yard and she was up above in her wheelchair, supervisin the operation the way she liked to do. Every now n then she'd holler down, "Six pins, Dolores! Six pins on every last one of those sheets! Don't you try to get away with just four, because I'm watching!"

"Yeah," I says, "I know, and I bet you only wish it was forty degrees colder and a twenty-knot gale blowin."

"*What?*" she caws down at me. "*What* did you say, Dolores Claiborne?"

"I said someone must be spreadin manure in their garden," I says, "because I smell a lot more bullshit around here than usual."

"Are you being smart, Dolores?" she calls back in her cracked, wavery voice.

She sounded about like she did on any day when a few more sunbeams than usual was findin their way into her attic. I knew she might get up to mischief later on, but I didn't much care—right then I was just glad to hear her makin as much sense as she was. To tell you the truth, it seemed like old times. She'd been

number'n a pounded thumb for the last three or four months, and it was sorta nice to have her back . . . or as much of the old Vera as was ever gonna come back, if you see what I mean.

"No, Vera," I called up to her. "If I'd been smart, I'd've gotten done workin for you a long time ago."

I expected her to yell somethin else down at me then, but she never. So I went on hangin up her sheets n her diapers n her warshcloths n all the rest. Then, with half the basket still to do, I stopped. I had a bad feeling. I can't say why, or even where it started. All at once it was just there. And for just a moment the strangest thought came to me: "That girl's in trouble . . . the one I saw on the day of the eclipse, the one who saw me. She's all grown up now, almost Selena's age, but she's in terrible trouble."

I turned around n looked up, almost expectin to see the grownup version of that little girl in her bright striped dress n pink lipstick, but I didn't see nobody, and that was wrong. It was wrong because *Vera* should have been there, just about hangin out onto the roof to make sure I used the right number of clothespins. But she was gone, and I didn't understand how that could be, because I'd put her in her chair myself, and then set the brake once I had it by the window the way she liked.

Then I heard her scream.

"*Duh-lorrrrr-isss!*"

Such a chill ran up my back when I heard that, Andy! It was like Joe had come back. For a moment I was just frozen to the spot. Then she screamed again, and that second time I recognized it was her.

"Duh-lorrr-isss! It's dust bunnies! They're everywhere! Oh-dear-God! Oh-dear-God! Duh-lorrr-iss, help! Help me!"

I turned to run for the house, tripped over the damned laundry-basket, and went sprawlin over it n into the sheets I'd just hung. I got tangled up in em somehow n had to fight my way out. For just a minute it was like the sheets had grown hands and were tryin to strangle me, or just hold me back. And all the while that was goin on, Vera kep screamin, and I thought of the dream I'd had that one time, the dream of the dust-head with all the long snaggly dust-teeth. Only what I saw in my mind's eye was Joe's face on that head, and the eyes were all dark n blank, like someone had pushed two lumps of coal into a cloud of dust, and there they hung n floated.

"Dolores, oh please come quick! Oh please come quick! The dust bunnies! THE DUST BUNNIES ARE EVERYWHERE!"

Then she just screamed. It was horrible. You'd never in your wildest dreams have thought a fat old bitch like Vera Donovan could scream that loud. It was like fire n flood n the end of the world all rolled up into one.

I fought my way clear of the sheets somehow, and as I got up I felt one of my slip-straps pop, just like on the day of the eclipse, when Joe almost killed me before I managed to get shut of him. And you know that feelin you get when it seems like you've been someplace before, and know all the things people are gonna say before they say em? That feelin came over

me so strong it was like there were ghosts all around me, ticklin me with fingers I couldn't quite see.

And you know somethin else? They felt like *dusty* ghosts.

I ran in the kitchen door n pelted up the back stairs as fast as my legs'd carry me, and all the time she was screamin, screamin, screamin. My slip started to slide down, and when I got to the back landin I looked around, sure I was gonna see Joe stumblin up right behind me n snatchin at the hem.

Then I looked back the other way, and I seen Vera. She was three-quarters of the way down the hall toward the front staircase, waddlin along with her back to me n screamin as she went. There was a big brown stain on the seat of her nightgown where she'd soiled herself—not out of meanness or bitchiness that last time, but out of plain cold fear.

Her wheelchair was stuck crosswise in her bedroom door. She must've released the brake when she saw whatever it was that had scared her so. Always before when she come down with a case of the horrors, the only thing she could do was sit or lay where she was n bawl for help, and there'll be plenty of people who'll tell you she *couldn't* move under her own power, but she did yesterday; I swear she did. She released the brake on her chair, turned it, wheeled it across the room, then somehow got out of it when it got stuck in the doorway n went staggerin off down the hall.

I stood there, just frozen to the spot for the first second or two, watchin her lurch along and wonderin what she'd seen that was terrible enough to get her to

do what she was doin, to walk after her days of walkin should have been over—what that thing was that she could only think to call the dust bunnies.

But I seen where she was headed—right for the front stairs.

"Vera!" I yelled at her. "Vera, you just stop this foolishness! You're going to fall! *Stop!*"

Then I ran just as fast as I could. That feelin that all this was happenin for the second time rolled over me again, only this time it felt like I was Joe, that I was the one tryin to catch up n catch hold.

I don't know if she didn't hear me, or if she did n thought in her poor addled brain that I was in front of her instead of behind. All I know for sure is that she went on screamin—"*Dolores, help! Help me, Dolores! The dust bunnies!*"—and lurched on a little faster.

She'd just about used the hallway up. I raced past the door to her room n clipped my ankle a goddam good one on one of the wheelchair's footrests—here, you can see the bruise. I ran as fast's I could, shoutin, "*Stop, Vera! Stop!*" until my throat was raw.

She crossed the landin and stuck one foot out into space. I couldn't've saved her then, no matter what—all I coulda done was pull myself over with her—but in a situation like that, you don't have time to think or count the cost. I jumped for her just as that foot of hers come down on thin air and she started to tilt forward. I had one last little glimpse of her face. I don't think she knew she was goin over; there wasn't nothing there but bug-eyed panic. I'd seen the look before, although never that deep, and I can tell you it didn't

have nothing to do with fear of fallin. She was thinkin about what was behind her, not what was ahead.

I snatched at the air and didn't get nothing but the littlest fold of her nightie between the second n third fingers of my left hand. It slipped through em like a whisper.

"*Duh-lorrrrr—*" she screamed, and then there was a solid, meaty thud. It turns my blood cold to remember that sound; it was just like the one Joe made when he hit the bottom of the well. I seen her do a cartwheel n then heard somethin snap. The sound was as clear n harsh as a stick of kindlin when you break it over your knee. I saw blood squirt out of the side of her head n that was all I *wanted* to see. I turned away so fast my feet tangled in each other and I went to my knees. I was starin back down the hallway toward her room, and what I saw made me scream. It was Joe. For a few seconds I saw him as clear as I see you now, Andy; I saw his dusty, grinnin face peekin out at me from under her wheelchair, lookin through the wire spokes of the wheel that had got caught in the door.

Then it was gone, and I heard her moanin and cryin.

I couldn't believe she'd lived through that fall; can't believe it still. Joe hadn't been killed outright either, accourse, but *he'd* been a man in the prime of life, and she was a flabby old woman who'd had half a dozen small strokes n at least three big ones. Also, there wasn't no mud n squelch to cushion her landin like there had been to cushion his.

I didn't want to go down to her, didn't want to see where she was broken and bleedin, but there wa'ant

no question, accourse; I was the only one there, and that meant I was elected. When I got up (I had to haul on the newel post at the top of the bannister to do it, my knees were so watery-feelin), I stepped one foot on the hem of my own slip. The other strap popped, n I raised up my dress a little so I could pull it off . . . and *that* was just like before, too. I remember lookin down at my legs to see if they were scratched and bleedin from the thorns in the blackberry tangle, but accourse there wasn't nothing like that.

I felt feverish. If you've ever been really sick n your temperature's gone way, way up, you know what I mean; you don't feel out of the world, exactly, but you sure as hell don't feel in it, either. It's like everythin was turned to glass, and there isn't anything you can get a solid grip on anymore; everythin's slippery. That's how I felt as I stood there on the landin, holdin the top of the bannister in a death-grip and lookin at where she'd finished up.

She was layin a little over halfway down the staircase with both legs twisted so far under her you couldn't hardly see em. Blood was runnin down one side of her poor old face. When I stumbled down to where she lay, still clingin onto the bannister for dear life as I went, one of her eyes rolled up in its socket to mark me. It was the look of an animal caught in a trap.

"Dolores," she whispered. "That son of a bitch has been after me all these years."

"Shh," I said. "Don't try to talk."

"Yes he has," she said, as if I'd contradicted her. "Oh, the bastard. The randy bastard."

"I'm going downstairs," I says. "I got to call the doctor."

"No," she says back. She reached up with one hand and took hold of my wrist. "No doctor. No hospital. The dust bunnies . . . even there. *Everywhere.*"

"You'll be all right, Vera," I says, pullin my hand free. "As long as you lie still n don't move, you'll be fine."

"Dolores Claiborne says I'm going to be *fine!*" she says, and it was that dry, fierce voice she used to use before she had her strokes n got all muddled in her head. "What a relief it is to have a professional opinion!"

Hearin that voice after all the years it had been gone was like bein slapped. It shocked me right out of my panic, and I really looked into her face for the first time, the way you look at a person who knows exactly what they're sayin n means every word.

"I'm as good as dead," she says, "and you know it as well as I do. My back's broken, I think."

"You don't know that, Vera," I says, but I wasn't wild to get to the telephone like I had been. I think I knew what was comin, and if she ast what I thought she was gonna ask, I didn't see how I could refuse her. I had owed her a debt ever since that rainy fall day in 1962 when I sat on her bed n bawled my eyes out with my apron up over my face, and the Claibornes have always cleared their debts.

When she spoke to me again, she was as clear and as lucid as she'd been thirty years ago, back when Joe was alive and the kids were still at home. "I know there's only one thing left worth deciding," she says, "and that's whether I'm going to die in my time or in some hospital's. Their time would be too long. My time is now, Dolores. I'm tired of seeing my husband's face in the corners when I'm weak and confused. I'm tired of seeing them winch that Corvette out of the quarry in the moonlight, how the water ran out of the open window on the passenger side—"

"Vera, I don't know what you're talkin about," I says.

She lifted her hand n waved it at me in her old impatient way for a second or two; then it flopped back onto the stairs beside her. "I'm tired of pissing down my legs and forgetting who came to see me half an hour after they're gone. I want to be done. Will you help me?"

I knelt beside her, picked up the hand that'd fallen on the stairs n held it against my bosom. I thought about the sound the rock made when it hit Joe in the face—that sound like a china plate breakin all to splinters on a brick hearth. I wondered if I could hear that sound again without losin my mind. And I knew it *would* sound the same, because she'd sounded like him when she was callin my name, she'd sounded like him when she fell and landed on the stairs, breakin herself all to pieces just like she'd always been afraid the maids'd break the delicate glassware she kept in the parlor, and my slip was layin on the upstairs landin in a little ball of white nylon with both straps busted, and that was just like before, too. If I did her, it'd sound the same as it had when I did him, and I knew it. Ayuh. I knew it as well's I know that East Lane ends in those rickety old stairs goin down the side of East Head.

I held her hand n thought about how the world is—how sometimes bad men have accidents and good women turn into bitches. I looked at the awful, helpless way her eyes rolled so she could look up into my face, n I marked how the blood from the cut in her scalp ran down the deep wrinkles in her cheek, the way spring rain runs in plow furrows goin downhill.

I says, "If it's what you want, Vera, I'll help you."

She started to cry then. It was the only time when she wasn't all dim n foolish that I ever saw her do that. "Yes," she says. "Yes, it *is* what I want. God bless you, Dolores."

"Don't you fret," I says. I raised her old wrinkled hand to my lips n kissed it.

"Hurry, Dolores," she says. "If you really want to help me, please hurry."

"Before we both lose our courage" was what her eyes seemed to be sayin.

I kissed her hand again, then laid it on her stomach n stood up. I didn't have no trouble that time; the strength'd come back into my legs. I went down the stairs n into the kitchen. I'd set out the bakin things before going out to hang the warsh; I had it in mind that it'd be a good day to make bread. She had a rollin pin, a great heavy thing made of gray marble veined with black. It was layin on the counter, next to the yellow plastic flour canister. I picked it up, still feelin as if I was in a dream or runnin a high fever, n walked back through the parlor toward the front hall. As I went through that room with all her nice old things in it, I thought about all the times I'd played that trick with the vacuum cleaner on her, and how she'd got

back at me for awhile. In the end, she always wised up and got her own back . . . ain't that why I'm here?

I come out of the parlor into the hall, then climbed the stairs toward her, holdin that rollin pin by one of the wooden handles. When I got to where she lay, with her head pointed down and her legs twisted under her, I didn't mean to take no pause; I knew if I did that, I wouldn't be able to do it at all. There wasn't going to be any more talk. When I got to her, I meant to drop on one knee n brain her with that marble rollin pin just as hard as I could and as fast as I could. Maybe it'd look like somethin that'd happened to her when she fell and maybe it wouldn't, but I meant to do it either way.

When I knelt beside her, I saw there was no need; she'd done it on her own after all, like she done most things in her life. While I was in the kitchen gettin the rollin pin, or maybe while I was comin back through the parlor, she'd just closed her eyes n slipped off.

I sat down beside her, put the rollin pin on the stairs, picked up her hand n held it in my lap. There are some times in a person's life that don't have no real minutes in em, so you can't count em up. All I know is that I sat n visited with her awhile. I dunno if I said anything or not. I think I did—I think I thanked her for lettin go, for lettin *me* go, for not makin me have to go through *all* of it again—but maybe I only thought those things. I remember puttin her hand against my cheek, then turnin it over and kissin the palm. I remember lookin at it and thinkin how pink n clean it was. The lines had mostly faded from it, and it looked like a baby's hand. I knew I ought to get up and telephone

someone, tell em what happened, but I was weary—so weary. It seemed easier to just sit there n hold her hand.

Then the doorbell rang. If it hadn't, I would have set there quite awhile longer, I think. But you know how it is with bells—you feel you have to answer em, no matter what. I got up and went down the stairs one at a time, like a woman ten years older'n I am (the truth is, I *felt* ten years older), clingin to the bannister the whole way. I remember thinkin the world still felt as if it was made of glass, and I had to be damned careful not to slip on it n cut myself when I had to let go of the bannister n cross the entry to the door.

It was Sammy Marchant, with his mailman's hat cocked back on his head in that silly way he does—he prob'ly thinks wearin his hat that way makes him look like a rock star. He had the regular mail in one hand and one of those padded envelopes that come registered mail just about every week from New York—news of what was happenin with her financial affairs, accourse—in the other. It was a fella named Greenbush took care of her money, did I tell you that?

I did? All right—thanks. There's been so much globber I can hardly remember what I've told you and what I haven't.

Sometimes there were papers in those registered mail envelopes that had to be signed, and most times Vera could do that if I helped hold her arm steady, but there were a few times, when she was fogged out, that I signed her name on em myself. There wasn't nothing to it, and never a single question later about any of the ones I did. In the last three or four years,

her signature wa'ant nothin but a scrawl, anyway. So that's somethin else you c'n get me for, if you really want to: forgery.

Sammy'd started holdin out the padded envelope as soon as the door opened—wantin me to sign for it, like I always did with the registered—but when he got a good look at me, his eyes widened n he took a step backward on the stoop. It was actually more of a jerk than a step—and considerin it was Sammy Marchant doin it, that seems like just the right word. "Dolores!" he says. "Are you all right? There's blood on you!"

"It's not mine," I says, and my voice was as calm as it woulda been if he'd ast me what I was watchin on TV and I told him. "It's Vera's. She fell down the stairs. She's dead."

"Holy Christ," he says, then ran past me into the house with his mailbag floppin against one hip. It never crossed my mind to try n keep him out, and ask y'self this: what good would it have done if I had?

I followed him slow. That glassy feelin was goin away, but it seemed like my shoes had grown themselves lead soles. When I got to the foot of the stairs Sammy was halfway up em, kneelin beside Vera. He'd taken off his mailbag before he knelt, and it'd fallen most of the way back down the stairs, spillin letters n Bangor Hydro bills n L. L. Bean catalogues from hell to breakfast.

I climbed up to him, draggin my feet from one stair to the next. I ain't ever felt s'tired. Not even after I killed Joe did I feel as tired as I felt yest'y mornin.

"She's dead, all right," he says, lookin around.

"Ayuh," I says back. "Told you she was."

"I thought she couldn't walk," he says. "You always told me she couldn't walk, Dolores."

"Well," I says, "I guess I was wrong." I felt stupid sayin a thing like that with her layin there like she was, but what the hell else *was* there to say? In some ways it was easier talkin to John McAuliffe than to poor dumb Sammy Marchant, because I'd done pretty much what McAuliffe suspected I'd done. The trouble with bein innocent is you're more or less stuck with the truth.

"What's *this?*" he asks then, n pointed at the rollin pin. I'd left it sittin on the stair when the doorbell rang.

"What do you *think* it is?" I ast him right back. "A birdcage?"

"Looks like a rollin pin," he says.

"That's pretty good," I says. It seemed like I was hearin my own voice comin from far away, as if it was in one place n the rest of me was someplace else. "You may surprise em all n turn out to be college material after all, Sammy."

"Yeah, but what's a *rollin pin* doin on the *stairs?*" he ast, and all at once I saw the way he was lookin at me. Sammy ain't a day over twenty-five, but his Dad was in the search-party that found Joe, and I all at once realized that Duke Marchant'd probably raised Sammy and all the rest of his not-too-brights on the notion that Dolores Claiborne St. George had done away with her old man. You remember me sayin that when you're innocent you're more or less stuck with the truth? Well, when I seen the way Sammy was lookin at me, I all at once decided this might be a time when less'd be quite a bit safer'n more.

"I was in the kitchen gettin ready to make bread when she fell," I said. Another thing about bein innocent—any lies you *do* decide to tell are mostly unplanned lies; innocent folks don't spend hours workin out their stories, like I worked out mine about how I went up to Russian Meadow to watch the eclipse and never seen my husband again until I saw him in the Mercier Funeral Home. The minute that lie about makin bread was out of my mouth I knew it was apt to kick back on me, but if you'd seen the look in his eyes, Andy—dark n suspicious n scared, all at once—you might've lied, too.

He got to his feet, started to turn around, then stopped right where he was, lookin up. I followed his gaze. What I seen was my slip, crumpled up in a ball on the landin.

"I guess she took her slip off before she fell," he said, lookin back at me again. "Or jumped. Or whatever the hell it was she did. Do you think so, Dolores?"

"No," I says, "that's mine."

"If you were makin bread in the kitchen," he says, talkin real slow, like a kid who ain't too bright tryin to work out a math problem at the blackboard, "then what's your underwear doin up on the landin?"

I couldn't think of a single thing to say. Sammy took one step back down the stairs n then another, movin as slow's he talked, holdin the bannister, never takin his eyes off me, and all at once I understood what he was doin: makin space between us. Doin it because he was afraid I might take it into my head to push *him* like he thought I'd pushed her. It was right then that I knew I'd be sittin here where I'm sittin before too much time passed, and tellin what I'm tellin. His eyes might as well have been speakin right out loud, sayin, "You got away with it once, Dolores Claiborne, and considerin the kind of man my Dad says Joe St. George was, maybe that was all right. But what did this woman ever do to you besides feed you n keep a roof over your head n pay you a decent livin wage?" And what his eyes said more'n anything else was that a woman who pushes once and gets away with it might push twice; that given the right situation, she *will* push twice. And if the push ain't enough to do what she set out to do, she won't have to think very hard before decidin to finish the job some other way. With a marble rollin pin, for instance.

"This is none of your affair, Sam Marchant," I says. "You better just go about your business. I have to call the island ambulance. Just make sure you pick up your mail before you go, or there's gonna be a lot of credit card companies chewin on your ass."

"Mrs. Donovan don't need an ambulance," he says, goin down another two steps n keepin his eyes on me the whole time, "and I'm not goin anywhere just yet. I think instead of the ambulance, you better make your first call to Andy Bissette."

Which, as you know, I did. Sammy Marchant stood right there n watched me do it. After I'd hung up the phone, he picked up the mail he'd spilled (takin a quick look over his shoulder every now n then, prob'ly to make sure I wasn't creepin up behind him with that rollin pin in my hand) and then just stood at the foot of the stairs, like a guard dog that's cornered a burglar. He didn't talk, and I didn't, neither. It crossed my mind

that I could go through the dinin room and the kitchen to the back stairs n get my slip. But what good would that have done? He'd seen it, hadn't he? And the rollin pin was still settin there on the stairs, wa'ant it?

Pretty soon you came, Andy, along with Frank, and a little later I went down to our nice new police station n made a statement. That was just yest'y forenoon, so I guess there's no need to reheat that hash, is there? You know I didn't say anything about the slip, n when you ast me about the rollin pin, I said I wasn't really sure *how* it'd gotten there. It was all I could think to say, at least until someone come along n took the OUT OF ORDER sign offa my brains.

After I signed the statement I got in my car n drove home. It was all so quick n quiet—givin the statement and all, I mean—that I almost persuaded myself I didn't have nothing to worry about. After all, I *hadn't* killed her; she really *did* fall. I kept tellin myself that, n by the time I turned into my own driveway, I'd come a long way to bein convinced that everything was gonna be all right.

That feelin only lasted as long's it took me to get from the car to my back door. There was a note thumb-tacked to it. Just a plain sheet of notebook paper. It had a smear of grease on it, like it'd been torn from a book some man'd been carryin around in his hip pocket. YOU WILL NOT GET AWAY WITH IT AGAIN, the note said. That was all. Hell, it was enough, wouldn't you say?

I went inside n cracked open the kitchen windows to let out the musty smell. I hate that smell, n the house always seems to have it these days, no matter if

I air it out or not. It's not just because I mostly live at Vera's now—or did, at least—although accourse that's part of it; mostly it's because the house is dead . . . as dead as Joe n Little Pete.

Houses *do* have their own life that they take from the people who live in em; I really believe that. Our little one-storey place lived past Joe's dyin and the two older kids goin away to school, Selena to Vassar on a full scholarship (her share of that college money I was so concerned about went to buy clothes n textbooks), and Joe Junior just up the road to the University of Maine in Orono. It even survived the news that Little Pete had been killed in a barracks explosion in Saigon. It happened just after he got there, and less'n two months before the whole shebang was over. I watched the last of the helicopters pull away from the embassy roof on the TV in Vera's livin room and just cried n cried. I could let myself do that without fear of what she might say, because she'd gone down to Boston on a shoppin binge.

It was after Little Pete's funeral that the life went out of the house; after the last of the company had left and the three of us—me, Selena, Joe Junior—was left there with each other. Joe Junior'd been talkin about politics. He'd just gotten the City Manager job in Machias, not bad for a kid with the ink still wet on his college degree, and was thinkin about runnin for the State Legislature in a year or two.

Selena talked a little bit about the courses she was teachin at Albany Junior College—this was before she moved down to New York City and started writin full time—and then she went quiet. She n I were riddin up the dishes, and all at once I felt somethin. I turned around quick n saw her lookin at me with those dark eyes of hers. I could tell you I read her mind—parents can do that with their kids sometimes, you know—but the fact is I didn't need to; I knew what she was thinkin about, I knew that it never entirely left her mind. I saw the same questions in her eyes then as had been there twelve years before, when she came up to me in the garden, amongst the beans n the cukes: "Did you do anything to him?" and "Is it my fault?" and "How long do I have to pay?"

I went to her, Andy, n hugged her. She hugged me back, but her body was stiff against mine—stiff's a poker—and that's when I felt the life go out of the house. It went like the last breath of a dyin man. I think Selena felt it, too. Not Joe Junior; he puts the pitcher of the house on the front of some of his campaign fliers—it makes him look like home-folks and the voters like that, I've noticed—but he never felt it when it died because he never really loved it in the first place. Why would he, for Christ's sake? To Joe Junior, that house was just the place where he came after school, the place where his father ragged him n called him a book-readin sissy. Cumberland Hall, the dorm he lived in up to the University, was more home to Joe Junior than the house on East Lane ever was.

It was home to me, though, and it was home to Selena. I think my good girl went on livin here long after she'd shaken the dust of Little Tall Island off her feet; I think she lived here in her memories . . . in her heart . . . in her dreams. Her nightmares.

That musty smell—you c'n never get rid of it once it really settles in.

I sat by one of the open windows to get a noseful of the fresh sea-breeze for awhile, then I got feelin funny and decided I ought to lock the doors. The front door was easy, but the thumb-bolt on the back one was so balky I couldn't budge it until I put a charge of Three in One in there. Finally it turned, and when it did I realized why it was so stubborn: simple rust. I sometimes spent five n six days at a stretch up to Vera's, but I still couldn't remember the last time I'd bothered to lock up the house.

Thinkin about that just seemed to take all the guts outta me. I went into the bedroom n laid down n put my pillow over my head like I used to do when I was a little girl n got sent to bed early for bein bad. I cried n cried n cried. I would never have believed I had so many tears in me. I cried for Vera and Selena and Little Pete; I guess I even cried for Joe. But mostly I cried for myself. I cried until my nose was plugged up and I had cramps in my belly. Finally I fell asleep.

When I woke up it was dark and the telephone was ringin. I got up n felt my way into the living room to answer it. As soon as I said hello, someone—some woman—said, "You can't murder her. I hope you know that. If the law doesn't get you, we will. You aren't as smart as you think you are. We don't have to live with murderers here, Dolores Claiborne; not as long as there's still some decent Christians left on the island to keep it from happenin."

My head was so muzzy that at first I thought I was

havin a dream. By the time I figured out I was really awake, she'd hung up. I started for the kitchen, meanin to put on the coffee-pot or maybe grab a beer out of the fridge, when the phone rang again. It was a woman that time, too, but not the same one. Filth started to stream out of her mouth n I hung up quick. The urge to cry come over me again, but I was damned if I'd do it. I pulled the telephone plug outta the wall instead. I went into the kitchen n got a beer, but it didn't taste good to me n I ended up pourin most of it down the sink. I think what I really wanted was a little Scotch, but I haven't had a drop of hard liquor in the house since Joe died.

I drew a glass of water n found I couldn't abide the smell of it—it smelled like pennies that've been carried around all day in some kid's sweaty fist. It made me remember that night in the blackberry tangles—how that same smell came to me on a little puff of breeze—n *that* made me think of the girl in the pink lipstick n the striped dress. I thought of how it'd crossed my mind that the woman she'd grown into was in trouble. I wondered how she was n where she was, but I never once wondered *if* she was, if you see what I mean; I *knew* she was. *Is.* I have never doubted it.

But that don't matter; my mind's wanderin again n my mouth's followin right along behind, like Mary's little lamb. All I started to say was that the water from my kitchen sink didn't use me any better than Mr. Budweiser's finest had—even a couple of ice-cubes wouldn't take away that coppery smell—and I ended up watchin some stupid comedy show and drinkin one of the Hawaiian Punches I keep in the back of the

fridge for Joe Junior's twin boys. I made myself a frozen dinner but didn't have no appetite for it once it was ready n ended up scrapin it into the swill. I settled for another Hawaiian Punch instead—took it back into the livin room n just sat there in front of the TV. One comedy'd give way to another, but I didn't see a dime's worth of difference. I s'pose it was because I wa'ant payin much attention.

I didn't try to figure out what I was gonna do; there's some figurin you're wiser not to try at night, because that's the time your mind's most apt to go bad on you. Whatever you figure out after sundown, nine times outta ten you got it all to do over again in the mornin. So I just sat, and some time after the local news had ended and the *Tonight* show had come on, I fell asleep again.

I had a dream. It was about me n Vera, only Vera was the way she was when I first knew her, back when Joe was still alive and all our kids, hers as well as mine, were still around n underfoot most of the time. In my dream we were doin the dishes—her warshin n me wipin. Only we weren't doin em in the kitchen; we were standin in front of the little Franklin stove in the livin room of my house. And that was funny, because Vera wasn't ever in my house—not once in her whole life.

She was there in this dream, though. She had the dishes in a plastic basin on top of the stove—not my old stuff but her good Spode china. She'd warsh a plate n then hand it to me, and each one of em'd slip outta my hands and break on the bricks the Franklin stands on. Vera'd say, "You have to be more careful than that,

Dolores; when accidents happen and you're not careful, there's always a hell of a mess."

I'd promise her to be careful, and I'd *try*, but the next plate'd slip through my fingers, n the next, n the next, n the next.

"This is no good at all," Vera said at last. "Just look at the mess you're making!"

I looked down, but instead of pieces of broken plates, the bricks were littered with little pieces of Joe's dentures n broken stone. "Don't you hand me no more, Vera," I said, startin to cry. "I guess I ain't up to doing no dishes. Maybe I've got too old, I dunno, but I don't want to break the whole job lot of em, I know *that*."

She kep on handin em to me just the same, though, and I kep droppin em, and the sound they made when they hit the bricks kep gettin louder n deeper, until it was more a *boomin* sound than the brittle crash china makes when it hits somethin hard n busts. All at once I knew I was havin a dream n those booms weren't part of it. I snapped awake s'hard I almost fell outta the chair n onto the floor. There was another of those booms, and this time I knew it for what it was—a shotgun.

I got up n went over to the window. Two pickup trucks went by on the road. There were people in the backs, one in the bed of the first n two—I think—in the bed of the second. It looked like all of em had shotguns, and every couple of seconds one of em'd trigger off a round into the sky. There'd be a bright muzzle-flash, then another loud boom. From the way the men (I *guess* they were men, although I can't say for sure) were swayin back n forth—and from

the way the trucks were *weavin* back n forth—I'd say the whole crew was pissyass drunk. I recognized one of the trucks, too.

What?

No, I *ain't* gonna tell you—I'm in enough trouble myself. I don't plan to drag nobody else in with me over a little drunk night-shootin. I guess maybe I didn't recognize that truck after all.

Anyway, I threw up the window when I seen they wasn't puttin holes in nothin but a few low-lyin clouds. I thought they'd use the wide spot at the bottom of our hill to turn around, and they did. One of em goddam near got stuck, too, and wouldn't *that* have been a laugh.

They come back up, hootin and tootin and yellin their heads off. I cupped m'hands around m'mouth n screamed "*Get outta here! Some folks're tryin t'sleep!*" just as loud's I could. One of the trucks swerved a little wider n almost run into the ditch, so I guess I threw a startle into em, all right. The fella standin in the back of that truck (it was the one I thought I recognized until a few seconds ago) went ass-over-dashboard. I got a good set of lungs on me, if I do say so m'self, n I can holler with the best of em when I want to.

"*Get offa Little Tall Island, you goddam murderin cunt!*" one of em yelled back, n triggered a few more shots off into the air. But that was just in the way of showin me what big balls they had, I think, because they didn't make another pass. I could hear em roarin off toward town—and that goddam bar that opened there year before last, I'll bet a cookie—with their mufflers blattin and their tailpipes chamberin backfires

as they did all their fancy downshifts. You know how men are when they're drunk n drivin pick-em-ups.

Well, it broke the worst of my mood. I wa'ant scared anymore and I sure as shit didn't feel weepy anymore. I was good n pissed off, but not s'mad I couldn't think, or understand why folks were doin the things they were doin. When my anger tried to take me past that place, I stopped it happenin by thinkin of Sammy Marchant, how his eyes had looked as he knelt there on the stairs lookin first at that rollin pin and then up at me—as dark as the ocean just ahead of a squall-line, they were, like Selena's had been that day in the garden.

I already knew I was gonna have to come back down here, Andy, but it was only after those men left that I quit kiddin myself that I could still pick n choose what I was gonna tell or hold back. I saw I was gonna have to make a clean breast of everything. I went back to bed n slept peaceful until quarter of nine in the morning. It's the latest I've slep since before I was married. I guess I was gettin rested up so I could talk the whole friggin night.

Once I was up, I meant to do it just as soon's I could—bitter medicine is best taken right away—but somethin put me off my track before I could get out of the house, or I would've ended up tellin you all this a lot sooner.

I took a bath, and before I got dressed I put the telephone plug back in the wall. It wasn't night anymore, and I wasn't half in n half out of some dream anymore. I figured if someone wanted to phone up and call me names, I'd dish out a few names of my own, startin with "yellowbelly" n "dirty no-name sneak."

Sure enough, I hadn't done more'n roll on my stockings before it *did* ring. I picked it up, ready to give whoever was on the other end a good dose of what-for, when this woman's voice said, "Hello? May I speak to Miz Dolores Claiborne?"

I knew right away it was long distance, n not just because of the little echo we get out here when the call's from away. I knew because nobody on the island calls women Miz. You might be a Miss n you might be a Missus, but Miz still ain't made it across the reach, except once a month on the magazine rack down to the drugstore.

"Speakin," I says.

"This is Alan Greenbush calling," she says.

"Funny," I says, pert's you please, "you don't *sound* like an Alan Greenbush."

"It's his *office* calling," she says, like I was about the dumbest thing she ever heard of. "Will you hold for Mr. Greenbush?"

She caught me so by surprise the name didn't sink in at first—I knew I'd heard it before, but I didn't know where.

"What's it concernin?" I ast.

There was a pause, like she wasn't really s'posed to let that sort of information out, and then she said, "I believe it concerns Mrs. Vera Donovan. Will you hold, Miz Claiborne?"

Then it clicked in—Greenbush, who sent her all the padded envelopes registered mail.

"Ayuh," I says.

"Pardon me?" she says.

"I'll hold," I says.

"Thank you," she says back. There was a click n I was left for a little while standin there in my underwear, waitin. It wasn't long but it *seemed* long. Just before he came on the line, it occurred to me that it must be about the times I'd signed Vera's name—they'd caught me. It seemed likely enough; ain't you ever noticed how when one thing goes wrong, everythin else seems to go wrong right behind it?

Then he come on the line. "Miz Claiborne?" he says.

"Yes, this is Dolores Claiborne," I told him.

"The local law enforcement official on Little Tall Island called me yesterday afternoon and informed me that Vera Donovan had passed away," he said. "It was quite late when I received the call, and so I decided to wait until this morning to telephone you."

I thought of tellin him there was folks on the island not so particular about what time they called me, but accourse I didn't.

He cleared his throat, then said, "I had a letter from Mrs. Donovan five years ago, specifically instructing me to give you certain information concerning her estate within twenty-four hours of her passing." He cleared his throat again n said, "Although I have spoken to her on the phone frequently since then, that was the last actual *letter* I received from her." He had a dry, fussy kind of voice. The kind of voice that when it tells you somethin, you can't not hear it.

"What are you talkin about, man?" I ast. "Quit all this backin and fillin and *tell* me!"

He says, "I'm pleased to inform you that, aside from a small bequest to The New England Home for Little

Wanderers, you are the sole beneficiary of Mrs. Donovan's will."

My tongue stuck to the roof of my mouth and all I could think of was how she'd caught onto the vacuum cleaner trick after awhile.

"You'll receive a confirming telegram later today," he says, "but I'm very glad to have spoken to you well before its arrival—Mrs. Donovan was very emphatic about her desires in this matter."

"Ayuh," I says, "she could be emphatic, all right."

"I'm sure you're grieved at Mrs. Donovan's passing—we all are—but I want you to know that you are going to be a very wealthy woman, and if I can do anything at all to assist you in your new circumstances, I would be as happy to do so as I was to assist Mrs. Donovan. Of course I'll be calling to give you updates on the progress of the will through probate, but I really don't expect any problems or delays. In fact—"

"Whoa on, chummy," I says, n it came out in a kind of croak. Sounded quite a bit like a frog in a dry pond. "How much money are you talkin about?"

Accourse I *knew* she was well off, Andy; the fact that in the last few years she didn't wear nothing but flannel nighties n lived on a steady diet of Campbell's soup and Gerber's baby-food didn't change that. I saw the house, I saw the cars, n I sometimes looked at a wee bit more of the papers that came in those padded envelopes than just the signature line. Some were stock transfer forms, n I know that when you're sellin two thousand shares of Upjohn and buyin four thousand of Mississippi Valley Light n Power, you ain't exactly totterin down the road to the poorhouse.

I wa'ant askin so I could start applyin for credit cards n orderin things from the Sears catalogue, either—don't go gettin that idear. I had a better reason than that. I knew that the number of people who thought I'd murdered her would most likely go up with every dollar she left me, n I wanted to know how bad I was gonna get hurt. I thought it might be as much as sixty or seventy thousand dollars . . . although he *had* said she left some money to an orphanage, and I figured that'd take it down some.

There was somethin else bitin me, too—bitin the way a June deerfly does when it settles on the back of your neck. Somethin way wrong about the whole proposition. I couldn't put m'finger on it, though—no more'n I'd been able to put m'finger on exactly who Greenbush was when his secretary first said his name.

He said somethin I couldn't quite make out. It sounded like *blub-dub-a-gub-area-of-thirty-million-dollars.*

"What did you say, sir?" I ast.

"That after probate, legal fees, and a few other small deductions, the total should be in the area of thirty million dollars."

My hand on the telephone had started to feel the way it does when I wake up n realize I slep most of the night on it . . . numb through the middle n all tingly around the edges. My feet were tinglin, too, n all at once the world felt like it was made of glass again.

"I'm sorry," I says. I could hear my mouth talkin perfectly well n perfectly clear, but I didn't seem to be attached to any of the words that were comin out of it. It was just flappin, like a shutter in a high wind.

"The connection here isn't very good. I thought you said somethin with the word *million* in it." Then I laughed, just to show how silly I knew that was, but part of me must've thought it wa'ant silly at all, because that was the fakest-soundin laugh I ever heard come outta me—*Yar-yar-yar*, it sounded like.

"I *did* say million," he said. "In fact, I said *thirty* million." And do you know, I think he woulda chuckled if it hadn't been Vera Donovan's dead body I was gettin that money over. I think he was *excited*—that underneath that dry, prissy voice he was excited as hell. I s'pose he felt like John Bearsford Tipton, the rich fella who used to give away a million bucks at a crack on that old TV show. He wanted my business, accourse that was part of it—I got a feelin that money's like electric trains to fellas like him n he didn't want to see such an almighty big set as Vera's taken away from him—but I think most of the fun of it for him was just hearin me flub-dubbin around like I was doin.

"I don't get it," I says, and now my voice was so weak I could hardly hear it myself.

"I think I understand how you feel," he says. "It's a very large sum, and of course it will take a little getting used to."

"How much is it *really*?" I ast him, and that time he *did* chuckle. If he'd been where I coulda got to him, Andy, I believe I woulda booted him in the seat of the pants.

He told me again, *thirty million dollars*, n I kep thinkin that if my hand got any stupider, I was gonna drop the phone. And I started to feel panicky. It was like someone was inside my head, swingin a steel cable

around n around. I'd think *thirty million dollars*, but those were just words. When I tried to see what they meant, the only pitcher I could make inside my head was like the ones in the Scrooge McDuck comic books Joe Junior used to read Little Pete when Pete was four or five. I saw a great big vault fulla coins n bills, only instead of Scrooge McDuck paddlin around in all that dough with the spats on his flippers n those little round spectacles perched on his beak, I'd see *me* doin it in my bedroom slippers. Then that pitcher'd slip away and I'd think of how Sammy Marchant's eyes had looked when they moved from the rollin pin to me n then back to the rollin pin again. They looked like Selena's had looked that day in the garden, all dark n full of questions. Then I thought of the woman who called on the phone n said there were still decent Christians on the island who didn't have to live with murderers. I wondered what that woman n her friends were gonna think when they found out Vera's death had left me thirty million dollars to the good . . . and the thought of that came close to puttin me into a panic.

"You can't do it!" I says, kinda wild. "Do you hear me? You can't make me take it!"

Then it was *his* turn to say he couldn't quite hear—that the connection must be loose someplace along the line. I ain't a bit surprised, either. When a man like Greenbush hears someone sayin they don't want a thirty-million-dollar lump of cash, they figure the equipment *must* be frigged up. I opened my mouth to tell him again that he'd have to take it back, that he could give every cent of it to The New England Home for Little Wanderers, when I suddenly understood

what was wrong with all this. It didn't just hit me; it come down on my head like a dropped load of bricks.

"Donald n Helga!" I says. I musta sounded like a TV game-show contestant comin up with the right answer in the last second or two of the bonus round.

"I beg pardon?" he asks, kinda cautious.

"Her *kids!*" I says. "Her son and her daughter! That money belongs to them, not me! They're *kin!* I ain't nothing but a jumped-up housekeeper!"

There was such a long pause then that I felt sure we musta been disconnected, and I wa'ant a bit sorry. I felt faint, to tell you the truth. I was about to hang up when he says in this flat, funny voice, "You don't know."

"Don't know *what?*" I shouted at him. "I know she's got a son named Donald and a daughter named Helga! I know they was too damned good to come n visit her up here, although she always kep space for em, but I guess they won't be too good to divide up a pile like the one you're talkin about now that she's dead!"

"You don't know," he said again. And then, as if he was askin questions to himself instead of to me, he says, "*Could* you not know, after all the time you worked for her? *Could* you? Wouldn't Kenopensky have told you?" N before I could get a word in edgeways, he started answerin his own damned questions. "Of course it's possible. Except for a squib on an inside page of the local paper the day after, she kept the whole thing under wraps—you could do that thirty years ago, if you were willing to pay for the privilege. I'm not sure there were even obituaries." He stopped, then says, like a man will when he's just discoverin somethin

new—somethin *huge*—about someone he's known all his life: "She talked about them as if they were *alive*, didn't she. All these years!"

"What are you globberin about?" I shouted at him. It felt like an elevator was goin down in my stomach, and all at once all sorts of things—little things—started fittin together in my mind. I didn't want em to, but it went on happenin, just the same. "*Accourse* she talked about em like they were alive! They *are* alive! He's got a real estate company in Arizona—Golden West Associates! She designs dresses in San Francisco . . . Gaylord Fashions!"

Except she'd always read these big paperback historical novels with women in low-cut dresses kissin men without their shirts on, and the trade name for those books was Golden West—it said so on a little foil strip at the top of every one. And it all at once occurred to me that she'd been born in a little town called Gaylord, Missouri. I wanted to think it was somethin else—Galen, or maybe Galesburg—but I knew it wasn't. Still, her daughter mighta named her dress business after the town her mother'd been born in . . . or so I told myself.

"Miz Claiborne," Greenbush says, talkin in a low, sorta anxious voice, "Mrs. Donovan's husband was killed in an unfortunate accident when Donald was fifteen and Helga was thirteen—"

"I know that!" I says, like I wanted him to believe that if I knew that I must know everything.

"—and there was consequently a great deal of bad feeling between Mrs. Donovan and the children."

I'd known that, too. I remembered people remarkin on how quiet the kids had been when they showed up on Memorial Day in 1961 for their usual summer on the island, and how several people'd mentioned that you didn't ever seem to see the three of em together anymore, which was especially strange, considerin Mr. Donovan's sudden death the year before; usually somethin like that draws people closer . . . although I s'pose city folks may be a little different about such things. And then I remembered somethin else, somethin Jimmy DeWitt told me in the fall of that year.

"They had a wowser of an argument in a restaurant just after the Fourth of July in '61," I says. "The boy n girl left the next day. I remember the hunky—Kenopensky, I mean—takin em across to the mainland in the big motor launch they had back then."

"Yes," Greenbush said. "It so happens that I knew from Ted Kenopensky what that argument was about. Donald had gotten his driver's licence that spring, and Mrs. Donovan had gotten him a car for his birthday. The girl, Helga, said *she* wanted a car, too. Vera—Mrs. Donovan—apparently tried to explain to the girl that the idea was silly, a car would be useless to her without a driver's licence and she couldn't get one of those until she was fifteen. Helga said that might be true in Maryland, but it wasn't the case in Maine—that she could get one there at fourteen . . . which she was. Could that have been true, Miz Claiborne, or was it just an adolescent fantasy?"

"It *was* true back then," I says, "although I think you have to be at least fifteen now. Mr. Greenbush, the car

she got her boy for his birthday . . . was it a Corvette?"

"Yes," he says, "it was. How did you know that, Miz Claiborne?"

"I musta seen a pitcher of it sometime," I said, but I hardly heard my own voice. The voice I heard was Vera's. "I'm tired of seeing them winch that Corvette out of the quarry in the moonlight," she told me as she lay dyin on the stairs. "Tired of seein how the water ran out of the open window on the passenger side."

"I'm surprised she kept a picture of it around," Greenbush said. "Donald and Helga Donovan died in that car, you see. It happened in October of 1961, almost a year to the day after their father died. It seemed the girl was driving."

He went on talkin, but I hardly heard him, Andy—I was too busy fillin in the blanks for myself, and doin it so fast that I guess I musta known they were dead . . . somewhere way down deep I musta known it all along. Greenbush said they'd been drinkin and pushin that Corvette along at better'n a hundred miles an hour when the girl missed a turn and went into the quarry; he said both of em were prob'ly dead long before that fancy two-seater sank to the bottom.

He said it was an accident, too, but maybe I knew a little more about accidents than he did.

Maybe Vera did, too, and maybe she'd always known that the argument they had that summer didn't have Jack Shit to do with whether or not Helga was gonna get a State of Maine driver's licence; that was just the handiest bone they had to pick. When McAuliffe ast me what Joe and I argued about before he got chokin me, I told him it was money on top n booze under-

neath. The tops of people's arguments are mostly quite a lot different from what's on the bottom, I've noticed, and it could be that what they were *really* arguin about that summer was what had happened to Michael Donovan the year before.

She and the hunky killed the man, Andy—she did everything but come out n tell me so. She never got caught, either, but sometimes there's people inside of families who've got pieces of the jigsaw puzzle the law never sees. People like Selena, for instance . . . n maybe people like Donald n Helga Donovan, too. I wonder how they looked at her that summer, before they had that argument in The Harborside Restaurant n left Little Tall for the last time. I've tried n tried to remember how their eyes were when they looked at her, if they were like Selena's when she looked at me, n I just can't do it. P'raps I will in time, but that ain't nothing I'm really lookin forward to, if you catch my meanin.

I *do* know that sixteen was young for a little hellion like Don Donovan to have a driver's licence—too damned young—and when you add in that hot car, why, you've got a recipe for disaster. Vera was smart enough to know that, and she must have been scared sick; she might have hated the father, but she loved the son like life itself. I know she did. She gave it to him just the same, though. Tough as she was, she put that rocket in his pocket, n Helga's, too, as it turned out, when he wasn't but a junior in high school n prob'ly just startin to shave. I think it was guilt, Andy. And maybe I want to think it was *just* that because I don't like to think there was fear mixed in with it, that maybe a couple of rich kids like them could blackmail

their mother for the things they wanted over the death of their father. I *don't* really think it . . . but it's possible, you know; it *is* possible. In a world where a man can spend months tryin to take his own daughter to bed, I believe anything is possible.

"They're dead," I said to Greenbush. "That's what you're telling me."

"Yes," he says.

"They've *been* dead, thirty years n more," I says.

"Yes," he says again.

"And everything she told me about em," I says, "it was a lie."

He cleared his throat again—that man's one of the world's greatest throat-clearers, if my talk with him today's any example—and when he spoke up, he sounded damned near human. "What *did* she tell you about them, Miz Claiborne?" he ast.

And when I thought about it, Andy, I realized she'd told me a hell of a lot, startin in the summer of '62, when she showed up lookin ten years older n twenty pounds lighter'n the year before. I remember her tellin me that Donald n Helga might be spendin August at the house n for me to check n make sure we had enough Quaker Rolled Oats, which was all they'd eat for breakfast. I remember her comin back up in October—that was the fall when Kennedy n Khrushchev were decidin whether or not they was gonna blow up the whole shootin match—and tellin me I'd be seein a lot more of her in the future. "I hope you'll be seein the kids, too," she'd said, but there was somethin in her voice, Andy . . . and in her eyes . . .

Mostly it was her eyes I thought of as I stood there

with the phone in my hand. She told me all sorts of things with her *mouth* over the years, about where they went to school, what they were doin, who they were seein (Donald got married n had two kids, accordin to Vera; Helga got married n divorced), but I realized that ever since the summer of 1962, her eyes'd been tellin me just one thing, over n over again: they were dead. Ayuh . . . but maybe not *completely* dead. Not as long as there was one scrawny, plain-faced housekeeper on an island off the coast of Maine who still believed they were alive.

From there my mind jumped forward to the summer of 1963—the summer I killed Joe, the summer of the eclipse. She'd been fascinated by the eclipse, but not just because it was a once-in-a-lifetime thing. Nossir. She was in love with it because she thought it was the thing that'd bring Donald n Helga back to Pinewood. She told me so again n again n again. And that thing in her eyes, the thing that knew they were dead, went away for awhile in the spring n early summer of that year.

You know what I think? I think that between March or April of 1963 and the middle of July, Vera Donovan was crazy; I think for those few months she really *did* believe they were alive. She wiped the sight of that Corvette comin outta the quarry where it'd fetched up from her memory; she believed em back to life by sheer force of will. *Believed* em back to life? Nope, that ain't quite right. She *eclipsed* em back to life.

She went crazy n I believe she wanted to *stay* crazy—maybe so she could have em back, maybe to punish herself, maybe both at the same time—but in

the end, there was too much bedrock sanity in her n she couldn't do it. In the last week or ten days before the eclipse, it all started to break down. I remember that time, when us who worked for her was gettin ready for that Christless eclipse expedition n the party to follow, like it was yesterday. She'd been in a good mood all through June and early July, but around the time I sent my kids off, everythin just went to hell. That was when Vera started actin like the Red Queen in *Alice in Wonderland*, yellin at people if they s'much as looked at her crosseyed, n firin house-help left n right. I think that was when her last try at wishin em back to life fell apart. She knew they were dead then and ever after, but she went ahead with the party she'd planned, just the same. Can you imagine the courage that took? The flat-out coarse-grained down-in-your-belly *guts?*

I remembered somethin she said, too—this was after I'd stood up to her about firin the Jolander girl. When Vera come up to me later, I thought sure she was gonna fire me. Instead she give me a bagful of eclipse-watchin stuff n made what was—to Vera Donovan, at least—an apology. She said that sometimes a woman had to be a high-ridin bitch. "Sometimes," she told me, "being a bitch is all a woman has to hold onto."

Ayuh, I thought. When there's nothin else left, there's that. There's always that.

"Miz Claiborne?" a voice said in my ear, and that's when I remembered he was still on the line; I'd gone away from him completely. "Miz Claiborne, are you still there?"

"Still here," I sez. He'd ast me what she told me

about em, n that was all it took to set me off thinkin about those sad old times . . . but I didn't see how I could tell him all that, not some man from New York who didn't know nothin about how we live up here on Little Tall. How *she* lived up on Little Tall. Puttin it another way, he knew an almighty lot about Upjohn and Mississippi Valley Light n Power, but not bugger-all about the wires in the corners.

Or the dust bunnies.

He starts off, "I asked what she told you—"

"She told me to keep their beds made up n plenty of Quaker Rolled Oats in the pantry," I says. "She said she wanted to be ready because they might decide to come back anytime." And that was close enough to the truth of how it was, Andy—close enough for Greenbush, anyway.

"Why, that's amazing!" he said, and it was like listenin to some fancy doctor say, "Why, that's a brain tumor!"

We talked some more after that, but I don't have much idear what things we said. I think I told him again that I didn't want it, not so much as one red penny, and I know from the way he talked to me—kind n pleasant n sorta jollyin me along—that when he talked to you, Andy, you must not've passed along any of the news flashes Sammy Marchant prob'ly gave you n anyone else on Little Tall that'd listen. I s'pose you figured it wa'ant none of his business, at least not yet.

I remember tellin him to give it *all* to the Little Wanderers, and him sayin he couldn't do that. He said *I* could, once the will had cleared through probate (although the biggest ijit in the world coulda told he

didn't think I'd do any such thing once I finally understood what'd happened), but *he* couldn't do doodly-squat with it.

Finally I promised I'd call him back when I felt "a little clearer in my mind," as he put it, n then hung up. I just stood there for a long time—must've been fifteen minutes or more. I felt . . . creepy. I felt like that money was all over me, stuck to me like bugs used to stick to the flypaper my Dad hung in our outhouse every summer back when I was little. I felt afraid it'd just stick to me tighter n tighter once I started movin around, that it'd wrap me up until I didn't have no chance in hell of ever gettin it off again.

By the time I *did* start movin, I'd forgot all about comin down to the police station to see you, Andy. To tell the truth, I almost forgot to get dressed. In the end I pulled on an old pair of jeans n a sweater, although the dress I'd meant to wear was laid out neat on the bed (and still is, unless somebody's broke in and took out on the dress what they would've liked to've taken out on the person who b'longed inside of it). I added my old galoshes n called it good.

I skirted around the big white rock between the shed n the blackberry tangle, stoppin for a little bit to look into it n listen to the wind rattlin in all those thorny branches. I could just see the white of the concrete wellcap. Lookin at it made me feel shivery, like a person does when they're comin down with a bad cold or the flu. I took the short-cut across Russian Meadow and then walked down to where the Lane ends at East Head. I stood there a little while, lettin the ocean wind

push back my hair n warsh me clean, like it always does, and then I went down the stairs.

Oh, don't look so worried, Frank—the rope acrost the top of em n that warnin sign are both still there; it's just that I wa'ant much worried about that set of rickety stairs after all I had to go through.

I walked all the way down, switchin back n forth, until I come to the rocks at the bottom. The old town dock—what the oldtimers used to call Simmons Dock—was there, you know, but there's nothin left of it now but a few posts n two big iron rings pounded into the granite, all rusty n scaly. They look like what I imagine the eye-sockets in a dragon's skull would look like, if there really were such things. I fished off that dock many a time when I was little, Andy, and I guess I thought it'd always be there, but in the end the sea takes everything.

I sat on the bottom step, danglin my galoshes over, and there I stayed for the next seven hours. I watched the tide go out n I watched it come most of the way in again before I was done with the place.

At first I tried to think about the money, but I couldn't get my mind around it. Maybe people who've had that much all their lives can, but I couldn't. Every time I tried, I just saw Sammy Marchant first lookin at the rollin pin . . . n then up at me. That's all the money meant to me then, Andy, and it's all it means to me now—Sammy Marchant lookin up at me with that dark glare n sayin, "I thought she couldn't walk. You always told me she couldn't walk, Dolores."

Then I thought about Donald n Helga. "Fool me

once, shame on you," I says to no one at all as I sat there with my feet danglin so close over the incomers that they sometimes got splattered with curds of foam. "Fool me twice, shame on me." Except she never really fooled me . . . her *eyes* never fooled me.

I remembered wakin up to the fact—one day in the late sixties, this musta been—that I had never seen em, *not even once,* since I'd seen the hunky takin em back to the mainland that July day in 1961. And that so distressed me that I broke a long-standin rule of mine not to talk about em at all, ever, unless Vera spoke of em first. "How are the kids doin, Vera?" I ast her—the words jumped outta my mouth before I knew they were comin—with God's my witness, that's just what they did. "How are they *really* doin?"

I remember she was sittin in the parlor at the time, knittin in the chair by the bow windows, and when I ast her that she stopped what she was doin and looked up at me. The sun was strong that day, it struck across her face in a bright, hard stripe, and there was somethin so scary about the way she looked that for a second or two I came close to screamin. It wasn't until the urge'd passed that I realized it was her eyes. They were deep-set eyes, black circles in that stripe of sun where everythin else was bright. They were like *his* eyes when he looked up at me from the bottom of the well . . . like little black stones or lumps of coal pushed into white dough. For that second or two it was like seein a ghost. Then she moved her head a little and it was just Vera again, sittin there n lookin like she'd had too much to drink the night before. It wouldn't've been the first time if she had.

"I don't really know, Dolores," she said. "We are estranged." That was all she said, n it was all she needed to say. All the stories she told me about their lives—made-up stories, I know now—didn't say as much as those three words: "We are estranged." A lot of the time I spent today down by Simmons Dock I spent thinkin about what an awful word that is. Estranged. Just the sound of it makes me shiver.

I sat there n picked over those old bones one last time, n then I put em aside and got up from where I'd spent most of the day. I decided that I didn't much care what you or anyone else believed. It's all over, you see—for Joe, for Vera, for Michael Donovan, for Donald n Helga . . . and for Dolores Claiborne, too. One way or another, all the bridges between that time n this one have been burned. Time's a reach, too, you know, just like the one that lies between the islands and the mainland, but the only ferry that can cross it is memory, and that's like a ghost-ship—if you want it to disappear, after awhile it will.

But all that aside, it's still funny how things turned out, ain't it? I remember what went through my mind as I got up n turned back to them rickety stairs—the same thing that went through it when Joe snaked his arm outta the well n almost pulled me in with him: *I have digged a pit for mine enemies, and am fallen into it myself.* It seemed to me, as I laid hold of that old splintery bannister n got set to climb back up all those stairs (always assumin they'd hold me a second time, accourse), that it'd finally happened, n that I'd always known it would. It just took me awhile longer to fall into mine than it took Joe to fall into his.

Vera had a pit to fall into, too—and if I've got anything to be grateful for, it's that I haven't had to dream my children back to life like she did . . . although sometimes, when I'm talkin to Selena on the phone and hear her slur her words, I wonder if there's any escape for any of us from the pain n the sorrow of our lives. I couldn't fool her, Andy—shame on me.

Still, I'll take what I can take n grit my teeth so it looks like a grin, just like I always have. I try to keep in mind that two of my three children live still, that they are successful beyond what anyone on Little Tall would've expected when they were babies, and successful beyond what they maybe could've been if their no-good of a father hadn't had himself an accident on the afternoon of July 20th, 1963. Life ain't an either-or proposition, you see, and if I ever forget to be thankful my girl n one of my boys lived while Vera's boy n girl died, I'll have to explain the sin of ingratitude when I get before the throne of the Almighty. I don't want to do that. I got enough on my conscience—and prob'ly on my soul, too—already. But listen to me, all three of you, n hear this if you don't hear nothing else: everything I did, I did for love . . . the love a natural mother feels for her children. That's the strongest love there is in the world, and it's the deadliest. There's no bitch on earth like a mother frightened for her kids.

I thought of my dream as I reached the top of the steps again, n stood on the landin just inside that guard-rope, lookin out to sea—the dream of how Vera kept handin me plates and I kep droppin em. I thought of the sound the rock made when it struck him in the face, and how the two sounds were the same sound.

But mostly I thought about Vera and me—two bitches livin on a little chunk of rock off the Maine coast, livin together most of the time in the last years. I thought about how them two bitches slep together when the older one was scared, n how they passed the years in that big house, two bitches who ended up spendin most of their time bitchin at each other. I thought of how she'd fool me, n how I'd go'n fool her right back, and how happy each of us was when we won a round. I thought about how she was when the dust bunnies ganged up on her, how she'd scream n how she trembled like an animal that's been backed into a corner by a bigger creature that means to tear it to pieces. I remember how I'd climb into the bed with her, n put my arms around her, n feel her tremblin that way, like a delicate glass that someone's tapped with the handle of a knife. I'd feel her tears on my neck, and I'd brush her thin, dry hair n say, "Shhh, dear . . . shhh. Those pesky dust bunnies are all gone. You're safe. Safe with me."

But if I've found out anything, Andy, it's that they ain't *never* gone, not really. You think you're shut of em, that you neatened em all away and there ain't a dust bunny anyplace, n then they come back, they look like faces, they *always* look like faces, and the faces they look like are always the ones you never wanted to see again, awake or in your dreams.

I thought of her layin there on the stairs, too, and sayin she was tired, she wanted to be done. And as I stood there on that rickety landin in my wet galoshes, I knew well enough why I'd chosen to be on those stairs that are so rotted not even the hellions will play

on em after school lets out, or on the days when they play hookey. I was tired, too. I've lived my life as best I could by my own lights. I never shirked a job, nor cried off from the things I had to do, even when those things were terrible. Vera was right when she said that sometimes a woman has to be a bitch to survive, but bein a bitch is hard work, I'll tell the world it is, n I was so tired. I wanted to have done, and it occurred to me that it wasn't too late to go back down those stairs, n that I didn't have to stop at the bottom this time, neither . . . not if I didn't want to.

Then I heard her again—Vera. I heard her like I did that night beside the well, not just in my head but my *ear.* It was a lot spookier this time, I c'n tell you; back in '63 she'd at least been *alive.*

"What *can* you be thinking about, Dolores?" she ast in that haughty Kiss-My-Back-Cheeks voice of hers. "*I* paid a higher price than you did; I paid a higher price than anyone will ever know, but I lived with the bargain I made just the same. I did more than that. When the dust bunnies and the dreams of what could have been were all I had left, I took the dreams and made them my own. The dust bunnies? Well, they might have gotten me in the end, but I lived with them for a lot of years before they did. Now you've got a bunch of your own to deal with, but if you've lost the guts you had on the day when you told me that firing the Jolander girl was a boogery thing to do, go on. Go on and jump. Because without your guts, Dolores Claiborne, you're just another stupid old woman."

I drew back n looked around, but there was only East Head, dark n wet with that spray that travels in

the air on windy days. There wasn't a soul in sight. I stood there awhile longer, lookin at the way the clouds ran across the sky—I like to watch em, they're so high n free n silent as they go their courses up there—and then I turned away n started back home. I had to stop n rest two or three times on the way, because that long time sittin in the damp air at the bottom of the steps put an awful misery in my back. But I made it. When I got back to the house I took three asp'rin, got into my car, n drove straight here.

And that's it.

Nancy, I see you've piled up purt-near a dozen of those little tiny tapes, n your cunning little recorder must be just about wore out. So'm I, but I come here to have my say, and I've had it—every damn word of it, and every word is true. You do what you need to do to me, Andy; I've done my part, n I feel at peace with myself. That's all that matters, I guess; that, n knowin exactly who you are. I know who *I* am: Dolores Claiborne, two months shy of my sixty-sixth birthday, registered Democrat, lifelong resident of Little Tall Island.

I guess I want to say two more things, Nancy, before you hit the STOP button on that rig of yours. In the end, it's the bitches of the world who abide . . . and as for the dust bunnies: *frig* ya!

Scrapbook

From the Ellsworth *American*, November 6, 1992 (p. 1):

ISLAND WOMAN CLEARED

Dolores Claiborne of Little Tall Island, longtime companion of Mrs. Vera Donovan, also of Little Tall, was absolved of any blame in the death of Mrs. Donovan at a special coroner's inquest held in Machias yesterday. The purpose of the inquest was to determine if Mrs. Donovan had suffered "wrongful death," meaning death as the result of neglect or criminal act. Speculation concerning Miss Claiborne's role in the death of her employer was fueled by the fact that Mrs. Donovan, who was reputedly senile at the time of her death, left her companion and housekeeper the bulk of her estate. Some sources estimate the worth of the estate to be in excess of ten million dollars.

From the Boston *Globe*, November 20, 1992 (p. 1):

A Happy Thanksgiving in Somerville
ANONYMOUS BENEFACTOR GIVES 30M
TO ORPHANAGE

The stunned directors of The New England Home for Little Wanderers announced at a hastily called press con-

ference late this afternoon that Christmas is coming a little early for the hundred-and-fifty-year-old orphanage this year, thanks to a thirty-million-dollar bequest from an anonymous donor.

"We received word of this amazing donation from Alan Greenbush, a reputable New York attorney and certified public accountant," said a visibly flustered Brandon Jaegger, head of the N.E.H.L.W.'s board of directors. "It appears to be completely on the level, but the person behind this contribution—the guardian angel behind it, I should perhaps say—is completely serious about his or her anonymity. It almost goes without saying that all of us associated with the Home are overjoyed."

If the multi-million-dollar donation proves out, the Little Wanderers' windfall would be the largest single charitable contribution to such a Massachusetts institution since 1938, when . . .

From *The Weekly Tide*, December 14, 1992 (p. 16)

Notes from Little Tall
By "Nosy Nettie"

Mrs. Lottie McCandless won the Christmas Cover-All at Friday Night Beano in Jonesport last week—the prize totaled $240, and that's a lot of Christmas presents! Nosy Nettie is *soooo* jealous! Seriously, congratulations, Lottie!

John Caron's brother, Philo, came down from Derry to help John caulk his boat, the *Deepstar*, while it was at drydock. There is nothing like a little "brotherly love" in this blessed season, is there, boys?

Jolene Aubuchon, who lives with her granddaughter, Patricia, finished a 2000-piece jigsaw puzzle of Mt. St. Helens last Thursday. Jolene says that she's going to

celebrate her 90th birthday next year by doing a 5000-piece puzzle of the Sistine Chapel. Hurrah, Jolene! Nosy Nettie and all at the *Tide* like your style!

Dolores Claiborne will be shopping for one extra this week! She knew her son Joe—"Mr. Democrat"—was coming home with his family from his toils in Augusta for an "island Christmas," but now she says that her daughter, famous magazine scribe Selena St. George, will be making her first visit in over *twenty years!* Dolores says she feels "very blessed." When Nosy asked if they would be discussing Selena's latest "think-piece" in the *Atlantic Monthly*, Dolores would only smile and say, "We'll find lots to talk about, I'm sure."

From the Early Recovery Dept., Nosy hears that Vincent Bragg, who broke his arm playing football last October . . .

October 1989–February 1992